W9-CMH-507

PRAISE FOR KELLEY ARMSTRONG

"Armstrong is a talented and evocative writer who knows well how to balance the elements of good, suspenseful fiction, and her stories evoke poignancy, action, humor and suspense."
The Globe and Mail

"[A] master of crime thrillers."
Kirkus

"Kelley Armstrong is one of the purest storytellers Canada has produced in a long while."
National Post

"Armstrong is a talented and original writer whose inventiveness and sense of the bizarre is arresting."
London Free Press

"Armstrong's name is synonymous with great storytelling."
Suspense Magazine

"Like Stephen King, who manages an under-the-covers, flashlight-in-face kind of storytelling without sounding ridiculous, Armstrong not only writes interesting page-turners, she has also achieved that unlikely goal, what all writers strive for: a genre of her own."
The Walrus

ALSO BY KELLEY ARMSTRONG

Rockton series
City of the Lost
A Darkness Absolute
This Fallen Prey
Watcher in the Woods
Alone in the Wild

Standalone Novels
The Masked Truth
Aftermath
Missing
Wherever She Goes

Completed Series (fantasy)
Otherworld
Darkest Powers
Darkness Rising
Age of Legends

Completed Series (mystery)
Nadia Stafford
Cainsville

WOLF'S BANE

KELLEY ARMSTRONG

Cover Design by Cover Couture
www.bookcovercouture.com

Photo (c) Shutterstock/Voraorn Ratanakorn
Photo (c) Shutterstock/Anntuan
Photo (c) Shutterstock/Stephen Moehle

ISBN-13 (print): 978-1-989046-06-7
ISBN-13 (e-book): 978-1-989046-07-4

For Julia

CHAPTER ONE

Kate

I'm crouched in a thicket, listening to the drawn-out howl of a wolf, blood calling to blood.

He's coming for me already? How is that even possible? I only dove into this hiding spot a few minutes ago. Maybe I misheard a dog from a neighboring farm.

I peer through the thick brush. The moon slides from behind a cloud and for a heartbeat, I see forest, acres of empty forest. Then darkness again. I stare into the night as I listen. The smell of spring-damp earth floats past on a sharp breeze. At a soft thump, I freeze, ears straining. Undergrowth crashes as a rabbit darts for cover. Then the forest falls silent again.

Okay, it really was just a neighbor's—

Another howl slices through the silence, raising every hair on my body. Even as it dies away, I feel it strumming through the air.

Unmistakably wolf.

Unmistakably him.

So stop listening and *do* something.

I swallow hard and concentrate, fingers digging into dirt. It's too late. He'll be here any second and—

Focus. Just focus.

I hunker down and slow my breathing. I might have time. I was careful choosing my spot, climbing through trees and dropping into my thicket so I didn't leave a trail for him to follow.

Paws thump over hard earth.

I squeeze my eyes shut, trying to focus and ignore the fact that those thumps grow louder with each slam of my heart.

He only knows the general direction of where to find me. He's coming from upwind. He won't smell me. I still have a chance. He'll run past, and then I'll have time.

I just need time.

I flatten onto my stomach, swathed in darkness and shadow. The footfalls slow to the soft pad of sure steps. I stop breathing. He's walking straight toward my hiding spot, as if I'm doing jumping jacks in the moonlight.

I hold my breath and hold my body too, as still as can be. He's still upwind and can't smell me. He doesn't actually know where—

A pale muzzle pushes into the thicket. Jaws open, sharp teeth behind inch-long fangs. Then eyes appear, a blue as bright as my own. My brother tilts his head, the question as clear as spoken words.

What's taking you so long, Kate?

I snarl. Logan withdraws with a snort and plunks down to wait. I growl, telling him to move farther away. He lifts his furry ass and transplants it exactly six inches.

Ever since we were kids, we've competed to see who can shift faster. The short answer is: Logan. Oh hell, the *only* answer is: Logan. I swear, he gets faster every year.

Tonight, I'd barely undressed before he was in wolf form.

I'd hoped to still Change quickly and then slip out and pretend I'd been just hanging around, waiting. That would work a lot better if he hadn't somehow known exactly where to find me, strolling over like there was a neon arrow flashing over my thicket.

Damn him.

I grumble for a few moments. Then I resume position, close my eyes and imagine sluicing through the long grass. Feeling the wind cut through my fur. Hearing every tiny creature shriek and scamper out of my path. Listening to the drum roll of my brother's paws as he races behind me, both of us drunk on exhilaration and adrenaline . . .

My skin ripples. Muscles shift, stretching and bunching as my skin prickles, fur sprouting.

I close my eyes, position my hands and feet and lower my head. When the first jolt of agony hits, it's as if this has never happened before, and I'm caught off guard, stifling a scream.

This too shall pass.

It's like getting a tooth drilled. Well, I presume it's like that because when I get a filling or a booster shot and the doctor says, "This is going to hurt," I almost laugh. A needle piercing my skin? Try having your entire body ripped apart and put back together twice a month.

What I mean is that the pain, however severe, is temporary. You grit your teeth, tell yourself this too shall pass.

It does. Waves of agony nearly knock me out, and then I'm standing on four legs, panting and shaking, my yellow fur gleaming in the moonlight.

Yes, I'm a yellow wolf. A werewolf's fur is the same

color as our hair, which for me means that if I'm seen, I'll be mistaken for a dog. Don't ask me how I know that. All-caps rule number one: DO NOT BE SEEN. But, yeah, it happens, for some more than others, and it's probably a good thing I'm blessed with golden retriever fur.

When a distant owl shrieks, my ears swivel to follow the sound. Most werewolves have excellent hearing in human form, and even better hearing as wolves. Logan and I hear just as well in both forms. We're . . . a little different.

There are only a few dozen werewolves in North America and almost all inherited the genes from their dads—it passes through the male line. It can also be trans-mitted through bites, but the survival rate for that is so low that there are only a few bitten werewolves . . . including both our parents.

So what happens when two bitten werewolves have kids? No one knew. When it comes to werewolves, statistics are nearly nonexistent. The human world doesn't know about supernaturals, so they're not exactly conducting studies. We could do it ourselves, but for us, survival is a whole lot more important than note-taking.

Growing up, I only wished for one thing, with every birthday candle, every four-leaf clover, every wishing-well coin. Make me a werewolf. I got my wish at the age of nine, a decade earlier than normal hereditary werewolves. As far as anyone knows, I'm one of two female werewolves in the world—mom being the other. I'm the first female hereditary werewolf *ever*. That's cool, but really, all I care about is that I got my wish: I am a werewolf.

When I step out of my thicket, Logan greets me with a welcoming snuffle. Seeing him, I don't know how anyone can mistake us for dogs. We look like wolves. We retain our human mass, which makes him a huge wolf, ghost white in the darkness, sleek furred and muscular.

As he snuffles me, I twist away and then surprise-pounce, which would work much better with any werewolf who *wasn't* my twin. Logan anticipates the pounce and feints out of the way, then twists and leaps at me. I duck and race around him so fast I swear I hear his vertebrae crackle as he spins to keep an eye on me.

Then I launch myself at him. I'm airborne, and he's diving, hitting the ground in a roll, expecting me to fumble when my target vanishes. But I wasn't jumping at him—I was jumping over him. With one massive bound, I clear his back, hit the ground and keep running.

It takes Logan a moment to recover from the fake-out. I bear down, my ears flat, muzzle slicing through the wind as the *thump-thump* of my brother's paws gallop behind me. Scents whip past. Damp earth and spring bluebells and the tantalizing musk of a distant deer. I don't slow. We can hunt later. Right now, I want to run, to feel the ground beneath my paws, the wind in my fur, my brother at my back.

The last is as important as the rest. Maybe more important now than ever. When I was little, Logan felt as integral to my life as a limb. Now, at sixteen, we've drifted, and I no longer feel whole. Yet whatever our problems, we shed them with our human forms. Out here, the rest of the world falls away and feels as it always has, and I am happy.

Ahead, the forest thickens. That'll slow me down, but it also adds the challenge of an obstacle course. I leap over a dead tree and weave through thick brush while trying to gauge whether Logan is far enough back for me to hide and pounce.

I slit my eyes and swivel my ears to listen. Logan had to slow down in the forest, and I grin at that. I might have a slight advantage in speed, but I have an even greater one in agility, his recent growth spurt leaving him with a body he can't quite operate yet. Behind me, there's a thump and a yelp, as if he cut a corner too sharp and plowed into a tree.

I grin and nimbly swerve behind an outcropping of rock. Ahead, I see the perfect cover—the deadfall of a massive evergreen. I'll hunker behind it, and when Logan vaults over, I'll tackle him.

Getting up speed for my own leap, I'm running full out when a whistle sounds, cutting through the quiet evening and sending me skidding to a stop.

The whistle comes again. It's the Alpha—who also happens to be our mom. If she's calling us in, something's happened. Something important enough to interrupt our run.

I throw back my head and howl. There's a question in that, and Mom returns two quick whistle bursts. No, Stonehaven isn't on fire or under attack by rogue wolves— she just needs to talk to us.

A sigh ripples behind me, and I twist to toss Logan a sympathetic snort. We exchange a mournful look and separate to Change back.

CHAPTER TWO

Kate

By the time I leave my thicket, Logan is already in human form, waiting for me. We were late getting back from our last day of school, and he's still wearing his uniform. Mom bought it new this term, and the pant legs already show a half inch of sock while the polo shirt strains over his shoulders and biceps. A year ago, Logan and I could share clothing. Now he could share Dad's. Not that he does, of course—my brother is decidedly more fashion conscious than our father.

As for me, I inherited Mom's build, which means I didn't wear a bra until I was fifteen, and I still need a belt to hold my jeans up because my hips sure as hell aren't doing the job. I also inherited her height. I've nearly caught up to her five-ten, and I'm hoping to pass it.

Strolling across the lawn, I smile when the house comes into view. As the name suggests, Stonehaven is made of stone, a mansion surrounded by acres of forest, the perfect home for werewolves. The Danvers always lived here, and they've always been werewolves.

I'm a Danvers by name—Jeremy Danvers having raised
Dad after he was bitten as a kid.

The back door clicks, and there's a canine yip as our
dog, Atalanta, comes running. We usually take her on our
runs, but she'd been sleeping after a jog with Mom. As she
races toward me, I break into a run. Logan bears down,
his footsteps thudding.

"Give it up," I call back. "You might be able to shift
faster than me, Lo, but you can't run faster."

And, of course, as I say that, I stumble. I recover, but
not before Logan yanks on the back of my T-shirt.

"Cheat!" I call.

"Cheating is party A starting a race without informing
party B."

"Blah-blah-blah."

From the back door, Mom smiles as she leans against
the doorframe to watch. She hasn't failed to notice the
growing gulf between Logan and me. I tell myself this too
shall pass, but it still hurts. Hurts me. Worries Mom. Yet
the gulf isn't so wide that we can't still reach over it, racing
across the yard like kids again.

Mom wears blue jeans, sneakers and an oversized plaid
shirt with the sleeves rolled up. She's tugged her white-
blond hair into a high ponytail. From across the yard, she
could be mistaken for a teenager. Up close, you'd guess she
was in her late thirties. She's actually fifty-one. Werewolves
age slowly. Dad's six years older, and girls at my school still
check him out, which is really gross. A moment later, he
appears beside Mom, in his usual outfit: worn jeans, a plain
white T-shirt, old sneakers, and a few days of beard scruff.

I skid to a stop, hand reaching to tag the doorframe.
"Home!"

"Really, Kate?" Logan says. "How old are we? Five?"

"I wasn't racing myself there."

"I was humoring you."

"Yeah, yeah. Good excuse." I swat his shoulder as he walks past, and he tosses me a very Logan smile, his lips barely moving but his eyes twinkling.

"I'm glad to see you both in good moods," Mom says as she and Dad back into the house, Atalanta tumbling after them.

I slow and eye her. "Because whatever you have to say is totally going to ruin it?"

"I hope not."

I slide a look Dad's way. His expression is studiously neutral.

"Shit," I mutter.

"Language, Kate," Dad says.

I flip him the finger. He only grins. Growing up, I heard those two words a lot from Mom. I wasn't the only one relieved when she finally stopped bothering. If Mom doesn't call me on my language, Dad no longer has to watch his. Let's just say I come by my profanity-propensity honestly.

We head into the study, site of all family conferences. It's my favorite room in the house. Pretty sure it's everyone's favorite—it's certainly where we usually hang out, despite the number of options, and I think that's why it *is* my favorite. It's where my family will be, and where I want to be, even if I'm just studying on the floor while Mom or Dad or Jeremy reads, not a word exchanged. I'm a werewolf, and this is my Pack, and I like having them around, however seriously uncool that might be.

Speaking of reading, that's what Jeremy's doing.

Without looking up from his novel, he lifts a hand in greeting. I high-five it. Logan just says, "Hey, Jer."

Technically, Jeremy is our grandfather since he foster-raised Dad. We never called him that or thought of him like that. He's just Jeremy, as much a part of our family as Mom or Dad.

I sit on the other armchair. Logan and Dad take the sofa. Mom stands by the fireplace, which means this is a "serious family discussion."

"Do you guys remember that youth conference I mentioned?" Mom says.

"You mean the bullet we dodged?" I say.

Mom came to us a couple months ago with this "cool new idea," sponsored by the supernatural interracial council. A leadership conference for supernatural teens, where we were supposed to hold hands, sing *Kumbaya* around a campfire and come to a better understanding of one another. I'd rather start my summer facing down hell hounds.

I have total respect for the council. Mom's the were-wolf delegate, and I'm named after the witch leader—Paige Katherine Winterbourne. The part I like, though, is the idea of supernatural races banding together to kick ass as a unified front. I can totally get behind that. The touchy-feely togetherness side, though? Really not my thing. And this conference was clearly all about the touchy-feely.

Mom had wanted us to go as werewolf representatives. I'd been considering it, by which I mean awaiting divine intervention in the form of a thunderbolt that burned down the conference center. At the same time, those in charge of the conference—who were *not* on the actual council—had debated whether they should allow werewolves.

Before they could make a decision, all the spots were miraculously taken. Yeah, among supernatural races, the only ones less welcome than werewolves are vampires. We're bloodthirsty monsters, don't you know, likely to slaughter you in your sleep if we get a case of midnight munchies.

Bullet dodged, like I said.

That's when I realize there's only one reason for Mom to be bringing this up now.

"Whoa," I say. "Wait, no. Don't tell me—"

"Two spots opened up."

"But they don't want us, remember?"

"They'd changed their mind about that, remember?"

"They changed it in the same breath as saying 'whoops, we're full," I say. "But now two kids canceled and the council found out, right? As sponsors, they're insisting we be allowed to take those spots, despite the fact the conference staff doesn't want us there."

"All the more reason for you to go. Prove them wrong."

Easy for Mom to say. She's not the one being asked to spend a week where she very clearly isn't wanted.

"I'm allergic to team-building exercises," I say. "Also crowds."

Dad snorts.

"Yeah," I say. "Wonder where I get that from. Maybe the guy who grumbled and stomped and snarled about going to New York last month to give a lecture . . . which he'd *agreed* to give."

"I agreed to a class of thirty," Dad says. "Not three hundred."

Logan's lips twitch in a smile. "Imagine if that got out. The most feared werewolf in the country can be laid low by the prospect of interacting with humans."

Dad twists fast, grabbing for Logan's arm. Logan dodges and swings to his feet. When Dad tries again, they end up locked together. Dad flexes, testing his hold, considering the possibility of still throwing Logan over his shoulder. He could do it, but not nearly as easily—or gracefully—as he once could.

"Shit," Dad murmurs.

"Yes," Jeremy says, gaze still on his book. "One day soon, Clay, you're going to try that and find your*self* flying onto the sofa. Your son is growing up fast."

"Nah," I say. "Dad's just growing old fast."

Dad spins on me.

I stay on the chair, lounging back. "Try it, old man."

Dad takes one slow step toward me, his eyes glittering. I grin, ready for the attack.

"Do I need to kick you out of the room?" Mom says.

"Yes, Kate," Dad says as he stops short, "behave yourself."

"I'd *like* to be kicked out of the room," I say. "But I think she meant you."

"Never." Dad feints left, grabs Mom and drops back onto the sofa, plunking her on his lap. "Continue."

Mom only rolls her eyes before turning to me. "Yes, I suspect there will be team-building exercises, but I'm sure the camping part would compensate for that."

"They could provide an open bar," I mutter, "and it wouldn't compensate for team-building exercises."

"Good thing there's no open bar then. And the other kids are supernaturals your own age, which might be good."

A chance for new friends she means. I drifted from my friend group in the last couple of years, and I haven't replaced them. Mom might also be hinting about boys, since I broke up with my boyfriend recently. I definitely have no plans to replace *him*. First serious boyfriend, first serious romantic humiliation.

"I'm good," I say, sinking into my chair.

Logan looks at Mom. "Is there any reason we both need to go?"

I nearly bolt upright. Logan go without me? We don't do that. We're the Danvers twins.

Does Logan *want* to go without me?

Mom glances my way. "As your mother, Kate, I'd like you to attend the conference. As your Alpha, I will not insist on it. Sending one representative is enough. Remember, though, that if you choose to let Logan go alone, it tells the supernatural world which of my children aspires to a leadership role . . . and which does not."

I squirm at that. Logan and I aren't competing for Alpha-hood. We'd co-lead before we'd fight one another. Yet I *do* want to be Alpha someday. I just don't think it requires "youth leadership" conferences.

Mom's right, though. Logan going alone sent a message. The wrong message.

I glance at my brother.

"It's up to you," he says, his voice neutral.

I flinch. He's hoping I'll stay home. We aren't in middle school anymore, the inseparable Danvers twins. Back then, I'd been the popular one, kids trailing after me like I was the Pied Piper, even when I just wanted to hang out with my brother. I was the girl who said what she liked and did what she liked, fierce and fearless, confident in her cloak of rebel-cool.

Then we hit high school, and it felt like everyone changed except me. I was still that girl, and suddenly, it *wasn't* cool. It was just different. Weird.

Some kids embrace their uniqueness. I used to, but then . . . Stuff happened, and the last month at school has been hell, and I'm exhausted from pretending I don't give a shit.

Now I'm listening to that neutral tone of Logan's, and I know what it means. He's okay with me staying home. Perhaps more than okay. Maybe, just maybe, it'd be nice to go someplace where he doesn't need to deal with the baggage of being Kate Danvers's twin.

"Maybe it's better if Logan goes alone," I say carefully. "If they have a problem with werewolves, I might just make things worse."

He frowns at me. It's a genuine frown of genuine confusion, and I love him for that . . . and miss him a little extra.

"One werewolf might be easier to accept," I say.

"Are we supposed to make this easier for them?" Logan says. "Also, if there's only one, then they can say I'm the exception." He meet my eyes. "It would be better with us both there but if you really don't want to go with me . . ."

"I will."

The words come before I can stop myself. If Logan wants me along, then I'm there. Then I remember where "there" is. An interracial leadership camp. Where I will be an outsider, unwanted and unwelcome at a time in my life when I have never felt more of either.

I open my mouth to take it back, to pretend that I meant something else, but Mom's face lights up. Then Dad twists to glance at me, mouthing a private "thank you," with a wry smile that says he knows I don't want to do this, and he appreciates me making the effort for Mom's sake. It pleases her, and so it pleases him.

Shit.

I take a deep breath. "When do we leave?"

Mom and Dad exchange a look.

"First thing in the morning," Mom says.

"What?"

"The actual conference started tonight. Your uncle Nick has business in Pittsburgh, so he's offered to drive you. You'll leave after breakfast."

CHAPTER THREE

Logan

Kate and I are napping, curled up in the back of Nick's car. We drifted off leaning on our respective doors, but I wake to Kate against my shoulder, my arm around her, as if in sleep we find what we've lost.

I keep my eyes half-closed and pretend I'm a kid again, dozing in Mom's car, smelling leather seats and Kate's strawberry shampoo, listening to her soft snores underscored by the thump of Nick's classic rock. I linger there, watching the West Virginia state sign pass as Kate lifts her head, mumbling something that sounds like "Where are the pancakes?" She rubs her eyes, groans and flips over to her own side of the car.

I take out my cell phone to save myself from awkward silence.

Awkward silence with my sister. There'd been a time when I couldn't imagine such a thing.

"Your mom told you two about the conference cell phone rule?" Nick asks.

"Cell phone rule?" Kate growls.

"Thanks, Elena," Nick mutters. He glances at us through the mirror. "Your cell phones will be locked up at the conference. You get them back for twenty minutes each evening."

"What the hell?" Kate shoots upright, seatbelt snapping. "That's bullshit."

"Yep," Nick says. "Your mom may have used that exact word. But it's the rule. So I'd suggest taking a few minutes to post your social media goodbyes."

Kate doesn't bother taking out her phone. After dumping her boyfriend, she wiped her social media accounts. My sister is known for her dramatic gestures, and if she's decided to play lone wolf for a while, I won't interfere. I just wish her social isolation didn't extend to me.

As I check my own messages, I see the advantages of my sister's choice. I have twenty Snapchats alone. Only half are from actual friends. Five are from girls I know by name alone. The first is a brunette I vaguely recognize, asking my opinion of her new bikini. At least she's wearing clothing. I get plenty of pics where they aren't.

I don't date. I don't have time. That's my excuse, and I know it's an excuse because it's not as if the girls who sext me are looking for a long-term relationship. Somehow, that's worse. They just want to be the one who lassos the class unicorn. Even those who seem interested in more than a hook-up don't chase me because they like me. They just like what they see.

I delete all those messages unseen. Then up pops one that's equally unwelcome.

Hey, Lo. Any chance of setting up that 'accidental encounter' with Kate? LMK.

Brandon. Kate's ex.

He's calling me Lo to be chummy, knowing only Kate uses that, but the bigger problem is him asking me to play mediator. I don't know why Kate dumped Brandon. It's none of my business, and I don't appreciate him playing on our sorta-friendship to win her back. Every time he does, I get a little more annoyed with my sister.

I text Brandon a variation on the "family stuff, going offline" story. Nick takes an exit ramp and within minutes we're rumbling along a dirt road into the forest. A few miles later Nick slows the car and squints at a sign with lettering worn and weathered to illegibility.

"Please don't tell me *that's* the camp," Kate says.

We follow her finger to the forest. It's *all* forest here, trees looming over the narrow dirt road. I shift and squint until I can make out a ramshackle cottage that looks as if a thunderstorm would flatten it.

"Yep, this is the place," Nick says, putting the car in Park.

"What?" Kate squawks. "Hell, no. If you think for one second—" She catches Nick's smile and scowls. "Ha-ha."

"I was told to park here and call. The camp must be nearby but . . ." He scans the forest. "Maybe that's not the right signpost."

"Call anyway," Kate says as she opens her door. "I need to stretch my legs, and I want to check out that cabin."

"The one you just complained about?" Nick says.

"I'd complain if I had to sleep in it. Exploring it is a whole other thing."

She climbs out, and I reach for my door handle, waiting for the inevitable, "Come on, Lo." Instead, she jogs into the forest without a backward glance.

I used to follow. She'd get in her moods, and I'd go after her, standing between Kate and the world—interpreter, mediator, buffer. But a moat stretches between us these days, and I can't seem to build a bridge. I'm not even sure I try.

That isn't like me at all. I'm the calm one, the logical one, the easygoing one. Or I used to be. These days, there's the me I used to be, the me I'm becoming, and the me that others see, and none of them are who I *want* to be, and I'm not even sure who *that* is.

As Nick places his call, I get out and inhale the sharp tang of pine. I roll my shoulders, working out the kinks. I sniff again, and my legs ache to run, even in human form. Just run into the forest and forget what I'm supposed to be doing here. Which also isn't like me at all. I'm nothing if not responsible. Boring, responsible Logan Danvers.

Maybe that's why Kate seems to prefer her own company these days.

A click as Nick pops open the trunk. As we walk to the back, he says, "The head counselor is meeting us here and walking you over."

I reach in for my bag, but he stops me, glancing at where Kate disappeared.

"You guys okay?" he asks.

I shrug. "She's not happy about being here, which means I need to listen to her bitch about it for the next week. Situation normal these days."

Nick frowns, and he shoots me this look that makes me feel like I'm five, caught doing something I shouldn't. Except when I *was* five, I never did anything I shouldn't, not unless Kate talked me into it.

"Your sister has been having a difficult time lately,"

Nick says. "Maybe you could be a little more under-standing?"

I replay my words and wince as I realize I sounded like an asshole.

Part of me wants to admit he's right . . . and part of me wants to snap back that she's not the only one having a "difficult time," and maybe *she* could be more understand-ing. Which tips me right into asshole-hood again.

Before I can speak, my phone buzzes. It's Brandon, asking if he can come over, my "going offline" message having sailed right over his head.

"That's not Kate's Brandon, is it?" Nick says, unable to miss the message on my screen.

"Yeah." I thumb the text away.

"You two are still hanging out after what he did to your sister?"

"What?"

"Mr. Sorrentino?" a woman's voice trills.

Nick turns, and the woman stops with a little "Oh." The woman is maybe thirty, wearing shorts, a Team Half-Demon T-shirt and a goofy smile as she stares at Nick.

Nick shakes the young woman's hand and says, "Nick, please," and then waits. The woman just keeps ogling.

"Logan Danvers," I say.

She turns then, finally noticing me, and her smile—thankfully—changes to one of regular greeting.

"Tricia MacNab," she says.

"Team Half-Demon, I see." Nick gives her an easy grin. There's zero flirtation in it, but she still perks up.

"It's for orientation. All the kids and counselors get one as a fun way to introduce ourselves and our types. And then after that, the shirts go away as we work on forgetting our differences."

"Forgetting them after you establish them?" I murmur, low enough that only Nick hears, and his lips quirk in a smile. Louder, I say, "I understand that you only found out we were coming this morning, so I know you won't have Team Werewolf shirts."

Please tell me you don't have Team Werewolf shirts.

Her smile quivers. Then she says with a nervous laugh, "No, we don't. But that's why I came to meet you here. We'd like . . . At least at first . . . I think it's best if we don't announce what you and your sister are."

I frown. "But we're here as the werewolf delegates."

"To help prove we're not all the big bad wolf," Nick says.

Tricia giggles, a little too high-pitched. "Oh, I know you aren't. But we're concerned it's a liability issue when we couldn't warn—I mean, *tell*—parents that there would be werewolves. You two will be our mystery campers as an exercise to prove labels don't matter. Once everyone's comfortable with you, we'll have the big reveal."

This makes no sense. If it's a liability issue—which is really insulting—then revealing it later might only make that worse. Hiding *everyone's* type would be the true exercise in breaking down barriers.

"Isn't someone going to figure it out?" I say. "This is a leadership conference. The other campers will know a thing or two about supernatural politics. Introduce them to twins named Kate and Logan, race unknown, and someone is bound to realize who we are."

Tricia waves off my logic with, "These are teens. They won't know werewolf politics. Hardly any *adult* supernaturals do."

Nick and I exchange a look.

"Did Paige approve this?" Nick asks.

Tricia stammers a non-answer about Paige not being directly involved in the day-to-day running of the camp. The day that Paige Winterbourne isn't directly involved in something is the day my sister voluntarily wears a Team Werewolf shirt.

According to Mom, Paige is coming tomorrow. Until then, I'll fend off Kate's outrage by pointing out the alternative—that we'd need to design our own Team Werewolf shirts, probably with glitter pens.

As Nick talks to Tricia, I offer to fetch Kate, giving me a chance to warn her. Nick nods, and I take off, jogging toward the dilapidated cabin. There's no driveway leading from the road. No path either as I have to cut through thick bush.

After meeting Tricia, my hopes for this conference might be in free fall, but at least we get this forest—endless and empty wilderness, with the Appalachians rising in the distance. Kate and I will have a blast here, exploring new terrain, Changing and running and hunting. Maybe this is what we need, a chance for the two of us to hang out together doing something we both love.

I remember what Nick said about Brandon. Did Kate talk to Nick about the breakup?

No, he must be just taking her side, presuming Brandon did something wrong. If Brandon hurt Kate, she'd tell me. I'd notice, too, right? We're twins. We can barely stub a toe without the other feeling it. If Kate was hurting . . .

If Kate was hurting, she'd withdraw. She'd go quiet and keep to herself, which is exactly what she's been—

The crackle of brush stops me midthought. I glance up, expecting to see Kate. Instead, I'm staring at a stranger, a guy who looks like a high-school senior. Roughly my height and my build, athletic and lean muscled. Dark skin. Hair styled in short locs.

He doesn't see me. He's poised in the forest, staring straight ahead, and his profile prods a ping of recognition, as if I know him. Except I don't.

I inhale deeply, but he's downwind, and the more I look at him, the more certain I am that I've never seen him before. It's just a weird sense of déjà vu.

That crackle I heard was the guy stepping from the forest's edge. Then he saw my sister and withdrew. Now he's watching her.

Kate doesn't notice him. She's crouched looking at something with her back to the newcomer.

He stands there, staring at Kate. That's nothing new. In the last few years, Kate has been approached by a half-dozen modeling scouts. She's tall and slender with blue eyes and long blond hair, the kind of girl who gets attention even as her old T-shirts, faded jeans and ratty sneakers insist she doesn't want it.

Except the look this guy's giving her is different. It's surprise and something like disbelief. I don't know what this look means, but my hackles rise and a growl tickles my throat. He should say something. Let her know he's there. You don't hide in the shadows, watching a girl who's alone in the forest.

I ease back and creep up behind him. I lose sight of the guy in the thick forest, but I know exactly where he is. I listen, in case he decides to retreat, but the forest stays silent.

As I draw near the spot, I pause and take a deep breath. Then I realize my fists are clenched and give my hands a shake. None of that. I'm just here to show him what it's like to have a stranger sneak up on you.

I pause, preparing. Then I step through with, "What the hell do you think you're—?"

I stop.

The guy is gone.

CHAPTER FOUR

Kate

A cabin in the woods. Such a perfect setting for a horror movie that there's even one named exactly that. That was an adequate cabin in the woods. This one is perfection.

No roads or trails run to it. I only spotted it from the road because two storm-felled trees cleared a narrow sightline. Otherwise, it would have been completely hidden. I almost wish it was. I wish I'd come back here to stretch my legs and stumbled over it like a girl in a fairy tale.

This is no candy house, though. It's wood. Rotting wood. Or that's what it looks like from a distance, but when I get close, I see the timber is only covered in moss and darkened by time. The roof sags, the windows are boarded up and the porch slants to one side. It's clearly abandoned, yet when I try the front door, it doesn't budge. I put a little werewolf strength into it, and the wood protests, telling me that if I huff and puff, I'll break it down, which is not what I want.

I walk to a window, hoping to pry off a plank enough

to see through, but it's boarded from the inside. I'm circling to the back when someone whispers behind me.

I don't turn around. I've grown up with werewolves, who love to practice their silent prowling. At the risk of bragging, I'm something of a master at the craft myself. One Pack member who doesn't play the game is Logan—it's beneath my brother's dignity—so this must be Nick.

I pretend not to hear him, even as the hairs on my neck rise. The wordless whisper comes again, tickling my ear, and in the middle of it, I spin, my fist spinning with me, to teach Nick a lesson about—

My fist whizzes through empty air.

There's no one behind me. The hairs on my neck go wild, that chill blasting straight down my spine.

I must have imagined the second whisper. It would have been Nick the first time, sneaking up to whisper and then creeping away. I stride to the corner of the house, and when I don't see him there, I race around to the next corner and . . .

I'm alone.

I rub the back of my neck.

There *is* such a thing as ghosts in our world. Only necromancers can hear and see them, though.

I straighten and march around the cabin in a full one-eighty. There's clearly no one out here, and when I listen hard, Nick and Logan's distant voices drift over from the road.

I turn back to the house. Then I take a slow, careful step toward it, barely breathing, straining to catch—

Something moves inside. A scratching sound, like nails against wood. Coming from *inside* the cabin.

Even as I shiver, I shake my head. Abandoned cabin with the sound of tiny claws? Mice, voles, rats, rabbits, squirrels . . . The list of potential culprits extends to half the creatures in this forest.

I put my ear to the wall. As I do, I glance down at the concrete foundation. I'm not sure why it catches my attention. Then it clicks. This is a wooden cabin, a very simple structure, one that should not have a concrete foundation.

Something else caught my eye, though. A pattern in the concrete. Ivy snakes up, obscuring the design. I crouch to tug the plant, but it holds fast. I pull harder and the vines bite into my fingers, like I'm trying to snap wires.

When I was younger, I'd have gotten frustrated and yanked . . . and then cursed and snarled because I cut my hands. Now I detangle the ivy bit by bit.

"What the hell do you think you're—?"

I jump, not at the voice but at the words. The voice I recognize in a heartbeat. Yet the tone and the language make me think I'm mistaken. I must be.

Logan stands behind me, glowering.

He isn't glowering not at me, though. He's glowering at . . . nothing. At empty space.

That shiver runs through me.

"Lo?" I say.

He spins.

"What do you think you're doing, wandering off—?" He blinks and rubs a hand over his eyes.

"Lo?" I walk over. "Are you okay?"

He nods, still eye-rubbing. "Sorry. I didn't mean to snap. I'm just tired. Tired and cranky obviously." A glimmer of a sheepish smile, my old Logan peeking through. "Sorry for yelling. I just . . ." He looks around. "Did you see someone back here?"

That chill again. "No. Did you?"

"Logan! Kate!" Nick shouts. "Time to go!"

Logan jerks his head in Nick's direction. "The head counselor showed up, and there's something I need to explain before you meet her."

After saying goodbye to Nick, we head into the forest for the mile-long hike to camp. As we walk, Tricia explains more about the conference. Five counselors, and the other four are college students. Two dozen attendees between the ages of sixteen and eighteen from all across the country. She launches into a description of the supernatural races we'll encounter, as if we haven't grown up in this world.

Over half the campers are half demons, like Tricia. That's no surprise. They're the most common race. Lots of demons out there, making lots of babies with lots of human women. A half-demon friend of ours calls them the X-Men of the supernatural world. Accurate. They all inherit one main power from their demon daddy—ice, fire, teleportation, telekinesis, and so on—and that's their half-demon type. Oh, and they look human. All supernaturals do. That's how we've remained hidden for so long.

Next comes the spellcasters. Witches and sorcerers are two separate sex-specific races. If you're a witch, you have only daughters who are also witches. If you're a sorcerer, you have only sons who are also sorcerers. They have different magical specialties but can cast each other's spells. There's a lot of friction between the faces, a very old grudge dating back to when the sorcerers threw the witches to the inquisition, and then positioned themselves as the more powerful race. Guys, right? While there's still tension, it's better now. Paige herself is married to a sorcerer, and they have a son. Yep, that's the exception to the rule—if a witch and a sorcerer have a baby, it can be either a girl or a boy, and technically, dual-race, which is very cool.

The camp also has a few necromancers. Like I said, they have the ability to see and communicate with the dead. They can also raise and control zombies, though most don't except as a last resort. Raising a zombie means dragging its ghost back into its rotting corpse, and that's just nasty. In a pinch, though, it's a helluva power.

While there are also minor races—like shamans and druids—this camp is just the major races. Or, before we came, four of the six major ones, which isn't exactly an all-race conference. For most supernaturals, those are the four that count.

As for the sixth, I cannot resist an innocent, "Any vamps?" Tricia only gives a nervous titter, as if the answer is too obvious for comment. Yep, no vampires. They might be the most famous race, but they're also the rarest and most . . . I'd say "feared," but I'm not sure that's the right word. Fear and discomfort mixed. They might look human, but they're still undead, semi-immortal, living for hundreds of years without aging, healing upon injury. They're even more "the other" than werewolves.

Also, with vampires, there's the blood sucking, which understandably makes people squeamish. Werewolves are predators, and some are man-eaters, but most have never tasted human flesh in their lives. Feeding on people is gross and unnecessary. For vampires, it *is* necessary, and while they can drink without killing, they must kill one person a year to maintain their own immortality.

As for how vampires get their powers, like werewolves, most are hereditary. Like necromancers, it's selective—every so often, someone in that bloodline dies and rises again. You can also become a vampire, but again, like werewolves, it's both tricky and rare.

Tricia prattles on about the races we'll meet, and I tune her out as soon as I realize she's not going to say anything I don't already know. Instead, I strain for my first glimpse of the camp. I've never been to summer camp, for obvious reasons. Well, they're obvious to werewolves, being the same reasons that had us scrambling to avoid the draft in every war. It's not that we didn't want to fight. Come on, we're werewolves; we're the first to jump *into* a fight. The problem is that we can't spend months living in close quarters with humans while lacking an easy way to Change. Add in the tensions of war, and you've got a horror movie right there.

For Logan and me, summer camp as kids would have been the same thing. We hadn't been in full control of our Changes yet, and we—okay, I—would have been tense and anxious, separated from my Pack.

There'd been a time, though, when I desperately wanted to go to camp. Days of horseback riding and lake-front swimming and archery lessons. Nights of bonfires, s'mores and ghost stories . . . That was my idea of heaven. Then Mom explained that she and Dad couldn't tag along, and it'd be me and Logan with total strangers. At that, my vision of heaven flipped to sheer hell.

So, Mom gave us our own summer camp. Rented a cabin on a lake for swimming. Brought Jeremy along for archery and art lessons. Assigned Dad fire-building and s'more construction. Mom supplied the ghost stories. The only thing missing was horseback riding lessons. Were-wolves smell like predators, and we confuse and frighten animals. Atalanta had been an experiment in raising a puppy to see whether early exposure helped. Thankfully, it did.

As much as I dread this conference, I can't deny a glimmer of excitement. I envision tiny cabins ringing a bonfire pit. Sure, I'm hoping for indoor plumbing—and please have indoor showers—but I'd like to rough it. Sleep with only thin timbers between me and the forest, the smell of trees perfuming my dreams.

Yes, this could actually be a really good week.

Then I see the camp.

"What the—?" I manage to clamp my mouth shut before I swear. Sure, I'm going to, eventually, but super-naturals expect werewolves to be illiterate brutes, and I'm not handing them ammunition quite so soon.

The cursing is understandable, though, because I have no idea what the hell I'm looking at. It doesn't belong in a forest, that's for sure. It's a huge white rectangle, as if someone dropped a giant shipping container in the middle of the forest. It squats there like a scar in the landscape, making me want to cover my eyes and turn around to refresh my retinas with trees and mountains and proper wilderness elements.

"Isn't it amazing?" Tricia gushes. "It's so . . ." She waves her hand, searching for a word.

"Unexpected?" Logan says, and I stifle a laugh.

She spins on him, saying, "Yes! Exactly! Art in the forest."

I bite my tongue before I say the forest doesn't need art. It *is* art.

"Is the camp nearby?" my brother says, in his most unruffled tone.

"This is the camp," she says. "You get to stay here. In

this . . ." She waves, once again at a loss for words. I could supply a few. Like *ugly mother-fucking crime against nature.*

Logan's look warns me not to say anything, but his eye-roll acknowledges I'm not the only one *thinking* it.

"Are there . . . windows?" Logan asks, staring at what seems to be a solid building.

"No," she says. "That's the genius of it. The lower floor contains the window-less bedrooms to keep them dark for sleeping. Then you go up to the second-floor common areas where the ceiling is solid glass. The symbolism is . . . *intense.*"

So is the heat, I bet. With the sun beating down on a solid glass roof.

She continues. "You are going to love it. We're so lucky to be the first people ever to stay here."

"It's a new building?" Logan asks.

"Completely new." She opens a metal door, and I realize I was only slightly off base thinking this thing looked like a giant shipping container. It's *made* from shipping containers. When I comment, Tricia trills, "Isn't that an amazing idea?"

It would be . . . in the city. In the forest, it's an unholy altar to the god of transcontinental commercialism. Also, it'll rust.

Tricia opens one solid steel door and ushers us into a dimly lit hall.

"It's awfully dark," I say, and refrain from adding *due to the lack of fucking windows.*

"We keep the lights low to add to the ambiance," she says. "Also, we're running on generators."

"Wouldn't you use solar?" I say. "Oh, wait, you'd need the roof for that, which you've used for a giant skylight, instead."

Logan gives me a look, but Tricia misses the sarcasm and says, "We do have solar, but the panels aren't working as well as expected." *Because they're on the damned ground, surrounded by trees.*

"So our conference is the first event here?" Logan says, my darling brother trying valiantly to steer the conversation back on track.

"Isn't it amazing?" She leads us toward a side hall. Well, no, after a moment of leading, she follows, because it really is dark, and we have werewolf night vision. "This whole valley was once owned by a single family who kept trying to sell the land, but they couldn't because of the legend."

I perk up so fast Logan chuckles. Before I can speak, he says, "I think my sister would like to hear that legend."

Tricia's lips moue in distaste. "Oh, I don't know it. It's a human legend."

"Human legends are very important," I say. "They give us insight into the myriad ways supernaturals unintentionally reveal themselves, forcing humans to invent personal folklore to explain those encounters while also revealing *themselves* through their fears and desires."

She stares at me as if I'm a talking parrot.

"Our Dad's an anthropologist," Logan says. "Kate caught the bug."

"Oh, that's so sweet. Are you hoping to go to college for anthropology, Kate?"

She emphasizes "hoping," imbued with what seems like genuine sympathy for this poor kid who dreams of college, a fantasy her bestial IQ will never permit.

"No," I say. "I want to be a doctor."

She looks over quickly, as if to see whether I'm joking.

"That's . . . a lofty goal," she says. "My brother had straight As, and he barely got into med school."

I solder my mouth shut, clamping down the words—

"Kate has a ninety percent average," Logan says. "It'll be higher next year, when she actually applies herself."

"Hey, for me, ninety *is* applying myself. Not like some people who can goof off and still get better grades than me."

"I didn't goof off this year. I just tried to find a better life-school balance."

Tricia stares at us, certain this is a joke.

"About this legend," I say. "Please tell me the camp wasn't built on an ancient burial ground. Because that shit's just old."

"Language, Kate," Logan says, and his lips quirk again, the two of us falling into rhythms so comfortable that my eyes prickle with grief for what we've lost.

"No, it isn't a burial ground," Tricia says. "The local tribes called the place by a word that means 'The Valley of the Disappeared.' People vanished. Leaving only signs that they'd been dragged off by wild beasts. I've heard the Pack used to live here, which may explain it."

"Oh, what a load of—" I begin.

"The Pack has never lived in West Virginia," Logan cuts in. "They settled in New York state and stayed there. They couldn't be responsible for an Indigenous name anyway, not when it would have originated hundreds of years before the Pack arrived. Though I would be surprised if there was such a name. That sort of thing tends to be apocryphal, lending what white culture perceives as an air of authority to a legend when, in fact, it trivializes Indigenous culture."

She laughs. "You kids today. You're all so 'woke.'" She

actually air-quotes *woke*. I try not to gag. I don't exactly succeed, and she turns to me with "Kate? Are you all right?"

"Tricia!"

Footsteps thunder down the corridor. It's a guy in his early twenties. He doesn't see us, too intent on his target.

"Fight," he pants. "There's a fight. Outside. We were doing a team-building exercise, and two people started going at it."

"Arguing?" she says.

"No, *fighting*. Hitting each other. With their fists."

"Better than swords," I murmur under my breath, only Logan hearing and appreciating it with a smile.

Tricia exhales. "Teenage boys. They're all testosterone and hormones."

"Testosterone *is* a hor . . ." I begin, and then trail off, shaking my head.

"It's not the campers," the guy says. "Well, one of them's a camper. Arjun. The other is Jared."

The guy starts to explain, something about a trust-building exercise gone awry, which is a total shock because I'd completely trust people I met less than twenty-four hours ago. Tricia waves off the guy's explanation and begins to follow him. Then she remembers us.

"Room three up ahead is yours, Logan. You're with Mason. Kate, you're in twelve with Holly. Turn around and go all the way to the end."

When she's gone, I look at Logan, hoping he'll say we can drop off our stuff and meet up to explore. But he just rocks on his heels, as if eager to escape my company. I hate thinking that. It sounds whiny. I feel like whining, though, as if any moment of connection has evaporated.

"So . . ." I say. "I'll see you around?"

He nods and goes before I can add anything. I watch him leave. Then I head back down the hall.

Ahead, I see an open bedroom door. Inside girls are laughing. I should pop my head in and say hello. Instead, I wonder whether I can sneak back to that abandoned cabin and set up camp there.

I won't do that, obviously. Still, I can't summon the energy to introduce myself. My best bet is to slip out the front doors and see whether there's another entrance closer to my room.

I jog to the door, and, distracted, I throw it with full werewolf strength. There's an *oomph* and, on the other side, a guy goes flying. I drop my duffel and scramble to help him. As I do, he peers up, his brow furrowing.

"Kate?" he says. "Kate Danvers?"

I take a better look at him and . . .

Oh, shit.

CHAPTER FIVE

Logan

I tramp down the hall, duffel bag slung over my shoulder. The door to my room is closed. I knock. No one answers, and I guess that makes sense, since it's afternoon and everyone will be at the team-building exercise.

I'm not sorry to have missed that. Kate may be the one vocalizing her objections, but she speaks for both of us. As pack animals, we're all about team dynamics, yet we know better than anyone that you can't build "team spirit" with total strangers in an hour. Trust and respect are things you earn.

My room is pitch dark, not surprising with the complete lack of windows in this ridiculous building. Again, my sister might be the one complaining, but she's doing it for both of us. This main floor feels like a creepy old basement. It even smells like one, musty and unnatural despite the new construction.

My night vision helps, and I can make out two twin beds inside. I open the door just enough to spot a light switch. I flick it and—

"What the fuck?" a voice snarls.

A guy jumps up from the bed across the room. He's over six feet tall, with broad shoulders. Pale skin. Wavy black hair. And a scowl that would beat any of Kate's.

He's not wearing a team shirt. That's the first thing I look for—some hint of his supernatural race. It's impossible to tell otherwise, and from the way this guy is scowling at me, I'd like to be forewarned before I get hit with a sorcerer's knock-back spell or an ice half-demon's touch.

He rips earbuds from his ears. "Did you hear me, asshole? What are you doing in my room?" He squints at me. "Who the hell are you, anyway?"

"Logan," I say, extending a hand. "Logan Dan— Logan Michaels," I amend, as I remember we're going incognito. Not that it'll help much. My mother is Elena Michaels. Still, Danvers is the better known werewolf name, the family having been around since the dawn of the American Pack.

My roommate, thankfully, doesn't figure it out. He just keeps scowling at me.

"Get the hell out of my room, Logan Michaels," he says.

"If your name is Mason, it's *our* room. I'm your roommate."

"The hell you are. I was promised a room to myself."

I toss my bag onto the empty bed. "If they want to move me, I'll go, but I get the impression my sister and I took the last available spots."

"No, you took an *unavailable* spot. Get the hell out of my room."

As my temper sparks, I remind myself this isn't a true territorial dispute. It's just a misunderstanding, and if they find me a new room, I will indeed move.

"This is my assigned bed," I repeat, as calmly as I can. "I'm here until I'm told otherwise."

I begin to unpack my bag, which isn't really necessary at this moment, but yes, my hackles are up. I'm asserting my claim to this particular patch of territory, discreetly but significantly.

"Put your shit back," Mason says. "You aren't staying."

"If I'm not, then I'll repack. Until then . . ." I drop onto the bed. "I was up at five. I'm going to take a nap."

He moves so fast I only see a blur, and my brain blurts, *Teleporting half-demon*. I roll off the bed and onto my feet, and I'm behind him before he realizes *I've* moved.

He swings around and snorts, and I have this image of a bull pawing the ground. I might laugh. Well, it's more of a snicker, which is smaller than a laugh but potentially more insulting.

Mason pulls himself to his full height and advances until he's close enough for me to see the vein pulsing in his neck. I look up into his face.

"Yes?" I say.

He hesitates at that, obviously accustomed to guys backing down from him. I meet his gaze and wait.

He steps even closer, heat rolling off him.

"If you're trying to intimidate me, don't bother," I say. "It won't go as well as you hope."

"Is that a threat?"

"A threat is what *you're* doing, encroaching on my physical space. A warning is what I issued, suggesting that threatening me is a very bad idea."

"Let me guess . . . you know karate," he says with a sneer.

"No, I'm not very good at martial arts."

"So what is your sport?" He looks me up and down and sneers. "Beach volleyball?"

"Yes. Now, I'm going to suggest you back off—"

The guy attacks. Again, it happens so fast I see only a blur. This time, he's too close for me to dodge. Close enough for me to hit, though. And . . . well . . . catching me off guard means I react on instinct, without holding back. He sails into the opposite wall.

He doesn't crumple to the floor. I'll give him credit for that. He stays on his feet, though he is propped against the wall, doubled over and gasping for breath. I didn't hit him in the stomach. I know better. It was a hard blow, though.

He lifts his head. "What the fuck are—?"

The words are a distraction, and halfway through, he charges. I can tell now that he isn't teleporting. He's just really fast, especially for a guy his size. I swing out of the way. He twists and lunges at me, and I can't back up—I'm against the wall. So I knock him to the floor and pin him there.

He's not a half-demon.

I don't know what he is, but something in his eyes sends a chill through me. He's spitting mad, his face contorting, and in that face, I see a fellow predator. Not a werewolf, though. His scent would give that away.

I pin Mason as he thrashes. After a moment, he stops and stares up at me.

"You're a werewolf," he says, almost breathing the words. He struggles up as I back off. "They put me in a room with a fucking werewolf?"

I manage a laugh. "Of course not. I'm a Ferratus half-demon." As the name implies, a Ferratus has skin like iron. They aren't necessarily stronger than humans, but if one hits you, you know it, and that seems like a reasonable explanation.

"Didn't you say you're here with your sister? Daddy Demon must have really liked your mom, knocking her up twice."

"We're twins."

"A multiple birth, just like wolves."

"Actually no, multiple births aren't any more common among werewolves than humans because only the father is typically a werewolf."

"*Typically?*" His eyes narrow as he looks at me. "Oh, no. Fuck no. Don't tell me you're—"

"I'm a Ferratus."

"Twin teenage werewolves. Multiple birth because double the werewolf blood. You're Clayton Danvers's kid." Mason throws up his hands. "It wasn't enough to lock me in a room with a fucking werewolf. I have to get the psycho's kid. This is someone's idea of a joke, isn't it? Lock up the freaks together."

"Freak?" I frown. "What are *you?*"

"Out of here, that's what I am. Not sticking around to get my throat ripped out in the night."

"I'm a Pack wolf. The Alpha's son. I don't kill people."

His eyes narrow. "So you admit it? You're his kid?"

"*Her* kid. My mom's Alpha. Dad's her Beta, which isn't actually a traditional Pack position, but that's what he calls himself because it sounds much less scary than 'Pack enforcer.'"

"Your dad could call himself Tinkerbell, and he wouldn't sound any less scary. You think I haven't heard the stories about him?" Mason grabs a duffel from under his bed and starts filling it. "I think you cracked my rib.

Not exactly the way to convince someone you aren't dangerous."

"You came at *me*. After I warned you. I was quite reasonable about the whole thing."

He shakes his head, and I catch a glimmer of something almost like a smile, but it's clearly an optical illusion because when he looks up again, he's scowling.

"You don't need to leave," I say. "I'll talk to the counselors—"

"The counselors hate my guts already. This is probably their idea of punishment. They think I need an attitude adjustment."

"I can't imagine why," I murmur.

He finishes packing his stuff and strides out. When he's gone, I exhale.

So, apparently, I lasted five minutes before giving away not only *what* I am but *who*. Off to a grand start.

I thump back on the bed and sigh again. When someone taps at the door, I spring up.

"Kate?" I call, hopefully.

The door's half open, and I can see no one's there. I exhale again, this time in disappointment.

Then I stop.

If I want to talk to Kate, I should go find her. It isn't her responsibility to reach out. It's just that she always *has*. Kate has been the alpha in our twin pack. Which doesn't mean I can't take the initiative and let her know *I'd* like to hang out together.

I head into the empty hall. Tricia said Kate was in room twelve at the far end of the hall. I pass the main entrance and then a partly open door with girls' voices wafting out. They don't notice me.

I continue on to the end, where I find Kate's door

cracked open an inch. I tap on it. No one answers, but I hear a voice inside.

I rap harder, and the door opens at my knock. Something flashes in the darkness, and a ball of flame flies straight at me.

CHAPTER SIX

Kate

When I was thirteen, I accidentally made out with a sorcerer named Allan Redman. It happened on summer break, as these things usually do. Logan and I had spent a few weeks in Portland with Paige, and we'd hung out with some other supernatural kids. Long story short, I met this thirteen-year-old sorcerer and accidentally made out with him.

Okay, technically, the making out didn't happen by accident. I knew what I was doing. A cute guy liked me and wanted to kiss me, and he was really sweet and nice, and I'd never kissed anyone, so he seemed like an excellent place to start. Get past the awkward first-kiss experience with a guy who lived clear across the country. But apparently, if you make out with a thirteen-year-old guy, he presumes it means something. Allan figured this was the start of a long-distance relationship, and while I didn't exactly run away screaming, I handled it badly, and he really had been a nice guy, and I've felt guilty ever since.

So who did I just knock flying with the door?

Allan Redman.

"Kate?" he says as I scramble to help him to his feet.

"Hey," I answer with a too-bright smile. "Fancy meeting you here. And by 'meeting you,' I mean slamming a door into your face and knocking you flat on your ass. I am so sorry. I didn't see you."

"Due to the bizarrely impractical lack of a door window?" he says with a slight smile.

"Exactly. No windows plus a distracted werewolf." I stop. "Shit. I mean, damn. Er, uh . . ." I look around. and lower my voice "They don't want anyone to know what Logan and I are."

"Ah, so that explains why you don't have a T-shirt. You lucked out."

He makes a face as he waves at his bright yellow Team Sorcerer shirt. The color doesn't do him any favors. He's grown up cute. Well, he was always cute, but once you pass thirteen, the next few years put you at the mercy of puberty. He's coming through it very nicely with an early summer tan, summer green eyes, a lean build and dark blond hair gathered in a ponytail. It's the tan that really doesn't go well with the yellow shirt.

"Yeah," I say. "I'd hate to see what color they'd use for werewolves. Blood red, probably. Anyway, you already know what Logan and I are so . . ."

"Your secret is safe with me."

"Thanks." I transfer my duffel to the other shoulder. "I should, uh, probably take this to my room. It was good seeing you. It'll be cool having someone here. And I'm sorry . . ."

Sorry for being a total bitch three years ago. That's what I almost say, but at the last second I manage to divert to, "Sorry for the door."

"You don't know your own strength," he says with a smile and winks.

"Exactly."

I give a little wave that I hope doesn't look completely pathetic, and then I jog along the side of the building. When I reach the back, I exhale.

Well, that was awkward.

I take a deep breath and continue on. There isn't a door on this side, so I keep circling until I find a door exactly opposite the front one. So much for an exit closer to my room.

I slip through and ease the door shut behind me, taking the light with it. My eyes need a moment to adjust to the dimness. There's no hall to my left, which would have let me loop around and bypass the giggling girls. The hall in front of me returns to where I started. There's also a corridor to my right, and when I look down it, I see twin rows of bedroom doors.

A giggle rings out near my bedroom hall, and the very pitch of it scrapes my spine. When one of the girls breaks into a nasally twang, I know she's imitating another camper. The others all laugh. I cringe. At one time, I had no problem dealing with mean girls. After the past month, though, I just can't face them.

Okay, let's head down this other hall and see what Logan—

I turn just as a guy steps from a bedroom. He glances my way. I see only a swing of what look like short braids. Then he zooms back inside so fast I glance down to make sure I'm not wielding an AK-47. Nope, just a very bulky duffel bag.

Okay, that was weird. He must have mistaken me for a girl he's avoiding, and I've had enough awkward today. I won't go that way after all. I turn to face the exit I just came through.

Really, Kate? Are you really doing all this to avoid walking past a room of mean girls? You used to be able to handle those just fine.

Used to, yes. Back when *handling the mean girls* meant sticking up for their targets. Post-Brandon, though, I *am* their target. Yet the girls down that hall don't know me. Time to channel the old Kate and handle this.

I turn and stride toward my bedroom hall. I make it two steps before running footfalls sound. It's the guy who vanished into his bedroom five seconds ago.

"Well, hello there, hottie," he says.

I blink, certain I've heard wrong. "Huh?"

"Oh, I'm sure you've heard that one before." His gaze slithers over me. "However, I definitely haven't seen you before, and I'm really hoping I'll see a whole lot more."

"What?" I can't even manage a good comeback—my brain is too busy trying to process his words because he can't be saying what he seems to be. Sure, I've been hit on before, but this is like watching the "Do Not" segment of a Flirting 101 video.

The guy has a southern accent with a faint cowboy twang. Texas, Arkansas, somewhere like that. He's about my age, and as much as it pains me to say it, he is very fine. Gorgeous mahogany eyes, dark skin, short locs. Even the bile-green Team Half-Demon T-shirt looks good on him, snug over a nice set of biceps.

His smile sends convulsive shivers through me . . . but not the good kind. It's the smarmiest hot-guy smile ever, the sort that says, "I know you're checking me out," when you just happen to glance his way. Also, he stinks. He's wearing cheap cologne at gag-inducing levels.

When he steps closer, I back up. I hate retreating, but I have to for the sake of my gastrointestinal health.

He doesn't seem to notice me withdraw. He's too busy staring as if I'm a double-fudge banana split.

"You are something," he says. "I know a lotta guys want a girl with more curvature." He gestures to my chest. "But long and lean is my thing, and you are *all* that."

"What? No. Just—"

"Have you ever thought of straightening your hair, though?" He eyes my curls with a nose-scrunch of distaste. "It's the only thing keeping you from being a total babe."

"Babe? Did you just call me a—" I clamp my mouth shut as I realize what this is. Negging. I've read about it in books; I've just never seen it in action, and I hoped that meant it didn't really exist, because I cannot imagine any girl actually falling for a guy who insults her.

"My hair is fine," I say. "My body is fine. Everything about me is fine . . . except for the fact that I'm currently standing downwind of an asshole."

He blinks. Then amusement flashes through his eyes, and I think he's going to laugh, as if this is all a joke, some kind of hazing ritual. But he erases the look with another blink and leans back, dark eyebrows rising almost to his hairline.

"You could just tell me you prefer girls," he says.

"What? I don't—" I stop myself. "Yes, yes, I do. If you are the alternative, then for the next week, I definitely prefer girls."

I walk away. He calls after me, "You don't need to be a . . . a . . ." He seems to stick on the next word. He actually gets as far as pronouncing "cu" before stopping himself, as if he can't go through with it. Instead, he mutters a half-hearted, "You don't need to be a bitch about it."

His footsteps stomp off, extra hard, echoing down the hall.

I shake my head. Just when I thought my day couldn't get weirder.

I want to write the guy off as a total douche, but between the over-the-top leering, the ridiculous negging and that flash of amusement, I can't help but feel that I just witnessed a performance. One he'd managed right up until he tried to utter that particularly heinous word and couldn't make himself finish the line.

A performance for *what*, though?

I back up to the guy's hall and take a few steps down it. I look for hidden cameras, listen for snickering guys, search for any sign that I've just been played. Footsteps sound, but they're on the other side of the building. I silently pad to the guy's bedroom and listen, ear pressed to the door. Nothing.

Okay, I officially have no idea what all that was about.

As I turn the corner to my own bedroom hall, a girl shrieks. And there's my brother lying flat out on the floor. Which wouldn't be quite so alarming if he wasn't also on fire.

CHAPTER SEVEN

Logan

When the fireball comes at me, I dive to the side, only to slide on the waxed floor and land flat on my back. I do manage to avoid the fireball, which slams into the wall . . . and drops onto me. At some point during this, a girl shrieks. I'm not exactly sure when that happens. I'm too busy catching fire.

A girl flies out of the room. I don't notice anything about her, still being *on fire* and all. She starts hitting me, and in retrospect, I suppose she was trying to put out the fire, but considering she's the one who lit me aflame, I can be forgiven for shoving her aside.

"I'm so sorry," she says as I rise. "The door swung open, and I was doing spell practice, and I just reacted."

"I knocked, which opened the door." I shake my shirt, now sporting a scorched bullseye. "I was looking for my sister."

"Your . . . ?"

"Sister," a voice says, and I look to see Kate walking toward us. "That'd be me. Sorry, I got a little lost." Kate brushes sparks from my shirt and then turns to the girl.

"Nice fireball. As your new roommate, I appreciate your security sense."

The girl's gaze flicks over my sister, and she eases back as something in her face closes. I glance over at Kate, making sure her shirt isn't splattered with blood. It's Kate —totally plausible. I don't see anything to make the girl recoil, though.

"I think there's been a mistake," the girl says. "I know one of the girls down there"—she hooks a finger—"said she had a friend coming later. I'm guessing that's you."

Kate's brows shoot up. "Uh, no." She looks down the hall. "The only person I know here is my brother. We just arrived. I was heading here, and then I detoured to duck around some girls down the hall. I heard giggling."

"You detoured for giggling?" I say.

"It was the *type* of giggling." Kate shuts the door behind us. "There's a certain pitch people get that means they're making fun of someone. When guys do it, they pitch down." She illustrates with a low *huh-huh-huh.* "When girls do it, they pitch up." She gives a shrill snicker that has her roommate snorting a laugh.

Kate continues, "I decided to skip the *Mean Girls* reenactment. Love the movie. Don't want to live it."

"Good call," her roommate says. "Luckily, steering clear of them is easy. I don't think they've attended a single session. Today, they're waiting for their friend . . ." She trails off and clears her throat. "They're waiting for someone."

"Wait," Kate says. "You thought I was one of them?"

"And you're not, which is great." The girl holds out a hand. "I'm Holly Nakamura, and as the shirt says, I'm a witch, in case the fireball didn't establish that."

Holly is our age and tiny, a foot shorter than me and

half my weight. Her black hair hangs straight past her shoulders, and she's wearing flip-flops and long shorts.

I extend my hand. "Logan. And this is my sister, Kate."

"Logan and Kate?" Her eyes widen. "You're the were-wolves." She squees and then claps her hand to her mouth. "Oh, my God. That was embarrassing."

"Hey, it's better than screams of terror," Kate says.

"Still embarrassing," Holly says. "Paige left a message asking me to keep an eye out for you. I just didn't think you'd look like . . ."

"Beach volleyball players?" I say.

Holly laughs. "Uh, yes."

When Kate's brows rise, I say, "That's what *my* room-mate called me. Right before he tried to throw me out of the room. I threw *him* down instead, and he figured out what I am. So much for going incognito. On the plus side, I seem to now have a private room."

"Who's your roommate?" Holly asks.

"Guy named Mason," I say.

She makes a face. "Ugh, yes. He's another one who's skipping out already, and in his case, no one's arguing. He practically bit my head off when I introduced myself last night. The Plastics down the hall got all worked up, thinking they'd found the camp bad boy. One went at him and . . . They might be bitches, but he was just nasty. I actually felt sorry for her. Then the counselors tried to make him sit through opening ceremonies. I don't know what he said to them, but they decided he could spend as much time in his room as he wanted. Well, when he *had* a room. Maybe we'll get lucky, and he'll go home."

Kate flops on the empty bed. "So he just took off?"

I nod. "Packed his stuff and left, vowing he wasn't

sleeping in the same room as a werewolf. After *he* was the one who came at me." I stop and glance at Holly. "In case you're worried, a werewolf roomie is perfectly safe. The only thing you'll need to worry about with Kate is snoring. If you need earplugs, I have extras."

Kate whips a pillow at me.

I catch and waggle the pillow at my sister. "Way to convince your new roommate you're a non-violent supernatural."

"Kate might be the one worrying about me," Holly says. "I *did* just set you on fire."

My sister grins. "Which means we're totally compatible roomies, considering I also knocked a guy on his ass, maybe ten minutes ago." She looks at me. "Remember Allan Redman?"

It takes a second. Then I say, "The sorcerer you accidentally made out with in Portland?"

Holly's brow furrows. "Accidentally . . . ?"

"I made out with him on purpose," Kate says. "But I didn't realize that, at thirteen, that implies the beginning of a romantic commitment. One of the biggest disappointments in my life. Not the kiss—that was fine. The disappointment was discovering I can't make out with guys and not have them think it means something."

Holly sputters a laugh.

Kate cocks a brow. "You disagree?"

"Actually, I don't. I've just never heard anyone say it. So you made out with Allan at thirteen . . . and then knocked him on his ass for it today?"

"Accidentally. I threw open the door and sent him flying. Fortunately, he already knew I was a werewolf, or that'd have given it away." She glances at me. "Have we met yet anyone who hasn't figured it out?"

"I already knew," Holly says.

"Right," Kate says. "You mentioned Paige."

"I'm one of her new Sabrinas."

Kate levers up. "Seriously?" She lifts her hand, and Holly gives her a high five that's slightly awkward, but if Kate notices, she says nothing, just starts chattering about the Sabrinas. Modern witches have little time for traditional covens, so Paige started a cyber-version. It became a coven for young witches, nicknamed the Sabrinas, after the comic-book teen witch.

As Kate chatters, Holly relaxes. I envy my sister's knack for this. It's not as if she intentionally seeks out the shyest person in the room. She just honestly finds that person the most interesting one. If I try her strategy, it ends up being two introverts in the corner, making really awkward conversation.

"This is awesome, isn't it, Logan?" Kate says. "We haven't met any of the new Sabrinas. I'll have to bug Paige to invite us to the next get-together."

"Sure," I say, and I mean it, but beside Kate's bouncing, I seem even more subdued, and I can tell by Holly's quick glance that my response is underwhelming.

"If you have any questions on werewolves, please do ask," I say to Holly. "There are a lot of misunderstandings, and we want you to be comfortable rooming with Kate."

"Which means not sleeping with one eye open," Kate says. "Or worrying about midnight munchies. We keep plenty of food for that, and even if we didn't, you're not in danger."

"I know," Holly says. "Or maybe I shouldn't say that if it gives me the excuse to ask questions." She flushes. "I'm a bit of a geek when it comes to supernatural races. Half the reason I signed up for the Sabrinas was to get access to the council's library. Which is *amazing*." She sighs and then colors again. "Sorry, my geek flag is flying high, isn't it?"

"They do have the best archives in the supernatural world," I say. "Have you read their copy of Hermann Werner's treatise?"

"Oh my God, *yes*. It's just . . ." Her arms flail. "His theories on the evolution of the hereditary races? Mind blown. It makes perfect sense, but no one's ever explained it that way before and . . ." She takes a deep breath. "I've just thrown a fireball through any shred of cool I ever possessed, haven't I?"

"To Logan, this *conference* is cool," Kate says. "He's all excited to dive in to the politics of supernatural interaction." She makes gagging noises.

"That's actually why I'm here," Holly says. "To learn more about other races and how we can better coexist."

Kate sighs. "You've been hanging out with Paige too long. I'll forgive you for the political stuff, though." She eyes Holly. "How do you feel about team-building exercises?"

Holly shudders. "That's why I'm hiding in my room. I told the counselors I have trust issues and mumbled something about a tragic backstory. Complete lie—I have the most happily boring family imaginable—but the counselors bought it."

"We'll get our own shirts," Kate says. "Team Anti-Team."

Before I can comment, a buzzer sounds.

"Please tell me that's a fire alarm," Kate says. "This architectural monstrosity is about to go up in smoke, and we'll have to camp in actual tents instead."

"Sorry, it's just the dinner buzzer," Holly says.

Kate hops off the bed. "Dinner?"

"That's one team event Kate can get behind," I say.

Holly smiles. "Then let's go eat."

I leave Kate and Holly in the dining hall. As hungry as I am, first I need to talk to the counselors about my roommate. They wanted to keep our racial identity a secret. That won't work. Holly and Allan already knew who we were, and Mason has figured it out for himself. The counselors need a backup plan.

I also need to tell them about my fight with Mason. Confess it, more like. Which is awkward when the reason they wanted to keep our race secret is that werewolves have a reputation for violence.

I weave through the dining hall, moving fast and avoiding the double takes as campers notice a new face in their midst. A couple of guys head my way, as if to introduce themselves. I pretend not to see them. And, yes, I feel guilty for that, but I have a mission, and I can't get sidetracked.

I follow Tricia by scent. Every person has one, and I recognize it when I smell it again. I follow the tendrils and find her at a table with the other counselors. One sports a Team Witch shirt, one has Team Necromancer, and the other two are Team Half-Demon like Tricia.

"Logan," Tricia says, beaming, "how are you settling in?"

"All right," I say. "But I really need to speak to you about something. I'm sorry for interrupting your dinner."

"Not at all." She pulls out a chair. "Sit."

"This is probably something we should discuss in private."

She waves at the others. "We're a team here. Whatever problem you're having, we'll solve it together."

I glance at the table of campers right beside theirs, discreetly pointing out that the counselors aren't the only ones who'll overhear. Tricia doesn't get the hint. She introduces me to her table-mates, and I cringe as they mirror her too-hearty grin. Those smiles are meant to show that they're fine with werewolves. To the wolf in me, though, they look like frightened rabbits, their eyes screaming, *Please don't eat me!*

"It's about my roommate," I say.

Tricia's smile falters.

"Who'd you get?" one of the half-demons says. "I thought the only empty spot was with . . ." His eyes widen. "No. You didn't put him in with . . ."

"It was the only open bed," Tricia protests.

"Mason?" the witch says. "You put him with Mason?"

"It's fine," I say quickly. "But Mason apparently expected to have a private room, and he wasn't happy. He came at me, and I defended myself, and he figured out what I am. I'm sorry. I wasn't expecting to be attacked by my new roommate, and he caught me off guard. Anyway, he packed his stuff and stomped off, and I wanted to explain the situation. Whoever you pair me with needs to know what I am and have the option of switching out. I don't want anyone to be uncomfortable around me."

"You put him with Mason?" the half-demon repeats, as if I haven't spoken. "It's bad enough we have to take these guys, and you put them together?"

I say carefully, "*These guys*? I understand you might have an issue with my race, and I hope that will change by the end of this conference, but clearly you're also referring to Mason. I noticed he didn't have a camp shirt, either."

They start talking amongst themselves as if I'm not here.

I clear my throat. "Perhaps we should discuss this with Mason? Do you know where he is?"

They keep talking. The gist of it is that the half-demon guy thinks Tricia was crazy putting Mason and me together, and Tricia thinks it was perfectly logical because no one else will want to room with us. I'm not sure which is more insulting.

So what is Mason? Which supernatural race?

There seem to be only two possibilities. Yet Mason very clearly isn't a werewolf or a vampire. I'd smell werewolf on him, and he was breathing just fine.

I want to give this conference a chance. I really do believe in the ideology. Right now, though, listening to our counselors bicker, it feels like a cut-rate summer camp rather than a leadership conference. Unless the idea is that we're so underwhelmed by our leaders that we develop our own skills by taking over.

Paige will arrive tomorrow. Until then, I need to be the adult here. Time to find Mason and discover what he is.

CHAPTER EIGHT

Kate

I've decided this camp won't be as awful as I feared. Yes, the building is an affront to all that's good and holy in architecture, and the counselors seem like walking millennial stereotypes, but that's the sort of stuff that'll make a good story later. For now, it doesn't affect me nearly as much as a shitty roommate would. Sure, it might turn out that Holly leaves wet towels on the floor or uses my toothpaste, but I like her, and she doesn't hate me, and that's far more important.

While having Allan here will be awkward, it gives me the chance to apologize and explain and renew a friendship. Given my track record for friendship lately, between Allan and Holly, I feel like I've hit a double home run already. I came here expecting to be ostracized, and I know I've gotten lucky so far, but that gives me strength and hope.

Besides relaxing on the werewolf front, I can already see adventures in my future. I want to return to that cabin for more exploration. There's a mystery there. I know it. Plus there's the legend that Tricia alluded to. Yet another mystery. There's also the guy with the locs—I want to know what was up with his performance. Lots of mysteries, meaning lots of opportunity for adventure.

It doesn't look as if we're going to need to hide the fact we're werewolves, which is a relief. Better yet, it's actually not *my* fault. Still, I'll be quick to take Logan's side and point out that Mason started the fight, and both Holly and Allan already knew what we were anyway.

My good luck rolls right into dinner. It's buffet style, which is perfect for werewolves. I know all the tricks for sneaking a third helping. You can't do that with plated meals.

The food is typical camp stuff. Fried chicken and lots of salads. Holly takes the latter, being a vegetarian. That leads to an awkward moment before she assures me she doesn't mind her dining companion consuming meat. For a werewolf, vegetarianism isn't an option—we need to hunt to satisfy our predatory instincts.

I'm filling my plate when a guy says, "Whoa, someone has an appetite."

I look up and meet his gaze with a level stare. That usually silences jerks. This one grins, as if he's caught the scent of challenging prey. Ugh.

When I get a better look at him, that "ugh" doubles. The guy is a living advertisement for Abercrombie & Fitch. He's blond, naturally. White, naturally. Blue-eyed, naturally. I'd make some snarky comment about him being a walking eugenics ad, except, well, as a white, blue-eyed blonde myself, I can't really make that joke. Or maybe I'm the best one to make it.

I add another chicken leg to my stack.

The guy gives me an appreciative once-over. "I sure don't see where you're putting it."

"Down the toilet, obviously, Hayden," says a brunette in a Team Witch T-shirt, who is clearly this guy's shopping buddy. From the looks of the others clustered behind them, these two are the alphas of an Aberzombie mob.

When the guy—Hayden—doesn't understand her comment, she rolls her dark eyes and motions jabbing a finger down her throat. "Trailer-park Barbie here is obviously a fan of the binge-and-purge diet."

"Hey," Holly says beside me, but they ignore her.

"You don't know that," Hayden says. "She might just have a high metabolism."

Another eye-roll from his twin-in-fashion-sense. "Any girl who tells you that is full of shit. And *not* full of food. Look at her. She can't be that skinny and even *look* at carbs."

"She's not eating carbs. She's eating protein. Lots and lots of protein. Because she's not skinny." Another appreciative once over. "She's fit. Hella fit. She can eat whatever she wants. I'll be first in line to help her work it off."

I love being talked about in the third person. I really do.

I clear my throat. "Hey, I don't think we've met." I balance the plate on one hand and thrust my other at the brunette. "I'm Kate Danvers. And your friend here is totally right about the metabolism thing. I can eat whatever I want because I burn it off shifting into wolf form, running through the forest and slaughtering small animals. It's kinda gross, but if it lets me eat this . . ." I pile three brownies on the edge of my plate. "It's worth it."

Hayden's face goes slack. "What?"

"She's joking," the brunette says. "There's no such thing as a female werewolf. Everyone knows that."

"Uh," the guy says. "Isn't the Alpha a female?"

"She is," I say. "Elena Michaels. Alpha of the American Pack. I call her Mom. My dad's better known, though. Clayton Danvers."

"Holy shit," one of Hayden's friends breathes.

"All the supernatural races in one place." I turn to Holly with a little bounce. "This conference is going to be fun, isn't it?"

Holly bites her lip, hard, as she takes in their expressions. "It is."

"My brother and I are so excited," I say. "Mom made sure we got our shots before we came, so you don't need to worry. We'll be just fine as long as we get enough food." I lift my overflowing plate with a convincing giggle. "Gotta keep the werewolves fed so they don't snack on their fellow campers."

Silence. Utter, dead silence, broken only by Holly's stifled snickers.

"See you around," I say with another bounce. "Oh, and a word to the wise, I hear there's a full moon coming up. I'd stay inside. Maybe lock your doors." I wink. "Can't be too careful."

As I walk away with Holly, I exhale and say, "Well, that was ill-conceived."

Holly laughs so loud half the dining hall turns. She claps a hand to her mouth and then says, "You have a way with words, Kate."

I sigh. "A bad, bad way with them. A way that finds them exploding from my mouth when I really need to keep it shut. Logan is going to kill me. I need to warn him."

I look around to see my brother deep in conversation with Tricia and other counselors.

"Looks like I'll be making a group confession," I

murmur.

Holly skirts into my path. "That seems like a serious conversation, and your brother doesn't look happy about it. Maybe you want to wait until he's alone."

She's right. Logan's face is dark, and whatever conversation he's having isn't making him happier. No one from the Aberzombie flash mob is racing over to tattle—they're all still clustered around the buffet table, watching us. This can wait. I grovel better on a full stomach.

"About what I said to those guys . . ." I begin.

"You were having a go at them. Werewolves don't change with the full moon. They don't kill people unless they lose control from a lack of shifting. Even that's rare because the Pack punishes man-killers, by death if necessary." She glances over. "How am I doing?"

"Very good. I'll have to set that group straight later. Maybe show off Logan as an example of a calm, rational werewolf."

"I wouldn't worry about it. Seems like the girls have already forgotten. They've spotted fresh prey."

I look over to see the brunette making a beeline for a guy sitting at a table. While he's not in a corner by himself, there's an empty seat on either side of him. A guy who doesn't know anyone well enough to join a group, yet his table-mates include him in their conversation.

All that matters to the brunette, though, is those empty seats. And the fact he's totally hot. Which isn't the first time I've thought about this particular guy.

He's the one who negged me in the hall.

"Poor Elijah," Holly says. "Mackenzie isn't giving up until she bags her prey."

"Elijah is the guy with the locs?"

"Yep, and Mackenzie is the brunette you just took

down. She's the leader of that pack you heard down the hall. She's also the one who set her sights on bad-boy Mason last night." Holly pulls out a chair, and we sit at an empty table. "When he brutally shot her down, she homed in on Elijah."

"Another bad boy?"

She wrinkles her nose. "Nah. Elijah is cool. I was struggling with my luggage—I seriously overpacked— and he gave me a hand. Didn't say much, but he seems nice."

"Very nice," I say.

She follows my gaze to Elijah and laughs softly. Before she can speak, a voice behind me says, "Causing trouble already, huh, Kate?"

I look over my shoulder. It's Allan, holding his plate and smiling, his green eyes twinkling. My gaze cuts to the buffet table, and he says, "Yep, I heard the whole thing. It was kinda awesome."

I sigh. "I have impulse-control issues."

That twinkle turns to a glint. "I seem to remember that."

My cheeks heat. "I, uh, I'd like to talk to you later if that's okay. I was kind of a bitch when, uh, we were younger. I didn't mean that. I just—"

"No explanation needed. You weren't a bitch at all." He motions at the empty seat across from Holly. "Mind if I join you two?" He looks at me. "And you can say no. I'm much better at understanding that word now."

He smiles when he says it, but I flush deeper. "Sit, please. I'm not sure if you guys know each other. Holly, this is Allan. Allan, Holly."

She looks up, her gaze rising to his face. Their eyes meet, and she blinks—witches recognize sorcerers on eye contact and vice versa. I thought Holly saw Allan's shirt but apparently not.

"Yep, he's a sorcerer," I say.

She looks flustered. "Of course. Sorry. Just . . . always a surprise, you know."

"Is it a problem?" Allan asks. "I'll sit elsewhere if—"

"No, of course not. Sit. Please."

He does, and we dig into our meals.

As we eat, I keep glancing over to Logan, but one second he's deep in conversation and the next he's gone. I'll catch up with him later and explain what happened with the Aberzombies. For now, I enjoy a very satisfying meal and equally satisfying conversation. Holly is totally cool, and Allan . . . well, I'm reminded of why I chose him for my first kiss. He's as friendly and sweet as I remember, and he makes what could be a horribly awkward situation smooth and easy.

After dinner, it's time for small-group sessions. While the conference is about fostering interracial relationships, they also want to give attendees a chance to chat within their own races about problems specific to them. That's great except that it means Logan and I will be talking to each other. At least it gives me a chance to discuss an issue we might currently be facing after my impulse-control failure at the buffet table.

I go in search of my brother. That's my plan, anyway. But as I'm leaving, I notice Elijah up ahead, telling another half-demon to start without him—the chicken didn't agree with his stomach and he needs a restroom pitstop. That alone wouldn't get my attention, especially when he does, indeed, pop into the restroom. But then I get stalled talking to Tricia for a few seconds, and as I'm breaking away, Elijah is already slipping from the restroom. He casts a furtive look around and jogs off in the other direction. Apparently someone is ducking the small-group sessions.

Not wanting a repeat performance from earlier, I hang back to avoid him. He pauses at the stairs going down to the first level, and his tensing shoulders warn me he's about to turn. I flatten myself into the recessed doorway, but he only glances around. Then his footsteps continue on, past the stairs, heading into a hall clearly marked Staff Only.

I give a quick look around. Then I follow.

CHAPTER NINE

Logan

In my quest to find Mason, I ask a few people whether they've seen him. Of course, I first need to introduce myself. As I slog through the "Hey, you're new? What race are you? Ooh, a secret, huh?" I find myself wishing I could be more like Kate, who'd plow past the small talk in a situation like this.

Two campers don't know who Mason is. Another two curl their lips and say that thankfully they haven't seen him, and then they launch into a speech about what a jerk he is. Clearly this is not a shortcut to finding my erstwhile roommate.

The obvious answer is to track Mason by scent, and I return to our room to pick up his trail.

His scent tells me he walked to the stairs, turned and headed out the door, then veered left. I spot a storage shed in that direction, jog over and bend to check. His trail continues inside.

The door has a padlock, but it's been left ajar. I push it open. This is a more traditional camp building. It even has windows, and I step into a quiet, still space that smells of fresh wood and canvas.

There's not much in the shed, and all of it is new, bought for this conference. Tents mostly, along with maybe a dozen sleeping bags. Presumably there's a small-group camping component to the conference. I'll have to tell Kate. She'll like that.

The tents and sleeping bags have been numbered so recently I can still smell the Sharpie fumes. One of each is missing. At the empty spot, I detect Mason's scent.

I could drop the matter here. If solo tent-camping is against rules, that's no concern of mine. I certainly won't tattle on him. Yet this isn't a state park campground. We're deep in the Appalachian foothills, and if you don't have a werewolf's tracking ability, it'd be easy to get lost. I smelled black bear earlier, and that won't be the only predator out there.

Mason isn't a little kid. If he makes stupid choices, that's on him. But if he's made a stupid choice because of me, I need to be exactly the kind of guy I suspect he despises—the overgrown Boy Scout compelled to warn him of the forest's dangers.

I follow his trail from the shed. As I do, I glance at the conference center. It's as silent as when we arrived. They should be out here, enjoying a late spring evening where they can make as much noise as they want with no one to disturb. Instead, they're locked up in a windowless box.

This can't be what Paige intended. Until she arrives, though, being alone out here is to my advantage. There's no one to stop me from slipping into the forest.

Tracking Mason is easier outdoors where I don't have to worry about someone spotting me with my nose in the dirt. I don't snuffle along like a bloodhound. Mason has followed a rough path into the forest, and I only need to drop every ten paces or so and make sure he hasn't left it. When he does, a half mile from camp, I can follow the trail of broken twigs and trampled undergrowth.

After that, I smell him on the breeze. He went maybe fifty feet off-trail before he found a suitable clearing and erected his tent. Or, I should say, he attempted to erect it. The structure lists to one side, and it'll collapse once he's in it. Clearly, Mason is not a guy with extensive camping experience.

Sitting on a log is the wannabe survivalist himself. He's eating a granola bar, water bottle in hand, his gaze down. When I approach, he doesn't even look up as he says, "Turn around and go back, mutt."

"I'm not a mutt. I'm a Pack werewolf."

He snorts. "Yeah, that's right. You're a werewolf prince. Can't mistake you for one of the plebs."

"Prince would imply a hereditary leadership, which we don't have. Admittedly, we do have an archaic system, though, given that we refer to non-Pack werewolves as mutts, which is meant to be as insulting as you implied. Mom would like to get rid of that word, but there's resistance even among those it refers to. Especially among those, actually. They see it as a badge of honor."

"Did you come out here to discuss werewolf politics?"

"We could," I say as I lower myself to the ground. "It's a favorite topic of mine."

He finally looks at me then, as if to see whether I'm kidding. He catches my eye, snorts again and shakes his head.

"Go away, Teen Wolf," he says. "Is that more politically correct?"

"I'm not sure *politically correct* is the right term but—"

"Fuck off, Logan Danvers. Better?"

I wrap my arms around my knees. "It is. And the answer is 'no thank you.' I understand the request, and I decline to comply."

His face hardens. Then he looks at the forest behind me. "How'd you find me?"

I arch a brow. "I'm a werewolf. I track scents."

He nods, slowly, as if assimilating this.

"I'm sure you realized that," I say. "What you actually meant was how did I track *you* when you shouldn't have a scent."

"Of course I have one. Everyone does."

"Not vampires."

There's a split-second delay. Then he takes a big bite of his bar, teeth bared as he rips it off, chews, swallows and pitches the rest at me.

"Check the wrapper," he says. "One hundred percent plasma-free."

I take out the last piece and pop it into my mouth.

"Hey!" Mason says.

"I missed dinner. You wouldn't happen to have more, would you?" I sniff the air, rise and find a stash beside the tent. I grab one and rip it open. "Thanks."

"That's my food, asshole."

"I think we already established that you're worried about me getting hungry. I don't want to scare you with my grumbling stomach. So, you're a vampire. Interesting."

"Did you just see me eat that bar?"

"Vampires can eat food. They just prefer not to because they have trouble digesting it, being dead."

"Do I look dead? Do I *smell* dead?"

"You *are* very pale, and you have the brooding-vamp persona down pat. If you're trying to hide your racial identity, you might want to act more cheerful. However, you do have a scent, and that stash of granola bars suggests you eat voluntarily, not just to fit in with humans."

"Weird, huh? It's almost like I'm"—he meets my gaze —"not a vampire."

"True. Except you are. Which makes this very odd."

He glowers at me. "I've heard of people being smarter than they sound, but you're the first person I've met who *sounds* smarter than he is. Let me guess. Private school?"

"See, here's the logical conundrum I'm trying to work out. You have a scent. You eat food. Your heart beats. You clearly are not dead. Yet I can tell you're a predator, and the only two supernatural predators are vampires and werewolves. I suppose I might not be aware of some minor predatory race, but that's highly unlikely."

Mason rolls his eyes. "Because you've read the Encyclopedia Britannica of Supernatural Races cover to cover."

"There is no such thing. However, I've read most of the interracial council's library. While I'd never rule out the possibility of a third predatory race, they'd be exceptionally rare, and the counselors know all about yours. They also commented on the danger of putting us in a room together. As predators, vampires and werewolves are naturally wary of one another, but it isn't the historical animosity of sorcerers and witches. I suspect the counselors have seen too many movies if they presume we're natural enemies."

"Or . . . I'm not a goddamned vampire."

"Vampires aren't damned by God. They're just another hereditary evolution."

He glowers at me.

I continue, "Vampires are the only race that other supernaturals hate and fear as much as werewolves. The counselor's comments suggest you and I fall into the same category. Ergo, since I can tell you're not a werewolf, by process of elimination, you must be a vampire."

"A breathing, eating, not-*dead* vampire." Mason shakes his head and pushes to his feet. "Enough of this bullshit." He unzips his tent and reaches in, grabbing his sleeping bag as if to start packing. One of the tent pegs wobbles.

"Watch——!" I begin.

The tent collapses on him.

I could help. That'd be the nice thing to do. But that would mean I'd miss out on the scene of Mason cursing and batting his arms with the tent draped over him. At least I'm polite enough to avoid laughing. Or avoid laughing loud enough for him to hear over his curses.

He staggers about, scrambling to get free, the tent draped squarely over his head. When he heads straight for the log, I leap up to catch him before he trips.

"Get your paws off me," he roars.

I let go. He falls face-first to the ground. More cursing. I helpfully tug the tent off his head. Blood streams from his nose. He swipes it and lifts his hand to me.

"*Not* a vampire," he says.

"Vampires can bleed if they've just fed," I say. "That might also explain the scent. I believe they have one if they've recently——"

"For fuck's sake, I am *not* a vampire!"

"Then what are you?"

He puts his face inches from mine. "None of your business."

Mason kicks the tent aside. Then he stomps to a backpack, hefts it and stalks into the forest.

"Don't forget your tent!" I call.

"It's all yours. I'm going back to camp."

I munch on another granola bar as his footsteps recede . . . in the wrong direction. I continue eating. Mason continues crashing through the brush.

I polish off the rest of the bar. Then I rise, brush crumbs from my shorts and start fixing his tent in case he returns. Otherwise, I'll go after him to make sure he gets back to camp. I'm just not in a hurry. If he gets lost and starts to panic, that brick wall might drop enough for me to find out—

"What the—?" Mason's voice rises, shrill, from deep in the woods. Then he bellows in pain, the sound cut short.

The forest falls silent.

I drop a tent peg and run.

CHAPTER TEN

Kate

Earlier, as we came upstairs for dinner, Holly said the other end of the hall belonged to the counselors. Bedrooms mostly. That's where Elijah's heading.

You messing around with a counselor, Elijah? Technically, none of my business, but you've piqued my curiosity. And I could use a little blackmail ammo in case you decide to continue your weird performance art with me.

He doesn't glance over his shoulder again, which seems odd. He was obviously being so careful before. Yet when my shoe scuffs the floor, he freezes. He turns then, but I'm still back by the stairs, where I can easily duck out of sight.

I'm surprised he heard that. Sound must really echo down here. It's definitely quiet. Also bright and sunny with the skylight ceiling. I'm envying the counselors' bedroom space until I realize that they'll be up at the crack of dawn, blasted awake by spring sunshine. Maybe my den-like main floor bedroom isn't so bad after all.

I track Elijah's footfalls. A doorknob turns with a squeak. A hard jangle, and the door creaks open on new and stiff hinges. Another creak, followed by a soft click as the door shuts.

If he's rendezvousing with a counselor, I definitely don't want to hear *that*. But if I can ID his hookup, that's a pellet of blackmail ammo to tuck in my back pocket.

The left side of the hall seems to be bedrooms. On the right, the first door is labeled Storage. A *thunk* comes from farther down the hall, still on my right. There's one more door on that side. I reach it and read the sign. *Office*.

Another *thunk*, like a desk drawer closing.

Elijah is rifling through the office. Huh. Now *that's* more interesting than hooking up with a counselor.

There's a keyhole, but the door's unlocked. I ease it open a crack. Elijah has his back to me. He is indeed rifling through a desk, and somehow I don't think he's looking for a pen.

As I watch, he finishes checking drawers. Whatever he's searching for, he can tell at a glance it's not there. He's moving fast enough that I don't think he expects to find it —he's just checking. When he zeroes in on the desktop computer, I nod in understanding. If I had to guess, I'd say he'd been looking for papers, seeking information that would be easier to get at than computer files. The twenty-something staff aren't going to keep much on paper, though.

Elijah flicks on the monitor. The computer pops to life with a login screen. He grunts and flips up the keyboard and then checks behind the monitor. Looking for a conveniently placed password.

I push open the door, and he jumps, spinning.

"Found you!" I chirp as I sail in. I waggle a forefinger. "You are playing hard to get."

He stares at me. Then he gives a strangled. "Wha —what?"

I stop in front of him and bounce on my toes. "I looked for you at dinner and saw you with those girls." Another finger waggle. "You better not be one of *those* guys."

"One of . . . ?"

"A player." I pronounce the word like a private school kid who's never said it before. "Hitting on all the single ladies. Because you"—I step closer and grab him by the shirtfront—"are mine."

He backpedals, and I release him with a giggle. "Kidding. I won't manhandle you. Not yet at least." I give an exaggerated wink.

"I, uh, don't understand . . ."

"You made it very clear earlier that you were into me, and I have decided the answer is yes. Let's do this thing."

"Do . . . ?"

"Hook up. Or at least make out."

He arches his brows. Just arches them, an unspoken question that he thinks he knows the answer to, but he's not guessing in case he's wrong.

"Player," I say, drawling the word in my usual voice, that chipper squeal gone.

"I don't know what you're talking about," he says, but his eyes twinkle.

"You played me. I played you back. Now, can we move on, or do we want to neg each other a bit more first?"

His brows knit. "Neg?"

"Flirting with me while pointing out my flaws to make me want to convince you that I'm good enough to date."

"There's a name for that shit?" He shakes his head.

"I've seen guys do it, and I just figured they were really bad at picking up girls."

"You weren't trying to hit on me," I say. "You were trying to scare me off, so I wouldn't follow you and see what you're up to."

One split second of confusion, followed by a wide grin. "You got me."

Liar. My explanation makes no sense, and he was far too quick to jump on it. Interesting. I'll drop it for now. I need more info before I figure out what he'd really been up to with this afternoon's performance.

"What are you doing in here?" I ask.

He shrugs, that overly nonchalant kind of shrug that precedes another fib. "Trying to get online, you know. They confiscated our phones, and I'm in a band, and we just posted our video to YouTube. I wanted to check our likes."

"Band, huh. What do you play?"

"Drums."

"What's in your trap set?"

He gives me this lopsided grin. "Four-piece mostly. Kick drum, snare, two rack toms, plus cymbals. I'll mix it up, but I'm fond of my four-piece. Keeps things simple." A knowing look. "Did I pass the test?"

I give a grudging nod.

He leans against the desk. "I'm guessing you're a drummer."

"I play a few instruments. All the loud ones."

He laughs at that, and his eyes . . . God, he has gorgeous eyes. I step back, telling myself I'm escaping the lingering cloud of body spray.

"I'll accept that you might play the drums," I say. "You might even be in a band."

"I *am* in a band. Comatose Honeymoon. And believe me, I couldn't make that name up."

"Maybe, but you aren't sneaking into this office looking for internet access to check your video stats."

He sighs. "You're going to turn this into a serious conversation, aren't you? I guess that means we aren't making out."

"Depends on whether you tell me the truth."

He gives a sharp bark of a laugh. "So that's my incentive?"

"Potential bonus."

He laughs again, his eyes on mine, warm and open. Then a look passes behind them, almost like regret, and he straightens. "As tempting as that might be, whatever I was doing, it's my business and—"

His head jerks up. I catch footsteps. I should have heard them first, and I kick myself. Apparently, those eyes and that smile distracted me, which is insanely embarrassing.

My consternation lasts a split second before I look for a place to hide. There isn't one. No closets. No back exits. No filing cabinet big enough to hide behind.

I grab Elijah's arm and yank him toward the door.

The footsteps are still a ways off. I peek into the hall. No one's in sight. I push Elijah out and follow, shutting the door behind us. When I turn, he's looking down the corridor, his lips parting in a "shit" that tells me we don't have time to duck out the way we came.

I glance in the other direction, but the hall ends ten feet away. Still, I grab his hand and pull him in that direction.

He resists. "That's a dead end."

I yank harder, hauling him along after me. Then I spin

him around, pushing his back into the corner as I lace my hands behind his neck. We're face-to-face for a heartbeat before his eyes close and his lips move toward mine. When I don't follow, his eyes fly open.

"Oh," he whispers. "You didn't mean we should . . ."

I didn't. I'd figured putting my arms around his neck would be enough of a hint about what was going on, to fool whoever is about to see us. But I shrug and murmur, "Sure, why not," and lift up to kiss him, pausing at the last second to be sure he's game. His lips meet mine just as the person must step into the hall, because sneakers squeak, and a female voice says, "Oh!"

I fully intended to stop there. The person approaching will see us and say something, and we'll leap apart with a fake-startled yelp and then sheepishly slip past her. Except Elijah doesn't stop. He pulls me to him, his mouth on mine, kiss deepening.

The newcomer retreats with a tapping of footfalls. I have no idea where she goes. I'm a little too busy to notice. Elijah's lips are on mine, his breath as sweet as fresh hay. There's a moment where I realize that's a really weird analogy, but the thought only flits past, banished by the kiss.

The kiss . . .

Hell and damn. It's a kiss that makes wonder whether I've been doing it wrong all this time.

His hands rest in the hollow just above my hips, his fingers encircling my waist, and there's a sturdiness there. Again, that's a weird word to use, but it's what it feels like, as if he's planted his hands there, firmly gripping me, to say this is where his fingers will stay, that they aren't going to suddenly inch toward another destination.

I wrap my arms around his neck, and the kiss goes

deeper still. I close my eyes as I swear I smell the tang of grass and trees, taste sharp water fresh from a cold stream, hear the sigh of wind in trees as I smell beyond his horrible body spray to a deep musk that lights my insides on fire.

My blood pounds as if I'm running, as if we're both in the forest and running, and within that sighing wind I hear the pant of a wolf at my side, the pound of paws, a soft growl, the musky smell of Elijah enveloping me and—

Holy shit.

I yank back, breaking the kiss, and I stare into his eyes. I blink. Then before he can react, I bury my nose in the crook of his neck, inhale sharply and breathe, "Werewolf."

CHAPTER ELEVEN

Logan

I run in the direction of Mason's bellow. I've been shouting for him, but I've heard nothing.

Nothing at all.

It must be an animal attack. A bear, because I can't imagine anything else out here big enough to hurt him into silence. No, that's not true. The even more likely answer is human. I'm just struggling to wrap my head around that because these woods feel so empty.

Nick had driven miles down an empty road. On the mile walk to camp, we saw no sign of anyone else out here.

If it *is* a person who attacked Mason, what could they have done to make him cry out in pain and then fall silent? I'd have heard a gunshot. If he was attacked with another kind of weapon, I should have heard more. A single blow could knock him out, but he wouldn't have had time to bellow in pain first.

A bear doesn't seem like the answer, either. Any animal attack, again, would take longer. Mason's bigger than me. A three-hundred-pound black bear *could* kill him, but not so quickly.

So what—

I brake suddenly, and my feet twist. In a year, I've shot up four inches and put on thirty pounds. Operating my new body is like playing a familiar video game with a new controller. Just when I think I've gotten the hang of it, I try to stop and nearly trip over my own feet. I drop to one knee before I catch myself, poised there in a sprinter's starting position, hands on the ground as I lift my nose to sample the air, and when I don't smell him, my eyes narrow.

I stopped because I've realized the answer to my problem. There's no logical solution to the puzzle of what attacked him. The answer, then, is "nothing." *Nothing* attacked him.

Mason is playing me.

What I heard was horror-movie fodder. An exclamation. A scream cut short as the monster rips out its victim's heart.

Mason strode into the forest and enacted a horror-movie sudden-death scene, one guaranteed to bring any decent person running. I've already proven I'd fall for it, having tracked him into the woods to make sure he's okay. Such a chump. Easy prey for an asshole like Mason.

Whatever Mason's plan, I'm prepared, and I'm going to flip this on him. He's the one who'll learn a lesson.

I should Change forms. Give him a real scare. Show him exactly what kind of risk he takes by threatening me.

As I realize what I'm thinking, I stop short. Sure, Change forms and then if he attacks, I'll defend myself with fangs and claws. Lethal fangs and claws.

I shiver and fight against the rage pulsing through me.

If I'm this angry now, I definitely can't afford to Change. I need to rein in my temper and confront Mason . . . as a human.

I rise, rolling my shoulders as I slough off my anger. I sniff the air again. There is a faint scent of Mason that I missed before. That scent means he *was* ahead of me, not that he's still there. Scent works like . . . well, I remember seeing old Charlie Brown comics, and there's this character called Pigpen drawn in a constant floating cloud of dirt. That's us, except the "cloud" is hair, dead skin, even breath particles, all of it laden with scent. Our scent floats downwind on the breeze. Once we walk away, it lingers there before drifting to the ground where it leaves a trail. I still smell Mason faintly on the wind, which means he *was* here but no longer is as his scent settles to the ground.

I move forward with extreme care, tracking those tendrils of scent while looking and listening for anything that shouldn't be in this forest. I resist the temptation to drop to my knees and sniff—that makes me an easy target. After about a hundred paces, I can no longer smell him. I've overshot. Somewhere nearby he veered off, probably after he cried out.

Now comes the tricky part where I *do* need to sniff-check the ground. His scent's too faint in the air to figure out exactly where he turned. I back up a few steps and look around. I'm in a small clearing, which makes this easier—I can see he isn't within attacking distance.

I do a weird crouch walk, head bobbing up like a prairie dog's, as I check left and right for attack. I listen, too, even more than I look, my ears straining.

It's oddly silent here. Disquietingly so. People say the forest is quiet, but that's just because they aren't really listening. There's always noise, birds chirping, animals scampering. Right now, even the light breeze seems to have died, and it is unnervingly still.

A predator is near.

That's what silence means. The birds and the animals hold their breath, waiting for the danger to pass.

Mason is near.

He's a vampire. He can scoff at me for drawing what seems like a ridiculous conclusion, but it's the only one that fits. I have eliminated the impossible, so my conclusion, however improbable, must be the truth. This silence only supports it. The clearing was quiet even before I entered, meaning another predator preceded me.

I find the spot where Mason's trail ends. Then I hit a problem. It doesn't go anywhere. He walked this far and stopped.

He must have retraced his steps. He knows I can track him, so he's wisely backed up.

After fifty feet, I realize I'm mistaken. There is no way Mason perfectly backtracked that far over his own trail. It's like drawing a line, taking the paper away, and trying to draw the exact same line again. There will be deviations. Yet this trail runs straight.

I return to where it stopped, and I sniff around, but his trail literally stops dead. I squint up. The nearest overhanging branch is ten feet to my left and another ten off the ground. No supernatural could spring into the air and grab it.

There are other scents. Deer, rabbits, fox and other small animals. No bear, though. No humans. Nothing spooked Mason. He stopped, let out an exclamation and a bellow of pain and then vanished.

Was I wrong about his supernatural type? I'd wondered earlier whether he could be a teleporting half-demon. That would explain the quick movements in our room. It would also explain this. He stops, screams for my benefit and then teleports.

Most supernaturals come into their powers post-puberty. For spellcasters, their powers kick in right around that time, and by our age, trained ones can cast decent spells, like Holly with her fireball. Necromancers start seeing ghosts around the same age. Werewolves are slower, with their secondary skills ramping up in adolescence and then culminating with their first Change around adulthood. Half-demons show sporadic power bursts in their early teens, but it's a slow build. Which is the long way of saying that if Mason is a teleporting half-demon, he can't have gone far.

There are three levels of teleporting half-demons, depending on their demon sire. At the lowest level, your dad was just some minor demon, probably not even in our records. At the highest level—an Abeo—your father was a lord demon. Even those guys aren't exactly transporting themselves halfway around the world. The lowest level—and most common subtype—can move a couple of feet, which sounds useless but makes them really hard to catch and hold. Demonology is a fascinating subject, and as may be obvious, I can go on about it at length.

The short version is that, at best, Mason could teleport fifty feet once he reached his full strength.

I hunt in ever-widening circles around his last-known point. Five feet, then ten, then twenty, and when I hit forty, I know something's wrong. There's no way a teenage half-demon teleported this far.

When I'm fifty feet away from the point of origin, I smell blood. I go still and sample the air.

It's definitely blood. Enough that I can smell it upwind.

I also smell Mason.

I lunge, ready to run. Then I pull up short, which makes me feel like the biggest asshole ever, but I don't trust the guy. So I proceed at a quick walk, surveying while listening and sniffing.

I see and hear nothing. I smell blood, though, and I smell Mason, the smell coming stronger until I spot Mason lying flat on his back in another clearing.

I stop, my breath coming fast as I gulp deep breaths to calm down.

It could be a trick.

It's probably a trick.

Be careful.

I approach one step at a time. At first, all I can see is a figure lying on the ground, almost hidden by the tall grass. It's the smell that tells me who it is. I spot swatches of clothing and sneakers pointed at the sky, telling me he's lying supine.

It's not until I'm barely a few feet away that I see the blood.

Blood covers his face and soaks his shirt, and I know then this is no trick. He's lying flat on his back, eyes closed, face and clothing covered in blood.

I race over and drop beside him. My hands fly to his neck, and I can't find a pulse. I know there was one earlier. Now there is not. No pulse. No heartbeat. No breathing.

Mason mocked me earlier for calling him a vampire when he was very obviously alive.

He isn't anymore.

CHAPTER TWELVE

Kate

"Werewolf," I breathe, the word coming on an exhale as I step back from Elijah. "You're a werewolf."

"Uhh . . ." He rubs a hand over his face as if still dazed from the kiss.

"That's why you're using that god-awful body spray. To cover your scent." I back up another step. "I saw you earlier, before we met. You walked out of your room, spotted me and bolted back inside. You recognized me. Then you sprayed on that shit and strolled out to make an impression—the kind of impression designed to send me running the other way every time I saw you."

"Uhh . . ." He glances down at his shirt, points at it and offers a weak, "Team Half-Demon?"

I sock him in the arm, hard enough to make him yelp. "That's how you heard the counselor coming before I did. That's how you heard me when I thought I was being quiet. And you broke open the office door, didn't you? It wasn't conveniently unlocked."

"Uhh . . ."

"Great. Just great. Logan and I are here to prove werewolves aren't muscle-bound brutes, and you are not going to help the cause. Can you say anything other than 'uhh'?"

He hesitates and then thrusts out a hand. "I'm Elijah."

"The werewolf."

"I don't usually introduce myself like that but . . ." He leans against the wall, all practiced nonchalance. "No law against being a werewolf."

"How about the one against misrepresenting yourself to Pack?"

His eyes roll. "No such thing. Nice try, though. I know the Laws, and I've never even bent one."

"Sure, because you haven't started Changing yet."

Those mahogany eyes narrow, as if I've insulted him.

"Your werewolf scent is faint. You'll notice mine is strong. I've been Changing since I was nine."

He crosses his arms. "Not possible."

I shrug. "I'm a prodigy. Now, about hiding from me . . . ?"

"I wasn't hiding. I was avoiding putting myself in the crosshairs of a Pack wolf, for the same reason I won't drive my mom's BMW. After getting pulled over twice in the first month, I decided it wasn't worth the hassle."

"If you don't cause trouble, we don't hassle you. If you've heard otherwise, then I'd appreciate the chance to clear that up. Right now, though, the problem is that you're misrepresenting yourself to the camp, too, pretending to be a half-demon. Let me guess: you told them you just haven't come into your powers yet."

"Technically true. I knew they wouldn't let in a were-wolf, so I lied, which is also not against Pack Law."

"Why are you here at all?"

He shrugs, leans against the wall again. "It seemed

cool. I thought it'd be nice to spend a week in the forest especially when I'm so close to my first Change."

"You do not want to be alone for that."

A laugh sounds from down near the dining hall.

"We should move this conversation outside," I say. "Better yet, help me find my brother, and we'll talk together."

"Or you can just drop the matter and let me go back to what I was doing."

"The computer is password protected. Unless you're a hacker . . ." I catch his expression. "You're a hacker."

"A game designer. With a little bit of hacking know-how."

"Well, you won't crack that password before the small group sessions break. I might be able to get you access to that computer another way—after you tell me why you want it. Now, let's go find my brother."

"And if I say no?"

I grab him by the T-shirt and start walking.

"I can slip out of the shirt," he says as he lets me drag him along.

"Please do," I say. "I'd appreciate the scenery."

He chokes on a laugh. "You are not what I expected, Kate Danvers."

"Less judging. More moving."

Logan isn't in his room. The scent pattern outside the door suggests he returned recently and left again. At that point, my hunt is delayed by Elijah, who wants to know how I can tell the scent is new.

"Your dad isn't in the picture, I presume?" I say.

He tenses, eyes darkening as his voice chills. "What

makes you presume that?"

"Tracking scents is the kind of thing your father should have taught you, so I'm guessing he didn't stick around. He wouldn't be the first werewolf to do that. It's against the Laws, though. If you father a son, you can't let him grow up without knowing what he is. What'd he do, send you a letter? We had a Pack member whose dad did that. Asshole move if you ask me."

He tenses again, but this time, his voice doesn't chill. "My father told me what I am, but he wasn't around to teach me. He died when I was five."

I rise, wiping my hands on my jeans. "Shit. I'm sorry."

"He knew it was coming, so he wrote notes explaining everything I'd need for when I got older. My mom and I were prepared."

"Your mom knew what he was?"

"Yes, and before you say it, he knew that was against the Laws. He didn't tell her. He was shot while in wolf form. Someone found him in the forest and called the local veterinarian, thinking he must be a huge dog. The local vet is my mom. She treated him—in wolf form—and put him into a kennel, planning to call wildlife services in the morning."

"And the next morning, she arrived to find a naked guy in that kennel."

"You got it. Dad tried to escape. Mom knocked him out with a shot of ketamine. Then she interrogated him."

"Interrogated?"

"Mom's kinda kick-ass, even if she doesn't have super-natural powers. No one was going to stand in the way of her solving that mystery. Dad eventually confessed, and they lived happily ever after. Well, happily for a couple of years, and then I came along unexpectedly—Mom figured she was too old for kids. Dad was even older, and when I was four, he started having heart problems. He knew he didn't have much time, so he wrote notes for me and made some videos. What I don't have, though, is access to other werewolves to ask questions about things like scent trails."

"But if your mom's human and you don't know other werewolves, how'd you end up at a camp for supernaturals?"

"You answer my questions, and I'll answer yours. You got the fatherhood one free."

I nod. "Fair enough. You can ask your questions later. First, I want to find my brother."

"Maybe he joined one of the small group sessions. I think I hear them getting out now."

He's right. Footsteps sound overhead, enough to suggest the groups are indeed breaking. We head down the hall and up the stairs. Elijah is making no move to ditch me now, and he follows at my heels as I move fast, dodging the exiting campers, looking for familiar faces.

Finally, I spot one down the hall.

"Holly!" I call as we draw near.

She perks up and looks over. I lead Elijah to her.

Holly looks from him to me and murmurs, "I thought you went looking for your brother. Found something better, I see."

She figures Elijah won't hear over the din, but his enhanced hearing means he does, and he stifles a chuckle. Fortunately, she misses that. I do a quick intro and then ask whether she's seen Logan. She hasn't, but she stops a few people to inquire. Of course, that turns into Holly needing to introduce me, and then people looking from me to Elijah, working out *our* connection. No one has seen Logan, though.

When I spot Allan, I ask him.

"I haven't," he says. "Is he missing?"

"Not really."

"Not *really*?"

"I'm just trying—"

Someone cuts between us, blocking my answer. When the kid passes, Allan waves us down into the dining hall, where we can speak more easily. Getting there makes me feel like a salmon fighting its way upstream. When we emerge in the dining hall, we pause to catch our breath.

"What the hell?" a voice says.

The brunette from earlier springs from the hallway crush. Mackenzie. Two of her hangers-on trail after her, both fixing me with self-satisfied smirks.

"What. The. Hell," Mackenzie repeats, because obviously she didn't enunciate dramatically enough the first time.

The question seems to be directed at me. Is she wondering why I'm still here after I've revealed I'm actually a ravenous killing machine?

She strides over and plants herself in front of Elijah instead. Then she looks from me to him and repeats, "What the hell?" her voice rising to a trill at the end.

Elijah inches closer to me and says, casually, "Hey, Mackenzie. What's up?"

"What's up is that I just overheard Tricia telling another counselor that she saw you and *her*"—she jabs her chin my way—"making out in the counselors' hall."

Allan masks his laugh with a sudden coughing fit. Mackenzie glares at him. Then she crosses her arms and steps up to Elijah. "Tell me Tricia was mistaken."

Elijah shrugs. "Sorry." His arm goes around my waist, pulling me against him so fast I stumble into his side. "We were hoping to keep it on the down-low for a while, get settled in before we let everyone know we're together but . . ." He shrugs. His hand moves around my shoulders, and he toys with one of my curls. "We couldn't help ourselves."

Mackenzie skewers me with a lethal gaze, spins on her heel and stomps off. Her flunkies both give me a once-over and a dismissive sniff before following.

When they're out of earshot, I spin on Elijah. He backs off fast, hands rising as if to avoid a blow, but instead I bounce and squeal, "OMG, Elijah, are you asking me to be your fake girlfriend? That is the sweetest . . ." I trail off and frown. "Wait, I don't remember you *asking*. You just presumed *I* want a fake *boyfriend*."

"Uhh . . ." He says. "Shit. I'm sorry. I wasn't thinking." He pauses, and then looks at me, brow rising hopefully. "*Do* you want a fake boyfriend? It might not be a bad idea. It's hookup central here, and it's barely been twenty-four hours since the conference started. Hormones gone wild. It's crazy."

So says the guy who just made out with a total stranger on the flimsiest of pretenses.

"I'm not looking for a hookup," I say. "Or a romance of any kind."

Elijah grins. "Excellent. Then it's settled. I'll be your fake boyfriend. You'll be my fake girlfriend. Everyone's happy."

His arm goes back around my shoulders. I pluck it off. "There's no one here except two people who know we aren't actually dating."

"Did Tricia really catch you two making out?" Holly says.

"Accidentally," I say.

Allan snorts a laugh so hard he doubles over.

"Caught accidentally?" Holly says with a smile. "Or made out accidentally?"

"We intended to be caught," I say. "That was the point. We were someplace we shouldn't be, and there was no escape, so we pretended to be there looking for a quiet place to make out. And then we ended up actually making out."

"Accidentally," Holly says through sputtered laughter.

"It happens," I say.

"Only to you, I think," Holly says. "I'm not judging. A little jealous maybe . . . but not judging."

"Did I miss something?" Elijah says.

"Holly?" someone says, coming in from the hall. It's a girl I don't recognize. She smiles at me and then turns to Holly. "Did I hear you were looking for the new guy?"

"Kate's brother," Holly says, nodding to me. "Yes."

"I saw him earlier. I ran down to my room to grab my notebook, and when I came back, he was heading out the back doors. I noticed because he's . . ." Her cheeks redden as she sneaks a furtive glance at me. "One of the girls pointed him out at dinner, so I noticed him leaving."

We thank her. Once she's gone, Elijah says, "See what I mean? It's like real-life Tinder here. You can't walk five feet without someone checking you out."

I pat his back. "That's just you. But don't worry. Your werewolf fake girlfriend will keep you safe from raging hormones. Except maybe mine. Now let's go see what trouble Logan's gotten himself into."

"You think he's in trouble?" Holly says.

"No, but we can always hope. It's been a long day, and I am in need of an adventure."

CHAPTER THIRTEEN

Logan

Mason is dead. He's lying on the ground, covered in blood, and he's dead. No heartbeat, no pulse, no breathing. He's still warm, though, and blood trickles from his nose. That's the only source of blood I see. It's a lot—far more than his earlier nosebleed—but it all seems to come from there with no obvious signs of injury.

I've taken first aid. If a Pack brother goes down, we need to treat him until we can get him to Jeremy. Kate hopes to fill the role of Pack doctor one day, but for now, Jeremy is our medic. Kate has learned all that she can from him, and I've sat in on every lesson. Now, finding Mason still warm with no sign of what stopped his heart, my brain switches into paramedic mode. His heart has stopped very recently, which means there's a possibility of reviving him.

I open his mouth and check inside. There's blood here, too, but it comes from a gash inside his cheek, as if he bit it. There's no sign of vomit or stomach bile. I clear the blood, and then I set him down, making sure he's flat and stable.

I have to be careful with chest compressions so, in my panic, I don't use more strength than necessary. Otherwise, I could crush his ribs. I count off thirty compressions and then switch to rescue breathing. Under normal circumstances, someone like me, not a medical professional—would stick to chest compressions and wait for help. But there's no ambulance coming, and it's highly unlikely there would be when I'm trying to resuscitate a downed Pack brother, so I'm trained in rescue breathing.

I tilt Mason's head back and put my mouth to his, and breathe into his lungs, pull back for thirty more chest compressions, and then press my mouth firmly to his, give two more breaths and—

Mason's eyes open. Or I presume they do because I'm too busy to be looking. I see a flicker at the edge of my vision, and then he gasps. I pull back, and he flails, shoving me hard.

"What the—" he says, breath raspy. "What the *hell*?"

Before I can respond, he hits me, his fists slamming into my chest as I'm already backing away.

"What the hell were you doing?" he snarls.

"Bringing you back to life, asshole." I back out of swinging range and glower at him. "I'm not into necrophilia."

He blinks, as if processing that.

"Making out with a dead guy?" I say. "We call that necro—"

"I know what the word means," he snaps. "You were . . ."

"Administering CPR. After finding you dead on the ground."

"Dead . . ."

"No heartbeat. No pulse. No breathing. We call *that* dead."

His face spasms with sheer panic.

"No," he whispers. "No, no, no."

His gaze flies to mine, his eyes round and terror filled. "Am I breathing now? Is my heart . . . ?" He pats his chest, eyes widening even more when he doesn't find what he's searching for.

The guy is sitting up, talking and moving and wondering whether he's actually alive. The obvious answer should be that he's mocking me.

But the look in his eyes is unmistakably terror, and there is only one reason he'd be asking this. One reason he might think he was sitting up, conscious and yet not alive. With that, I get the answer to my question, one I hadn't considered because it doesn't quite make sense. It's the only logical solution, though.

I don't confront him with that. The guy is freaking out, and I would never be so cruel. I'll get my answers later. He needs his answers first.

"Are you breathing?" I say.

His gaze locks on mine again, and his eyes narrow with a flicker of the Mason I know.

"You're breathing," I say. "I can hear it. I can see your pulse from here. But if you need reassurance, hold your breath."

He doesn't do that, but he does pause, getting a grip long enough to realize I'm right. He is breathing. He is alive.

His whole body goes limp with an exhale, and his fingers dig into the grass, as if to steady himself.

"You didn't die and come back as a vampire," I say. "That's what you were afraid of, isn't it?"

He doesn't answer, just keeps breathing, deep ones, as if needing to hear them, reassuring himself as he calms down.

"You're a hereditary vampire," I say. "Not a vamp yet, but you will be after you die. You'll rise again for your second life."

He just keeps breathing. He's not interrupting through, so I keep talking.

"That should have been the obvious answer," I say. "But from what I understand, you don't know if you have the gene until you die. Is there some advance I don't know about? A test? That should be possible with DNA."

"You like to talk, don't you?" Mason says. There's no snap to his words. His head is down, hair hanging as he catches his breath.

"Not usually," I say. "My sister's the chatty one. But if you get me on a subject that interests me, I'll make an exception."

"Thanks for the warning."

"You know you have the marker. That doesn't explain the secondary powers, though. Hereditary vamps don't get any powers until after their natural death. But you have a vampire's speed. Also the brooding. You've got the brooding down pat."

"Ha-ha."

"I believe, having saved you from death—sorry, from undeath—that I deserve an answer to my question. From the way you reacted, you're obviously in no hurry to begin your second life."

He grunts. Then he pushes his hair back and straightens. "Yeah."

"I presume that means yes, you're a hereditary

vampire. As for how you know that and why you seem to display secondary powers . . ."

He sighs. Leans back, arms braced on the ground, gaze fixed somewhere else. "Yeah, I'll turn when I die. Yeah, I'm in no fucking hurry for that to happen. Yeah, I know what I am. A lab rat."

"Lab rat?"

"Genetically modified supernatural."

"The Edison Group?"

His head whips my way.

I continue. "I know about Project Genesis and Project Phoenix. Genesis was about minimizing side effects. Phoenix was about resurrecting extinct supernatural races. Neither included vampires, though."

"Valhalla."

"Project Valhalla?" I consider that. "Valhalla being the Norse afterlife. I'm guessing that branch has something to do with eternal life, which would logically involve vampires. You're only semi-immortal, but it's as close as we get in our world. I know that's one danger vampires face—amateur supernatural scientists experimenting on them to unlock the key to invulnerability and semi-immortality."

"Yeah, well, the Edison Group aren't amateurs. I'll become a vamp when I die, and I have some of the secondary powers now. As for what else will happen? I have no idea. That's the joy of being a second-generation lab rat. Especially when all the first-generation ones escaped before they could be tested. Thanks, guys!"

"You can't blame them."

He snorts and pushes to his feet. "Enough chitchat. If you can point me in the direction of camp, I'll get my not-yet-undead ass out of here."

"Hold on. You were *dead*, Mason. You're covered in blood. What happened?"

"I got hit, remember?" He points to his nose, but his gaze shunts to the side.

"That's much worse than it was earlier."

He shrugs. "Something hit me from behind."

"And bloodied your nose? That's on the front of your face." Before he can respond, I say, " You called, 'What the—?' and then you bellowed in pain. That means you saw something and *then* you got hit."

"I'm fine now, and I just want to get back—"

"To the camp you couldn't wait to escape? Sorry, saving your life grants me an all-access pass to answers."

"I don't think that's how it works."

"You can give me answers or you can thank me. I suspect you'd rather stick to answers. You saw something, and you got hit in the face, but that wouldn't stop your heart. It also doesn't explain why your trail ends fifty feet that way." I point. "And why you ended up dead on the ground over here."

"What?" His brow knits. "No, I got hit right here . . ." He trails off as he looks around.

"This isn't the same clearing," I say. "What did you see?"

"I don't know, like I said. I spotted something flying at me. A person? An animal? It was a blur, and I thought it was you. I turned, and before I could see what it was, something hit me from behind, and I slammed face-first into . . ." He shrugs. "Something. I don't know what."

"Can you tell me—?"

"Christ, has anyone told you how annoying you are? You're a werewolf. Go be the strong, silent type. Very silent. Please."

I draw my knees up, arms around them. "You died, Mason, and we need to discuss—"

"You're not a werewolf at all, are you? You're some kind of shifter who turns into an annoying yappy dog."

"You've had a scare. A huge scare, one that you consider embarrassing. Then you thought you were dead, and your response to that was even more embarrassing, not at all in keeping with the tough-guy persona you're working so hard to perfect. To recover, you're insulting me. I understand that. I won't accept it, but I understand it. If you must compare me to a dog, I'd suggest you go with pit bull. I have questions, and I'm not letting you go until you answer them."

He bristles, shoulders squaring. "Yeah?"

"Yes, and if you'd like to turn that into a physical threat, please feel free. Attacking me went so well for you the last time."

"I don't know what happened. For all I know, the Edison Group planted a goddamn genetic time bomb in me. When I turn eighteen, it'll explode and turn me into a vamp."

"That doesn't explain how you ended up fifty feet away."

He throws his hands up. "Maybe I turned into a bat and flew."

"Vampires don't—"

"I know that. If they're going to screw with my genetic code, might as well give me *one* cool power. But no, I'm sure I'll just become a regular old vampire. You get super-strength, super-senses, the ability to change into a wolf. I get to live alone for hundreds of years, just me and my chalice of blood. What a deal."

I'm opening my mouth as a stick cracks, and I turn sharply.

"Oh, thank God," Mason mutters. "Saved by a psycho killer in the forest."

I creep forward, but whoever's coming is making no effort to stay quiet. I hear several sets of footfalls and the low murmur of a male voice I vaguely recognize. Then someone answers in a voice I'd know anywhere.

"Kate," I whisper, exhaling in relief.

I motion for Mason to wait, and I jog to meet my sister. As I round a tree, I see her walking with Holly and Allan.

I'm opening my mouth to greet them when I notice movement in the trees. Someone's following them. Stalking them. I tense, ready to charge.

Then I see who it is. The guy from the cabin. The one I'd caught watching Kate. Rage fills me, and I charge before he can disappear into the forest again.

"Logan," Kate says, grinning. Then she sees my face. "Uh, Lo?"

I tear past her. The guy freezes. He wheels, as if to flee, and I leap, taking him down.

CHAPTER FOURTEEN

Kate

I'm tracking Logan through the forest. As I do, I give Elijah a few tips. At one time, no Pack wolf would have helped an outsider, even one as young as Elijah. In fact, Pack wolves used to hunt them for sport. Ah, the good old days, when werewolves really did earn their rep as brutal thugs.

The Pack hasn't done anything like that in decades. We're always on the lookout for good recruits, especially someone like Elijah, young and lacking werewolf-family ties. So in helping him, I might be cracking open the door to recruitment. Either way, answering his questions is the right thing to do. The Pack won't offer a lifetime of free wolf-tech support—you gotta sign up for that—but we're the experts. The more Elijah knows about werewolf life, the less likely he is to get into trouble in the future.

As I track, it quickly becomes apparent why Logan is out here. He's following his cranky roommate. I have to sigh at that. From everything I heard, the guy is a total douche, but that won't stop Logan from worrying that he's driven his roommate into the cold, heartless forest, where he'll be devoured by rabid foxes.

Elijah wonders whether it was the other way around— the roommate followed Logan, who might have just headed out for a post-dinner stroll through the woods.

"That Mason guy isn't just a jerk," Elijah says. "He's creepy. I got seriously bad vibes from him. Made my hackles rise."

I point out that the roommate's trail seems older, and I show Elijah how to tell that. Allan and Holly wander off to check out a flowering tree. I'd follow, but Elijah holds me back with questions.

Once they're gone, Elijah says, "Are you really okay with the fake-girlfriend ruse? I realize I screwed up back there, springing it on you, and I get the impression maybe you and Allan . . ."

"We made out a few times."

"Uh . . ."

"We were thirteen. I haven't seen him since, so this is a little awkward, but he's being cool about it, and I really am fine with the fake-boyfriend thing. Like I said, I'm not looking for a real one. I'll take the make-out sessions, though."

"Uh . . ."

I sock his arm. "I'm kidding. I'm not going to insist on quasi-sexual favors in return for helping you. I'm told that's wrong."

He laughs and shakes his head. "You are . . ."

"So awesome I render you speechless? Thank you."

"We are going to need to do more than just *say* we're dating, though, so . . . if you really are on board with . . . the rest."

"The occasional semipublic make-out scene? I'm there. Also for any necessary practice sessions."

He smiles and opens his mouth to say something, but I see Holly and Allan ahead, deep in whispered conversation. Holly notices us and stops talking. Allan opens his mouth, spots us and closes it. He smiles, and it's an easy smile, but I can tell we've inadvertently interrupted a private conversation. Nothing flirtatious—I don't catch any hints of that between them—but definitely not for our ears. Spellcaster stuff, I guess.

The four of us continue walking, and I am relaxed in a way I haven't been in years, at least not outside my Pack. I'm with people who know what I am, and I'm being my weird self, and they're cool with it. Add in the fact that I'm walking through the forest as evening falls, drinking in the smells and sounds of unexplored territory, and I am giddy with joy.

The only thing that would make things even better would be if I can convince Logan to sneak out for a run tonight. We could invite Elijah along. He can't Change, obviously, but if he doesn't know other werewolves and his dad died when he was five, it would help him to see us in wolf form and know what to expect. It would also help to see us willingly Change when we don't have to—proof that as hellish as the transformation is, it's worth the pain.

Logan will agree to let Elijah come along. My brother is all about education, and no one is more generous or patient. He'll enjoy meeting Elijah, and I'm sure they'll get along. Everyone gets along with Logan.

I'm already planning the excursion when I hear my brother's voice. He's talking to another guy, presumably Mason. As I change direction, Elijah says, "I'm going to detour here for a sec. Gotta take care of some business."

"Trees need watering?" I say.

He chuckles. "Exactly."

"Catch up, then."

We keep going. Allan says something, and Logan must hear him. He appears through the trees, jogging our way. I lift a hand in greeting. Logan slows, as if he's not sure it's us. Then he breaks into a run.

"Logan," I say. Then I see his face, hard with rage as he barrels toward us. I stop short. "Lo?"

He tears past me. I'm trying to figure out what's wrong when I see Elijah walking toward us. He stops, his gaze fixed on Logan, his mouth opening.

Logan lunges at Elijah.

"Logan!" I shout.

My brother knocks Elijah to the ground. I race over. Elijah lies there, winded, staring up with a gasped "Wha—?"

"I saw you this morning," Logan growls. "Hiding in the woods by that cabin. Spying on my sister. Now you're stalking her?"

"Whoa!" I say. "No, he's with us, Lo."

Logan's head swings my way, mouth opening. Then he stops. His head drops closer to Elijah, and he inhales.

"Werewolf?" His hand bunches the front of Elijah's T-shirt. "You're a *werewolf*?"

"What?" Allan says. "No, Elijah's a half-demon."

"The shirt is a lie," I say. "Yes, he's a werewolf. I brought him to introduce—"

Logan hauls Elijah to his feet before I can finish. "You're a werewolf, and you're stalking my sister?"

"Logan," I say sharply, "he's with us."

My brother's face only hardens more. "Now maybe, but he wasn't when I saw him at the cabin."

I frown at Elijah. "You were at the cabin? Ah, okay, that makes sense. You didn't recognize me at a glance. You'd seen me earlier."

I turn to Logan. "He's not stalking me. I kinda stalked him—figuring out what he was up to after dinner. I discovered he's a werewolf, and he's going to explain why he's here, but I wanted to find you first. Now, please let him go. The caveman-brother routine really doesn't suit you."

"Yes," Elijah says, though gritted teeth. "The fact I'm not fighting is a sign of respect, not submission. If you want to throw down, just say the word."

Logan actually hesitates, and I say, "Lo!"

My brother grumbles as he releases Elijah, who mutters, "Well, someone's trying to fill Clay Danvers's shoes. Here's a tip. Try talking first. If that fails, *then* toss your weight around. Some werewolves do understand the concept of civil conversation."

Logan only grunts, and I try not to stare at him. Elijah is right. Logan's acting like Dad, and that's not my brother, at all.

I shake it off and peer at the clearing where I'd heard Logan. "Were you talking to Mason, the ex-roomie?"

"Yeah, he's . . ." Logan turns to the empty clearing. When he realizes Mason has fled, his sigh sounds more like himself. No snarl of anger. No cursing. Just a put-upon sigh.

"That's what I get for saving his life, apparently," Logan says, and then calls into the emptiness. "You're welcome!"

"Saved . . . ?" I say. "What?"

Logan waves a hand toward the empty clearing. "Something happened. Mason's heart stopped. I found him without vital signs, so I conducted CPR."

"You saved his life?" I throw my arms around Logan's neck. "Oh my God, that's *amazing!*" I pull back and look at him. "Wait, you brought him back from the dead, and he just walked away?" I head for the clearing. "You guys wait here. This asshole is about to die twice in one day."

"It won't work," Logan calls after me. "He has the hereditary vampire gene. When he dies, he'll come back as a vamp."

I turn slowly. Logan looks around at the others, staring at him.

"Uh, yeah," Logan murmurs. "That probably wasn't my secret to share. I'd appreciate it if you didn't let him know I tattled."

"You save the guy from early vamp-hood and he walked away. Now you're worried about pissing him off?" I turn to Elijah. "Elijah? Forget the guy who just knocked you down. Meet my real brother."

I expect Logan to smile, maybe a little sheepishly, but he looks uncomfortable. I hurry on. "Okay, so vamp-boy is gone, and we're all grateful for that. He did not strike me as the life of the party."

Elijah mutters, "Guess I know why he made my hackles rise."

"Yep," I say. "Mr. Predator Competitor. It's instinct. Now, since he's gone, on to the question of you, starting with why you're here."

Elijah sighs. "It's a long story."

"Good thing we aren't in a hurry, then." I plunk down on the grass. "It's a gorgeous night for campfire tales. I don't suppose anyone brought a lighter."

"I have fireballs," Holly says.

"And I'm going to be the responsible one," Allan says,

"and point out that if we build a fire, the counselors will see smoke, and we'll all catch shit."

"Spoilsport." I point at Elijah. "You. Sit. Talk."

CHAPTER FIFTEEN

Kate

Elijah lowers himself beside me, his fingers grazing mine as I lean back on my arms. It's only a quick and unintentional brush, but Logan notices, and his eyes narrow. Even after Elijah is settled in—with his hand a good six inches from mine—Logan mentally measures the distance like a teacher at a middle-school dance.

I lean over and lay my head on Elijah's shoulder. Logan's eyes narrow even more, and I have to chuckle at that.

"Get used to it, Lo," I say. "Elijah and I need to practice our public displays of affection. I've agreed to be his fake girlfriend for the remainder of the camp."

"What?" Logan says, and there's genuine outrage in his voice, which is adorable.

"So, Elijah," I say. "You're at this conference, posing as a half-demon because . . ."

"Because werewolves weren't invited."

My look tells him that isn't an answer to the actual question.

He continues, "When my dad died, he left a couple of

names for me. Two werewolves who might be able to help once I grew up. One's dead. The other blew me off but had a friend who heard about my situation and got in touch. He wasn't looking to play werewolf Big Brother. I've discovered werewolves aren't exactly the most helpful race, which is why I really do appreciate you giving me those tips, Kate."

"*Pack* werewolves can be plenty helpful," I say. "That's the point of being in one."

Elijah doesn't get the recruitment hint, but Logan does, and his eyes darken with fresh outrage.

Really, Lo? Aren't you the one who always takes Mom's side about wanting a bigger Pack . . . while I'm with Dad for keeping our borders tight?

Maybe he thinks I'm going to extend an invitation a few hours after meeting a new werewolf. Sure, Elijah's hot, and he's an amazing kisser, but I don't think Mom will accept those as recruitment qualifications.

"Well, I do appreciate it," Elijah says. "My dad wasn't exactly a fan of the Pack."

"Let me guess," Logan says. "He got his ass kicked for breaking the Laws, and he told you stories about how it was all a big mistake, the Pack bullies throwing their weight around."

"No," Elijah says, his voice chilling. "My father never had any run-ins with the Pack. But they were responsible for the death of someone he cared about. Someone who did not deserve it. At all."

"Older wolves have good reasons for not trusting us," I say quickly. "The Pack did some nasty shit back in the day. So, you had contact with another werewolf who didn't want to mentor you . . ."

"Yeah, but he gave me the name of this half-demon he

knew. He thought she might be able to help. She offered to put me in touch with the Pack, but I said hell no. We talk sometimes. It helps having contact with another supernatural. She mentioned this conference because she thought it'd be great for me. Except when she checked, the organizers kiboshed the idea on account of my race. No vamps. No weres. No exceptions."

"Uh . . ." Allan says.

"Yeah, apparently it was just me. Anyway, I *have* been interested in making contact with supernaturals my own age, so she agreed to vouch for me as a half-demon who hasn't come into his powers yet."

"That explains why you're here," I say, "and why you're playing for Team Half-Demon. It does not explain why you broke into the office and were trying to log on to the computer. And don't tell me you were checking your YouTube stats."

"Nah, I just . . ." He shifts, shrugging. "It's gonna sound weird and paranoid."

"I like weird. I *live* weird."

We exchange a smile, and there's a softness in his eyes as they crinkle at the corners.

"Get to the point," Logan says curtly. I frown his way, but he pretends not to see it.

Elijah turns to Holly and Allan. "You guys arrived yesterday, too. Does anything seem different today? Weirder?"

They glance at each other.

"It's a camp full of teens with supernatural powers," Holly said. "You'll have to be more specific about the weird."

Elijah shrugs, looking a little abashed. "Maybe it's me, then. When we got here, it was awkward and tense like any new situation. Today, though, you'd think it'd be better. We'd all be relaxing. Instead, I feel like someone's sitting in a control tower, cranking up the dial. I was saying earlier that this place is a hotbed of teen hormones with everyone looking to pair up. *Aggressively* looking to pair up. Then there's the actual aggression—the shouting matches and fistfights. People snapping over anything. It's as if everyone's looking for an excuse to fuck or fight, you know? I can *feel* the tension. My hackles go up and stay up for no reason I can tell."

Silence. Elijah looks at Allan and Holly. "I'm imagining it, aren't I?"

"I've only been here a few hours," I say. "But we arrived to a fight between a counselor and a camper, and Tricia didn't seem all that shocked."

"It's definitely hormone central," Allan says. "I've been hit on by three girls since I got here. I was hoping it was just my new shampoo. I mean, sure, we *are* at camp. It's like Las Vegas for teens. What happens here stays here. But as Elijah says, it seems *aggressive*. As if there's a hook-up competition with an awesome prize, and no one told me about it."

I glance at Holly, whose cheeks redden. "Uh, sorry. I can't help. No one's been hitting on *me*."

"Because no one's seen you," Allan says. "You spent the entire day in your bedroom. I saw you talking to Mackenzie at breakfast, and then you took off . . ." He stops and swears under his breath. "What'd she say to you?"

Holly's cheeks go redder, and when she says, "Nothing," it's an obvious lie. Holly hurries on with, "I just wanted to get in some spell practice, and I lost track of time."

"Well, you didn't miss much. Mackenzie and her clique were being total bitches to everyone all day. Spoiling for a brawl, with words that cut deeper than knives."

I know exactly what that feels like. I'd rather be sucker-punched than sliced with the tongue of a teenage girl. I nod Allan's way and then look at Elijah. "You believe they're spiking the Kool-Aid with testosterone?"

"Nah, I just think it's weird and suspicious. I've been feeling edgy myself. I was at that cabin this morning running to burn it off. I've heard of experiments being run on teen supernaturals. This would be the perfect laboratory. I don't know what I hoped to find in their files. I just wanted a look."

"There *is* another explanation," I say. "This land isn't empty for no reason. I heard that people tried to build on it and . . ." I flutter my fingers and waggle my brows. "Strange things happened. People disappearing. People turning up horribly dead."

"As opposed to nicely dead?" Elijah says.

I stick out my tongue at him. Allan and Holly laugh. My brother does not.

"Oh, man," Elijah says, leaning back. "Please don't tell me the conference center was built on an ancient Native American burial site."

"I beat you to that line about eight hours ago," I say.

"Then can I be the first to point out that we're a bunch of teens at a summer camp, wandering around the forest at night?"

"It's not night yet. And we won't die unless we sneak off to have sex."

"Huh." He lifts one brow. "In the interest of testing that theory . . ."

Logan levers forward so fast we all jump.

Elijah lifts his hands. "Chill. It was a joke. How about you get to know me before you're all up in my face?"

"Get to know you," Logan muses. "Let's see. The first time I saw you, you were hiding in the forest, ogling my sister."

"Ogling?" Elijah sputters. "I'm not saying Kate isn't worth an ogle, but the first time I saw her, my only thought was 'That girl smells like a . . . Holy shit, that's Kate Danvers.' And then I bolted."

"The second time," Logan continues. "You seemed to be stalking her through the forest."

"I wasn't—"

"And now I find out you've talked her into some kind of *fake girlfriend* arrangement."

I chuckle. "It didn't take much talking. A bit of kiss—" I stop fast, seeing Logan's expression. "We decided it was a perfectly logical solution to the hormone-overload situation. Which is what we're discussing." I look at Elijah. "What did you think of that cabin?"

He hesitates and looks around the group. "At the risk of sounding crazy again, I had a weird experience there. I didn't see the place at first. I was jogging past when I could have sworn someone whispered in my ear. Only no one was there. As I was shaking it off, I turned and saw the cabin."

"A creepy hidden cabin?" Holly says. "Am I going to sound weird if I say that's cool?"

"Not at all." I push to my feet. "In fact, I'm going to use this flimsy excuse to suggest we take a field trip and check it out."

CHAPTER SIXTEEN

Logan

Elijah.

As we head to the cabin, Kate walks beside this guy, chattering like they've known each other for years.

Sure, he's good looking. I'm not the sort of guy who pretends they can't see that for fear it means they're gay. I might *be* gay. Bisexual at least. All I know is that I'm not attracted to people in the way Kate is, where you see someone and think, *They're hot, and I'd like to make out with them.* There's nothing wrong with that. Sometimes I wish I *did* feel like that. At least it'd be normal. But I can't imagine wanting to make out with a random girl or guy. I want to spend time with them first, decide whether I'd like more.

I've reached that point twice—once with a female friend and once with a male one—but the attraction was never strong enough for me to act on it. I wasn't ready for the emotional impact a relationship would have on my life. I need the emotional with the physical, and I haven't met someone worth the time or effort.

But this isn't about me. It's about Kate. So I can recognize that Elijah is a good-looking guy, and I know my sister has no problem checking out boys who catch her eye. That's all she usually does, though. Checks them out, like admiring the scenery. When she dates, other qualities trump looks. But Elijah has her full attention, and I'm trying to figure out why while fearing I know the answer.

My sister has never met another werewolf our age. Elijah seems to think there's something hormonal going on at this camp, and I'd like to say he's full of crap, but it might explain what's going on between them.

What makes me suspect his motives is that he's a non-Pack werewolf, and Kate is the Alpha's daughter. Also Elijah is attending this conference under false pretenses. Maybe he came here with an ulterior motive.

Like what?

I can't answer that. I just know that I don't like him and that I feel like a jerk saying that. When I first saw him, though, I'd had a flash of déjà vu. I know we've never met. I'd recognize his scent. But I look at him, and there's this niggling sense that I've seen his face before. That bugs me.

I also want to know what's up with this fake-girlfriend business. He's charmed Kate into pretending to be his girlfriend, and that feels territorial. As if he's claimed her, and even though it's not a real relationship, other guys will steer clear. Other guys like Allan, who I always liked.

Now Allan's left on the sidelines, Brandon's blowing up my phone trying to reunite with my sister, and she's off gallivanting with this guy.

Gallivanting? I sound like an eighty-year-old on his porch, shaking his cane at some punk sniffing around after my great-granddaughter.

I'm just . . . confused. My sister isn't a heartless man-eater, laughing as she leaves a string of broken hearts in her wake. But first Brandon and now Allan, and I just feel bad for them.

So I blame Kate for that? As if she has a responsibility to like the guys who fall for her? No, of course not.

I don't even know what I'm saying. I'm just cranky because I don't like Elijah while realizing there's no reason for it, and that might be proof I *am* indeed being affected by something hormonal at this camp.

I'm also cranky because he's up there, laughing and talking to my sister, and that used to be me, and I miss it. I miss her. Earlier today, sitting in her room with Holly, I'd felt like her brother again, as if this conference might be what we needed to get back to that. Then along comes Elijah . . .

"Logan!" Kate calls, spinning around. "Did you ever learn the legend about this place?"

"Was I supposed to?" I say.

She smiles, thankfully missing the cranky snap in my words. "No, it wasn't a research assignment. I'm just wondering if you heard anything."

"You mean those stories about the land and why it hasn't been developed?" Allan says. "Sure, I know those."

"What?" Kate says, spinning on him. "We were just talking about that, and you didn't share?"

He smiles. "You never asked."

She hooks her arm through his, and says, "Asking now." Allan lights up, like the sun just turned his way. I glance at Elijah, expecting to see his face harden, but he only smiles at Kate's exuberance.

"Don't keep her in suspense," Elijah says. "She might burst."

"Well, it's not one story," Allan says. "It's a whole lotta them."

"Gimme," Kate says.

Allan takes a deep breath. "Okay, well, most of the land is owned by a mining company. It's West Virginia. There's coal in them there hills. Except, as it turned out, there wasn't a *lot* of coal. So the mining operation was short lived, cut even shorter when the mine collapsed, trapping everyone inside."

"And even today," Elijah intones. "You can hear the men tap-tapping on the shaft, telling the rescuers they're still alive. Only there was no way to get to them, so their loved ones had to listen to those taps, until finally"—his voice drops—"they fell silent. But if you go there when the moon hangs low, you can still hear the *tap-tap-tap* of the miners' ghosts."

"You've heard this story," Allan says.

"I've heard many, many variations on this story," Elijah says.

"It's still a good one," Kate says.

"Never said it wasn't." Elijah looks at Allan. "You wouldn't know where we could find this mine, would you?"

"Field trip!" Kate says.

"Uh, yeah," Holly says. "Field trip for you two. I'm going to hear tap-tapping in my sleep now."

"I'll keep you awake so you won't have nightmares," Kate says. "I'll tell you creepy urban legends *all night*. I'm kind of an expert."

Holly flashes Kate a thumbs-up. "Awesome." She turns to me. "Mason didn't leave his tent out here, did he? I might be looking for new lodgings."

"Oh, you don't want to stay out here," Allan says.

"Not all the ghosts are confined to the mine. There are plenty more stories. The rumor is that an ancient curse caused that mine accident. Experts at the time said the collapse was highly suspicious."

"Because the mine wasn't producing, as you pointed out," I say. "And it suffered a catastrophic disaster. I suspect these two things are not unconnected."

"Fie on you and your logic," Kate says. "Tell us the real story, Allan. Or at least the more interesting version."

"Well, like I said, the mine owners got the land cheap."

"Because the coal had run out," I say.

Kate claps a hand over my mouth. "Continue, Allan."

"They got it cheap because no one else wanted it. Now, legend says that when settlers first came to West Virginia, they found this area brimming with game. The native hunters avoided it. They called it—"

"Wait, I know this one!" Kate says. "Tricia said it was a Native American word that means 'The Valley of the Disappeared.'"

Allan frowns. "I heard it meant 'Forest of the Unwelcome.'"

"Nah," Elijah says. "It actually translates to 'white folks will believe any shit if we stick a fake Native American word on it.'"

Allan snaps his fingers. "Yes, that was it. So the local tribes avoided it because it was haunted. Or, possibly, because it's just one patch of rich forest in a massive wilderness of rich forest, and they found better places to live. Whatever the truth, the settlers thought they hit the jackpot. They settled a tiny community where they began clear-cutting for crops. You can still see the clearing down by the river bend, but the village itself is long gone."

"Please tell me the entire population disappeared one night, never to be seen again," Kate says.

"You've heard this one before, too?" Allan says.

"Roanoke," Kate and Elijah say in unison, and then grin at each other, like five-year-olds discovering they both like the color blue.

"Stories like Roanoke aren't that uncommon," I say. "People discovered problems with the location they'd settled in, often in the middle of a long winter, and they moved on."

"Leaving everything behind?" Kate says. "Even kettles whistling over the fire?"

"First, I doubt early settlers had whistling kettles. Second, no one was around to confirm that kettles were whistling when they left."

Kate makes a face at me and turns to Allan. "Is that what happened? Everyone vanished?"

"That's the short version. If you rush ahead to the ending, you don't get the full story."

"Sorry." Kate motions zipping her lips and then gestures for him to go on.

"The settlers began clearing farmland near the river bend. It was, by all accounts, a veritable Eden. Clean water, good soil, plenty of game and fish. One of the families wrote their adult daughter, telling her to come join them with her husband and new baby. They arrived in early autumn, well before the first frost. The four homesteads were empty. Deer carcasses and fish hung outside, buzzing with flies and maggots. All that remained of the village—"

"Was a single word, carved in a tree. Ro—" Elijah claps a hand over his own mouth. "Sorry."

"Bloody wolf prints," Allan says.

That gets Kate's attention. "What?"

"Paw prints from a massive canine, tracked through all four homes. Prints bigger than a man's hand."

Kate looks at me. "That must be the origin of the werewolf stories Tricia told us." To the others, she says, "She said there's a rumor that the Pack used to live here, and we're responsible for all the disappearances and deaths. We pointed out that the Pack has only been in America for a few hundred years, and they've always lived in New York State. She didn't seem to believe us."

I say, "Also, werewolves wouldn't carefully remove all the bodies while leaving bloodied paw prints everywhere."

"I'm not even sure how that'd work," Kate says. "Bloody paw prints require walking through pools of blood first. Is that the story, then? Four families disappear, leaving behind *only* bloody paw prints? No pools of blood?"

"Wait, I have the answer," Elijah says. "A mysterious man came by one evening, ragged and starving. They fed him, and he gave them the secret to life in the forest, how to become the ultimate hunters. He bestowed on them all the gift of werewolf blood, and they walked out into the forest to live new and wondrous lives."

Kate shakes her head. "Half right. The mysterious man comes by one evening, ragged and starving, and claims he's a god, so they feed him their own son to test him, and in punishment, he turns them all into wolves."

"Lycaon," Elijah says with a grin. "Nice one."

They high-five each other as Holly and Allan stare.

"According to Greek mythology, Lycaon was the first werewolf," I explain. "He was a king who didn't believe that an old traveler was Zeus, so he served his son to the god for dinner because Zeus is supposed to be all-knowing.

Zeus figured it out and transformed the entire family into wolves. It's the basis of the word lycanthropy."

"Wait," Allan says. "This king tested Zeus by feeding him his *son*?"

"Welcome to the weird and wonderful world of mythology," Elijah says. "Is that the story then? The villagers disappeared, never to be seen again?"

"Of course not," Allan says. "They're seen every year on the anniversary of their disappearance, hitchhiking along the nearest highway, trying to find their way home. I thought you knew your urban legends."

More high fiving. Holly sneaks an eye-roll my way, a shared look between the two sane people in this group.

"Anyway," Allan says. "The disappearing village was just the beginning of the stories. Anyone who tried to settle here either vanished or died horribly, as if torn apart by some great beast. At some point, the land was sold to the mining company. After the accident, stories of the curse got around, and no one wanted to purchase the land. It was passed down a few generations until the Cortez Cabal bought it and gifted a portion to the group running the conference. From what I hear, the Cabal plans to build their own conference and vacation center here."

"So we're the guinea pigs," Elijah says. "Making sure the land isn't cursed."

"There's no such thing as cursed land," I say. "You've been mocking Allan's stories because we've all heard them a hundred times. Standard urban legend fare."

"Which doesn't explain the weird stuff in camp," Kate says. "Or what happened to Mason. Or the fact that both Elijah and I heard whispers near that cabin."

Elijah looks at her. "You did, too?"

"What?" I say. "You never mentioned that."

Spots of color blossom on my sister's cheeks. "You'd have listed all the logical explanations and made me feel silly."

Elijah's gaze knifes my way. Yes, I'm quick with the logical explanations but only to open a debate with my sister, the sort of heated discussion we used to love, the verbal equivalent of our tussling matches. When she says this, I feel the stab of it far more than Elijah's look. Did she honestly think I'd mock her?

Isn't that what I've been doing?

Not exactly, but I am tossing a wet blanket over their fire. They're having fun, goofing around, and I am indeed that cranky old man rapping his cane. Worse, I actually am interested in these stories, silly as they may be. They're mysteries to be solved, something else Kate and I used to do together. And now . . .

My gaze cuts to Elijah, as if he's an invader on my turf. Which is ridiculous. She just met him, and they're getting to know each other, and they've connected over this shared interest. I need to lower my hackles and stop being such an ass.

"What did you hear at the cabin?" I ask Kate. I try to sound interested—I *am* interested—but I overdo it, and the lilt in my voice sounds vaguely mocking. I clear my throat. "Whispers? Like Elijah did?"

She shrugs. "Just that thing where you're certain you hear someone, but when you turn, no one's there. I was walking around the cabin, and I thought Nick snuck up on me. I was wrong."

"Because Nick and I were still at the car. Yet someone else *was* there." I glance at Elijah.

Elijah starts to protest, but Kate says, "No, I turned fast enough to catch whoever might have whispered. Then

I jogged around the cabin. I was definitely alone. I brushed it off as a weird experience." Her chin lifts as her gaze focuses on something in the distance. "And we're finally here just as dusk falls."

"Perfect timing," Allan says. "Let's go check it out."

CHAPTER SEVENTEEN

Logan

The first time I was here, I didn't take a good look at the cabin. I'd been focused on finding Kate, and then I'd been distracted by seeing Elijah watching her. Now when I look at it, my gut says there's something wrong. Kate would jump on this as proof of the otherworldly. But my brain looks for—and finds—logical explanations to that reaction.

For one thing, the cabin is oddly constructed. On the surface, it looks rustic, the sort of cottage people with a little construction know-how might build from locally sourced materials. Getting back to the land, and all that. The foundation is concrete, though. While that's common in modern buildings, it doesn't fit for a cabin like this. Concrete means it's been erected as a permanent structure, at odds with the homespun and temporary look of the place.

Yet that homespun look is also an illusion. From a distance, it seemed run down. The wood, while covered in moss, shows no signs of rot or insect infestation. The windows are boarded up . . . from the inside. That's intentional, someone taking care to secure the building against casual hikers who might yank off a board for a peek inside.

The porch lists, making the whole place appear to sag. Yet it's just the porch, which seems like an afterthought, tacked on by a weekend warrior. Even *that* is an illusion, though. I helped build a deck last year, and whoever did this one understood proper construction techniques, which show in the important places while the rest is deliberately sloppy. Like a false face on a Wild West saloon. Except instead of adding a false face to make the place look fancier, someone's added one to make this cabin look run down, not worth a second glance.

"It's warded." Holly's voice comes from around the side of the building.

I follow to see Kate and Holly in the same spot I'd found Kate this morning when I caught Elijah ogling her. And, yes, the fact he'd just realized who she is explains the staring, but in my mind, I still see ogling.

Kate had been looking at the cabin foundation, obscured by ivy. Now Kate has untangled part of that, and both she and Holly are crouched examining the concrete. I walk over to see etchings in it.

"Warding?" I say.

Holly nods. "It's witch magic."

"Because it's defensive," I say. "Historically, defense magic is associated with witches and offense—or attack—magic is sorcerers. That's not entirely accurate. An energy-bolt, for example, can be used offensively . . ." I trail off, feeling my cheeks warm. "And neither of you need a lesson in magic."

"I'm interested," Elijah says as he walks around the corner with Allan. It's an olive branch. I realize that. But instead of relaxing, I tense, as if patronized, though there's none of that in his tone.

Speaking of defensive . . .

Holly nods. "The majority of protective magic is witch. Sorcerers believe they don't need it. Typical guys." She turns to Allan and arches a brow. "Am I right?"

"Uh . . ."

"*Someone* needs to learn witch magic," she says to us.

"I know, I know," Allan says. "To totally change the subject, did I hear you say these are wards?"

Holly nods. "Witch magic carved right into the foundations."

"*Are* they carved?" I ask as I crouch beside her. "It looks as if they were drawn in while the cement was wet."

"I'd say so." Elijah runs a finger down the inside of a stroke. "See how this is smooth? When we got a pool put in, I decorated the border with our cat's paw prints."

"You have cats?" Kate says.

"A cat and two dogs. I mentioned my Mom's a vet, right?"

"The animals are okay with you being a werewolf?"

He shrugs. "At first, my dad couldn't be around pets, but Mom used a few vet techniques to overcome that. The ones we have now were all born after me, so I'm not some strange guy who smells like a predator."

"Same as our dog," Kate says. "She grew up with our scent. Sorry. I didn't mean to interrupt your story. You decorated the pool cement with cat tracks."

"Right. I was trying to freak out Mom, make her think the cat ran around in the wet cement, only she knew it was me. Probably because the prints spelled 'Mr. Cuddles was here.'"

Kate arches her brows. "How old were you?"

"Not the point."

"Wait, you named your cat . . . Mr. Cuddles?"

He mock glowers at her. "Also irrelevant. But I will point out that the name was a joke. No one touched him unless they felt like donating blood. He was *not* a cuddler."

"Shocking, really, when his owner went around sticking his paws in wet cement."

"Back to the *point* of this story. So, when Mom figured it out, she said I'd missed the chance to put my own name in the cement. I grabbed a stick, but by then the cement was almost hard. I spent the rest of the day carving my name in it. All that is to say that this"—he points at the warding—"was done while the cement was wet. Doing it afterward is like chipping away rock. Our pool cement looks like it was autographed by someone named Eliza."

Kate laughs and then runs her fingers over the symbols. "What's this one for, Holly?"

"I'm honestly not sure," Holly says. "I recognize it as a ward, but most I know are general alert systems. Like a supernatural security alarm. This is a heavy-duty ward against something very specific."

"And it was put in the concrete when the place was built," I say. "Drawn in this one spot."

Kate removes more ivy. Then she starts walking, untangling bits as she goes. She continues around the back of the house. Elijah jogs after her, as if following, but his footfalls pass her and keep going.

"It's not just that one spot," Kate calls back.

"It goes around the whole house," Elijah says.

They're right. In some places, it's hard to see the ward with the angle of the falling light. It's there, though, circling the entire cabin.

"Keeping something inside?" Elijah says, as he peers at the boarded windows.

"No." Holly looks around the forest. "This is to keep something out."

We can't get into the house. Or, to be more accurate, we choose not to. Kate or I could break down the door or snap a window board, but that would leave obvious signs of entry.

"Tomorrow," Kate says, when we give up on finding an easy way in. "We'll find tools and come back tomorrow. Pry open the door or a window."

"A polite break-in," Allan says.

"A *fixable* break-in," Kate says. "Cover our tracks, and cover our asses."

"Kate's right," I say. "This place might look abandoned, but that's an illusion. Someone owns it, and that warding suggests the owner is a supernatural. I'd rather not be the stereotypical teens destroying property to satisfy idle curiosity."

"I wouldn't say it's idle," Holly says. "There's enough weirdness to suggest something's going on, and this cabin being warded isn't a coincidence. But I agree that we don't have a valid reason for breaking down the door. Also, night is falling fast, and those wards tell me we aren't the scariest things out here."

"Agreed," Allan says. "Let's get moving."

We encounter nothing on our way back. I'm not sure whether that's a relief or a mild disappointment, like hearing the music build in a horror movie and then nothing actually jumps out. We arrive at the conference center to find Tricia and another counselor walking the perimeter.

"Where were you guys?" Tricia says as we exit the woods.

"Enjoying nature," Kate says. "There isn't nearly enough of that on the schedule. We have a whole forest here . . ." She waves. "And not a single outside activity after dinner."

"Perhaps because we also have a camp full of teens who've never set foot in a forest. We're restricting outdoor activities to daylight hours."

Kate's mouth opens to argue. At my look, she settles for muttering under her breath.

"I'm sorry we were gone so long," I say. "We were concerned about Mason. Have you seen him?"

"Get inside," she says. "You've missed the nighttime snack, so don't go looking for food."

Kate's mouth opens again. This time, I cut her off with, "That's fine. We'll just use our cell phones before we go to bed."

I say it without challenge, but Tricia wheels on me, as if my voice drips sarcasm.

"You missed that, too," she says. "Maybe tomorrow you'll follow the rules."

I hesitate. Then I say, carefully, "If we can just have one of our phones for a quick text—"

"Or what? You'll sic Mommy on me? You might be the Alpha's son, but you don't get special treatment here, Logan Danvers. Now take you sister and your new"—a dismissive wave at the others—"starter Pack, and go to bed."

She stalks off with the other counselor. We watch her

go, and then Elijah says, "Starter Pack? Are we collector cards? And does anyone else feel like we just got sent to bed without supper? How old are we?"

"Not to mention the fact she just outed us," Kate mutters. "If you guys didn't know we're werewolves, you would now. After she was the one who wanted us keeping it quiet."

"That was . . . odd," I say.

Kate pats me on the back. "You're just figuring that out, Lo? This whole conference is odd. But Mom will figure we were having too much fun to call. Paige can settle all this tomorrow. Everything seems quiet tonight. Let's hope it stays that way."

CHAPTER EIGHTEEN

Kate

We split up after that. Logan and Allan head down the center hall. Elijah motions for me to wait, and I do, with Holly, until the other two turn the corner.

"Anyone up for a kitchen raid?" Elijah asks.

My hand shoots up so fast he laughs.

"Figured that," he says.

"I do have food in my room," I say. "In case you're only suggesting a raid out of necessity. Mom doesn't send us anywhere without a foot-locker's worth of snacks."

"I've got some, too," he says. "A box of beef jerky."

"Beef jerky?"

He mock-scowls. "No judgment, remember? I'm a Texas boy. Rural Texas, ma'am. I love me some beef jerky and some chewing 'bacco." He pauses. "Okay, just the jerky."

I look at Holly. "See how he did that? Mentioned the chewing tobacco, and suddenly, I'm thinking the beef jerky isn't that bad. So, how about you? Up for a kitchen raid?"

Her expression says she's reluctant to seem like a poor

sport, but tonight was already enough rule-breaking for her.

"We'll grab you a snack," I say. "And we won't be long. Is that okay?"

"Sure. I'll be reading for an hour or so anyway. It's only . . ." She checks her watch. "Ten thirty? They really do think we're children, don't they?"

"Apparently. I will see you in an hour max, then, and I'll bring snacks."

Elijah reaches for the lock on the kitchen door, and I put out a hand to stop him.

"You can't keep snapping those," I say. "It's like breaking in to that cabin. Not the subtlest way to trespass."

He lifts his hand, revealing a key.

"Ah," I say. "Carry on."

"Hey, I'm a teenager *and* a werewolf," he says. "First thing I want to establish in any new situation? Where's the food, and how do I get it?"

He opens the door. We're at the far end, on the other side of the dining hall. Everyone has been sent to bed for the night, and there's no one even on this side of the building. We tiptoe across the floor—so we don't alert fellow campers sleeping below—but talking in low voices is safe.

I survey the pantry as Elijah rifles through the cupboards. When he's done, he finds me assembling stacks of graham crackers, marshmallows and chocolate. I put them in the toaster oven and watch the marshmallows expand. Then I pop them out before the dinger can sound.

I try to hand Elijah one. He eyes it with suspicion.

"S'mores," I say. "An essential part of any camping experience."

"If you say so." He takes one and examines it.

"Oh, come on," I say. "You must have made s'mores around a campfire. Didn't you ever go camping?"

"Camping is a white-folk thing. There's a reason God invented mattresses, and I don't question His wisdom."

"Uh-huh. Didn't you tell me you'd been to summer camp before?" I hop onto the counter and settle in next to the bag of s'more fixings, building another between bites of the one I've already baked.

"Bible camp, which did not involve the pagan sacrifice of hot dogs and marshmallows to the god of fire." He snatches the last s'more as I reach for it.

"I take it you like them?" I say.

"I'm still deciding. More testing is required." He crunches half of the s'more in one bite. "I will admit I was disappointed by the lack of marshmallow-roasting at Bible camp. And the overabundance of prayer, which is all well and good but could be done just as easily by actually getting out into the forest and admiring the Creator's creations. The staff did not agree. There's poison ivy out there, you know. And mosquitoes. Better to lock yourself in the cabin and pray really, really hard for the whole horrible experience to end."

"Sounds like those counselors would have gotten along well with these ones."

"No shit, huh? In the middle of all this wilderness, and we barely step outdoors. Why not just hold the conference between a McD's and a Starbucks. Which is what I told my mom after that first Bible camp. I'd rather be in the city than stuck in a cabin, staring out at forest I'm not allowed to explore like I can at home."

"You said you live in the countryside?"

"Yes, ma'am, tiny town about an hour outside Austin."

"Is it just you and your mom?"

He nods and puts my s'more stacks into the toaster oven. "She was forty when she met my dad. By that time, she figured she wasn't having kids. She was okay with that. Mom always went her own way. Grew up in the kind of town where there isn't a local vet because folks can barely afford medical care for their kids. Everyone wanted her to become a doctor, but her passion was animals. She didn't want to leave her family, though. So she commutes to a clinic in suburban Austin. It wasn't exactly the kind of life that encouraged dating. She liked it, though, and if it meant no husband and kids, that was fine."

"Then she met your father."

Elijah opens the oven before it dings. "Met my dad, had me, lost him, and kept on going. She dates, mostly city guys that she doesn't bring around. Not stepdaddy material. Just"—he waggles his brows—"dates."

"Totally understandable."

We've baked three s'mores, and we both reach for them at the same time. I grab one and try to snatch up a second, but my fingers graze the hot pan, and I yelp, dropping both. He scoops them up and shakes them at me. I grab for one, but he backs up, and I slide off the counter . . . just as he's coming back to give me the s'more, sandwiching me between him and the cupboards.

Elijah grins down at me. Then he puts a s'more half way into his mouth and arches one brow. I lift up the inch I need to be on eye level with him. Then I take one dainty bite from the edge of the s'more. His brow rises higher. I keep nibbling until our lips brush, and then I kiss him, tentative at first, in case this isn't what he intended. His hands slide down to the hollow above my hips, and he chomps down his half of the s'more before kissing me back.

After the first kiss, I expect this one to be a disappointment. That one had layered the thrill of danger with the buzz of the unexpected, making out with a cute stranger in an empty hall, hoping whoever was approaching didn't realize we'd broken into someplace we shouldn't be. Add in the realization that Elijah was a werewolf, and it's obvious the kiss held an extra something I shouldn't expect to find again.

Yet I do. He kisses me back, and sparklers explode in my brain, firing and popping and writing his name in the night sky. At first, I taste chocolate and marshmallow and graham cracker. Then that fades, and he tastes of things I never associated with tastes at all. He tastes of the forest. Of sunshine and shadow, forest and meadow, fast-running water and lazy ponds. Of the run and the chase and the hunt and the gloriousness of those moments when the human world slips away, when I am a creature whose skin I fully inhabit. In Elijah's kiss, I feel my wolf blood strumming through my veins, rising to meet his.

Elijah's kiss is deep, hungry even, as if he's reaching for something, reaching into me and embracing what he finds there. I smell him, the musk of wolf mingled with his own scent. I feel him, the heat of his body blazing against mine. Yet that hunger stays in the kiss, held fiercely in check. His hands remain on my waist, fingers splayed and as hot as fire-brands where my T-shirt rides up, his skin meeting mine. He grips me firmly, but not as if he's forcing his hands to stay where they are, not as if he needs to keep them from wandering up or down. Just like during our first kiss, the firmness feels as if it's for my sake, telling me his hands aren't going anywhere, that I won't feel them creeping and need to tense, pulled from the kiss, ready for the "no" that becomes a war of wills and boundaries, my body a battlefield.

His hands stay exactly where they are, letting me relax and enjoy the kiss until we run out of breath and separate, laughing softly as we pant for air.

"Wow," I say. "You are really good at that."

He hesitates and then lets out a whoosh of a laugh. "I was going to say the same thing about you. Pretty sure it's not me."

"Mmm, I think it is. But like with the s'more, I believe more testing might be in order."

I'm teasing, but he doesn't need another hint. He pulls me against him for another amazing kiss that only breaks when my stomach growls, and he chuckles against my lips before backing up.

"Making out is very strenuous," I say. "Burns *so* many calories."

"S'more s'mores?" he says.

"I think this requires protein."

"I have jerky."

"So you've said, and you may keep it."

I return to the pantry and come out with a jar of peanut butter. I take two Hershey bars and give one to Elijah. Then I open mine, break off a piece and dip it into the peanut butter. We sit there, dipping and eating.

"You said you have a dog," he says.

I nod. "A shepherd-border-collie cross. Atalanta. Not named after the city."

"Because that would be Atlanta. Atalanta is a huntress from Greek myth. I'm sure you hear that mistake a lot.

Try having a dog named Lagahoo. People come up with all kinds of weird mispronunciations for that."

"Lagahoo?" I grin. "You named your dog 'werewolf'? That's Caribbean, right? A variation on the French loup-garou."

His grin matches my own. "Very good. It is, indeed. Dad grew up in Jamaica, but his family was from Trinidad. That's where the *lagahoo* comes from. Someone dropped her in our front yard when she was a puppy, and Mom decided I was old enough to have a dog of my own."

"Atalanta was abandoned, too. I found her in our old playhouse one winter, and I convinced Dad to let me give her to Logan as a Christmas present. Only, as it turned out, Logan had found her first and *put* her *in* the playhouse as a Christmas present for me. I didn't realize that until years later because I was so excited about getting him a puppy that he didn't have the heart to tell me he'd rescued her for me."

"That's kinda awesome."

I take another scoop of peanut butter on chocolate. "My brother *is* awesome. I know you didn't see him at his best, but—"

A door bangs, right outside the kitchen, and we both freeze.

CHAPTER NINETEEN

Kate

When a door bangs in the hall, we go still at first. Then footsteps sound, coming our way. Elijah wheels for the pantry, but I catch his arm and mouth, "No hiding spot." He hesitates only a moment before realizing I'm right. Once we're in that pantry, there's no place to go. If someone else is coming for food, they'll head straight for the pantry.

The question is: What other option do we have? Only one. I run and duck behind the kitchen island. Elijah frowns, and I know what he's thinking—that it's hardly a perfect spot. But he slips over and crouches beside me, and I whisper a plan.

The footsteps approach. They stop at the door. It creaks open. We've left the lights off—we can see well enough with the moon filtering through the skylight overhead. Whoever it is doesn't hesitate at finding the lock undone. Footsteps enter. The person pauses. I wait for the click of the lights, but the room stays semidark. The steps sound again, heading for the pantry.

The setup of the room puts the pantry on the intruder's right. To get to it, though, they'll step past the island, meaning if they look left, they'll spot us. I track the intruder's steps as I creep toward the left side of the island. As soon as the footsteps pass the right edge, I zip around, and Elijah follows.

We've left the pantry door open, but the person doesn't seem to notice that. When the footsteps move into the pantry, I lean out, just a little, and inhale deeply. I don't pick up a scent, which is odd.

I creep out from my hiding spot. We're on a direct path to the door here. We just need to get to it while our fellow camper is inspecting the snack options. I dart soundlessly across the room. Elijah follows, bare feet padding as he carries his sneakers. I'm opening the kitchen door when I hear Elijah stop. I look back to see him frowning in the direction of the pantry. He mouths something I don't catch.

I wave for him to get over here. He starts my way . . . and the footsteps head from the pantry. I look around wildly, but there's no place to go. I yank open the door and swing out, but that leaves Elijah in the kitchen, and I'm not going to abandon him.

I reopen the door and step through, ready to take my punishment as Elijah says, "Kate?"

He's standing in the middle of the room. And he's alone.

I look around. Then I circle the island, checking the pantry as I do.

"We didn't both hallucinate those footsteps," he says.

I shake my head.

"And we heard them stop right about here." He stands on the right side of the island. "No one could have gotten past you."

"No one did."

"I don't know much about magic," he says. "Any spell that can do this?"

"A blur spell distorts your form," I say. "That's sorcerer magic. A cover spell hides you. That's witch magic. You'd need to use both to slip past and then disappear." I clear my throat and say louder, "If someone's in here, it's cool. We just came for a snack, same as you."

No answer. I turn on the light, and Elijah paces off the room while I watch from the corner, looking for a blur of movement. We don't see one. We check the pantry, too.

It's not foolproof. We could have missed that telltale blur. When we finish, I call, "You know the lock's on the outside, right? I can lock you in here."

Silence.

"Do you smell anyone?" Elijah asks.

I shake my head. Then I think of something, walk to the door and drop to all fours. I sniff the ground. The only recent scents I pick up are mine and Elijah's.

Hairs prickle on the back of my neck.

"No one but us, right?" he says.

I nod. "It's not a ghost, though. They couldn't open the door."

"So . . ." he says.

"I'll talk to Holly tonight and Logan tomorrow," I say. "Maybe I'm missing a spell or a subtype power. One of them will know. For now . . ." I scoop up the rest of the chocolate bars and return the peanut butter to the pantry. "Time to clean up and clear out."

I slip into my room fifty-five minutes after telling Holly I'd return in an hour. I'd have been sooner, but when I noticed I had fifteen minutes left, Elijah found a way to fill ten of them.

I slip back into our room to find Holly reading. I toss her a Hershey bar. She looks from it to me and back again.

"Is this what you ate?" she asks. "Because I want whatever you had. You can flick off the lights—your face is glowing enough for me to read by."

"You can have what I did, but I'd rather not offer up Elijah. Give me a room number, and I'll fetch you a proper midnight snack."

"I don't think it'll have the same effect." She flips onto her side, head braced on her arm. "You really like him, don't you?"

"He's really likable. A nice guy in a very nice package. Also, an amazing kisser." I thump onto my bed and sigh at the memory.

"So that line you gave him about not looking for a boyfriend. Changed your mind yet?"

"It wasn't a line. I'm on dating hiatus." I tug off my shoes. "I'm still in recovery from the last one. First longterm boyfriend. First longterm burn."

"Jerk."

I smile at her. "Thanks. I want to be one of those girls who bounces back and says it's his loss, but I'm not bouncing. Not mooning over him, either. I just . . . I got hurt worse than I expected."

"What happened?" She sits up. "Sorry. You don't have to tell me, obviously."

But I want to. The thought surprises me. The only person I've told is Nick, because he's the one I've always gone to for stuff like this—he dated a *lot* before he got married.

I couldn't talk to Logan—he and Brandon moved in the same school circle, and that was awkward. If Logan had asked pointblank, though . . .? But he didn't, and I won't deny that stung.

I'd have liked to tell Mom, but then Dad would find out, and while he wouldn't exactly hunt Brandon down for what he did, he'd want to, and I just wasn't ready to upset them both with a problem they couldn't fix for me.

"It was sex," I say as I lay back on the bed. "He wanted it, and I didn't—not yet. He just . . ." I look over at her. "He wouldn't stop pushing. Even kissing felt like a constant battle to keep his hands from sliding up my shirt."

"Asshole."

"Right? I eventually did let him go farther, because I wanted to, but he just plowed through that like it was a hurdle on the way to his real goal. He didn't care about all the steps in between. I did."

"You wanted to slow down and enjoy the journey, and he was powering through to the finish line."

"Exactly. He was convinced I'd eventually give in. It wasn't as if I have hangups about sex. Maybe the fact I was open about it led him to believe he could talk me into it."

She gives me a hard look. "That sounds like taking responsibility for his *in*ability to hear the word no."

"I don't mean that. I just . . . It felt like there must be a solution to this situation, and I wasn't seeing it, and that was my fault. I tried to talk to him, and he'd just say sure, yeah, he understood that I wasn't ready, and that was fine, but then the next day, he'd go right back to pushing for more. Eventually, he came up with a solution of his own. He found a girl who said yes."

"Seriously? What a jerk."

"In theory, no. If he felt he needed sex, then it was his prerogative to end our relationship and find someone else. The problem was the he skipped the 'ending it' part."

She turns so fast her bed squeaks. "He cheated on you?"

"Didn't even try to hide it. He went to a party and screwed around with a girl from school and then told me about it. Letting me know someone else gave him what he wanted. Like that would make me see the error of my ways."

"What the—?" She bites off the curse and throws her hand out, a tiny fireball igniting. "Take this. You know where to put it."

I laugh. "Thanks. If I had one of those at the time . . ." I trail off and sit, pulling my knees in. "No, that's a lie. I'd like to say I told him off or even threw him across the room. I didn't. I just . . . I went into shock. I barely got home before I broke down."

"I wouldn't have made it out of the room," Holly says softly, extinguishing the fireball. "I can pretend I'd use that fireball on him, but I would have been crying too hard to say the spell. I'm sorry. He's a total asshole, and I'm really sorry."

I nod, knees clutched tight. I'm looking at them, but she leans out and catches my expression. "There's more?"

I hesitate. Then the words come, the ones that wouldn't even with Nick, that were too humiliating to tell him.

"People knew," I say. "People at the party. The girl he picked . . . Of all the girls he could have chosen . . ."

"Uh-huh," she says, and I know I don't need to explain.

"He told her that I wouldn't have sex with him," I say. "So she offered to, thinking that would be her way to win him. Except he didn't want a relationship with her. When he tried getting back together with me, she told everyone that they'd had sex and why. She's the head of this clique I've had trouble with since I started high school, and this was exactly the sort of thing they'd been looking for. They started taunting me, sending stuff to my social media, even writing on the bathroom walls. At first, they said I was a frigid bitch, a prick tease. Then they decided I must be a lesbian. Then maybe, since I'm not exactly full-figured, I must actually be a guy, and I was afraid Brandon would find out. And then . . ."

Tears run down my cheeks, and I swipe them away, horrified.

"And then . . . ?" Holly says, so gently my tears only flow faster. "You don't need to tell me. But if it would help . . ."

"My brother," I spit out the words fast before I can change my mind. "They started saying I wouldn't sleep with Brandon because I had a crush on . . ."

My gorge rises, and I can't say the words. I don't need to. Holly's sharp intake of breath tells me she gets it.

"Those *bitches*. Those fucking bitches. I have never said that word before, but they deserve it."

"Bitches?" I say, laughing softly through my tears.

She doesn't return the laugh. "Why would they say . . . ? Oh, wait. Let me guess. The other accusations didn't bother you enough. Calling you gay. Calling you trans."

I shake my head. "I don't consider those insults, either. They didn't hurt me."

"So they had to find something that would." She goes quiet briefly before asking, "What did Logan say?"

My laugh comes harsher now. "I sure as hell wasn't telling him."

"But what about the rest of it?"

What about the rest? What about the fact that Logan still talks to Brandon. Still hangs out with him and their mutual friends. Still hangs out with the girl and her clique.

"We're fine," I lie. "But that's the reason I'm not looking for a new boyfriend. I'll take the fake one, though. Now, speaking of Elijah and totally changing the subject, something weird happened in the kitchen, and I'm hoping you might be able to solve this particular mystery . . ."

CHAPTER TWENTY

Logan

Allan's room is down the hall from mine, so we walk back together. Behind us, my sister talks with Elijah and Holly, their voices faint. I lower mine when I say, "Have you spoken to Kate? I know she felt really bad about . . . before."

He stiffens a little and tries for a smile, but it comes out strained as he says, "That's cool. I know . . ." He clears his throat. "What happened back then . . . It just happened. If I'd known where it would lead, I would have talked to her first. I certainly wasn't trying to trick her."

"About what you expected in a relationship?"

He looks over, and his gaze searches mine.

"That was the problem, right?" I say. "You wanted more than she was ready to give. Relationship-wise."

"Is that what she said?"

"Sure." I frown. "Did you think it was something else? It wasn't. She really did like you. Just not as a long-distance boyfriend."

He laughs softly, relaxing. "That's what she said. I just wasn't sure if she'd heard . . . anything else that changed her mind. I definitely did come on way too strong back then. Your sister is just . . ." He shrugs. "When a girl like that shows interest, you go for it. Gotta take your shot while you can. I overdid it, and I'm sorry she felt bad."

We walk a few more steps. Then I say, "About that guy she's with."

"Elijah?" The corners of Allan's mouth twitch. "You don't like him much, huh? It must be weird, him being a non-Pack werewolf. He seems cool, though. They make a cute couple."

"They aren't a couple." I shake my head. "Kate hasn't been herself lately, especially with guys. She ended it with her boyfriend, and now he's blowing up my phone because she won't talk to him."

"Better get used to it. Your sister is kinda unforgettable. Guys aren't going to get over her in a heartbeat. I sure didn't."

Footsteps sound, but it's only Holly, and she doesn't see us as she heads the other way to her room. Kate and Elijah's steps go up the stairs.

Are they dodging curfew?

I push back a dart of annoyance and turn to Allan. "If you're still interested in her, just hold on. This thing with Elijah is only Kate goofing around. It'll pass."

He shakes his head. "I'm looking forward to getting to know Kate again but only as a friend. Kate's . . . She's like a flame. Once you see it, you can't stop looking at it, can't stop wanting to get closer."

"But then you get burned."

"Nah, not that. She just isn't right for guys like me. I'd constantly be waiting for her to find someone more exciting, more high-energy, more like her. Around Kate, I feel like a plodder, as if she's revving on all cylinders and I'm struggling to keep up, wishing she'd slow down." He glances over. "You know what I mean."

I do. He isn't the only one who feels dull and plodding in Kate's company. She doesn't try to overshadow me, but she does, simply by existing. I cannot help but fade beside the flaming whirlwind that is my sister.

Is that what bothered me, seeing her with Elijah? He has that same spark, that same energy.

But this isn't a competition. Even when she was dating Brandon, she always had time for me. It was after she stopped dating him that the problem started.

"Anyway," Allan says. "You don't need to worry about me being on the losing side of a love triangle. I'm glad to see her again. Glad to see both of you. This camp seems a whole lot more interesting tonight than it did this morning. From what I've seen, though, Elijah is far more her speed, and I have no intention of getting in his way."

I walk into my room and flip on the light. A grunt sounds from the other side, and Mason lifts his head from the pillow. It takes him a moment to find his scowl. When he does, he rumbles, "Turn off the damn light. Some of us are sleeping."

"It's ten thirty."

"Well, dying takes a lot out of a guy. Now turn it off, and go chase sticks until you're tired."

I flip off the main light . . . after I find and flick on a penlight from my bag.

Mason groans. "Aren't you guys supposed to have night vision?"

"Yes, but I need some small illumination to activate

the rods in my eyes. The door closes tightly and blocks what little light might come from the hall."

I strip my shirt off. He grunts and flips over, facing the wall. I shake my head at that and then pull off my shorts and climb into bed.

"I'm decent now," I say as I slide under the sheet. "And you don't need to worry anyway. I keep my boxers on."

"You better. You also better keep on your side of the room. If I wake up to find you anywhere near me, we're going to have a problem."

"You really have a very misinformed view of werewolves, don't you?"

Another mutter. As I see his expression, my eyes narrow. "You *aren't* worried I'll devour you in your sleep, are you? You're warning me to stay on my side and keep my boxers on." I shine my penlight at him. "Is this about me performing rescue breathing on you?"

He turns over, eyes shaded from my light. "I'm just saying—"

"It was *rescue breathing*. To save your life. I wasn't playing Prince Charming, waking you with a kiss. Even suggesting that I was thinking about anything other than reviving you is immature, ridiculous and insulting."

"I didn't say you were gay."

"And that's not why it's insulting. I don't care if you think I'm gay. I care if you think I'd take advantage of someone in that condition."

His head lifts, his expression in shadow. "So you *are* gay?"

"Are we really going there?"

"It's a simple—"

"I have no idea what I am," I snap. "And it doesn't

matter. I was saving your life, and I haven't even gotten a thank-you."

"You have no idea what you are?" He pushes up onto one elbow. "What kind of bullshit is that? Do you date guys, girls or both? Do you hook up with guys, girls or both?"

"I don't have time to date, and I don't have any interest in 'hooking up.'"

"But theoretically . . ." he says.

"Theoretically, I have no idea because I haven't met anyone who interests me."

"So you're ace?"

"I don't think so, but again—and I'll keep saying this —*I don't know*. I'm certainly not going to hash out my sexuality with you. If you're homophobic—"

"I'm not."

"Could have fooled me," I mutter. "I will be interested in whoever I'm interested in, and I can guarantee, with one hundred percent certainty, that I am *not* interested in you. You are safe from my appetites of all varieties."

Three seconds of silence tick past. "So you *do* have appetites?"

I groan and flick out my penlight. "Good night, Mason."

I wake to the click of the door opening. I wasn't sleeping. Not really. It's been a roller-coaster day, and every time I start to drift off, I remember something I might have done wrong, something I might have said wrong, and I jolt awake, gut twisted by anxiety imps. So when the door opens, I'm conscious enough to know it isn't Mason rising to use the bathroom. I can hear his steady breathing in the silence.

The door creaks, new hinges sticking. Light slips through the opening, and I open my eyes, confirming that Mason is in his bed, sound asleep. Just as I think that, his breathing hitches and his eyelids flutter, predator's instinct kicking in.

His gaze meets mine, and his mouth twists, as if he's going to snarl something about me watching him while he sleeps. Then he stops, and his eyes slide toward the door.

Footsteps pad inside. Bare feet, moving as carefully as the intruders can manage, but to me, those steps are as loud as boot thuds. A whisper, cut short as the speaker is shushed.

Mason's eyes slit as he watches. I focus on my other senses. Hearing tells me there are three people in my room. Scent suggests they're all male. None are anyone I've met in more than passing.

Fellow campers, presumably here to play a midnight prank. Put our hands in water hoping we'll piss the beds. Stick a harmless snake in our beds and stand back to watch the fun. Juvenile stunts, and I'd have hoped we'd be past that at our age, but apparently not.

Mason stays still, watching and waiting. I almost pity the pranksters. They're just hoping for a fun gag to laugh at over breakfast, and Mason is going to make them wish they'd never opened that door. I'll be stuck playing mediator, making sure the situation doesn't get out of hand.

I sigh under my breath. Maybe I should have just left Mason for dead. Of course, then he'd have risen as a vampire, and these guys would be in danger of more than black eyes and bruised egos.

They start to close the door only to discover it would

plunge them into darkness. They leave it open a few inches.

One whispers, "The blond," and all three creep to my bed. I try not to sigh again. At least if I'm the target, Mason won't interfere, and we can just get this over with.

I might be rolling my eyes, but I'm accustomed to the immaturity of teenage boys. I learned that when I found myself somehow assimilated into the popular clique at school. It wasn't where I wanted to be, but it saved me from dealing with the jocks. I've always had trouble with jocks. They used to mock me for being small; now they harass me to join their teams. Dad had the same thing—if you start looking like an athlete, suddenly you're an asshole because you won't support your school by joining a team.

One good thing about being at a private school is that the jocks and the popular guys are not necessarily the same people. So, while some people in my clique can be juvenile and self-absorbed, it's a safe place for me. Which means I know guys like these, and now I just have to suffer through their prank.

They step up beside the bed. My eyes are open the barest crack.

"Anyone bring a silver bullet?" one says.

I tense so fast I'm surprised they don't notice.

According to the lore, you only need a silver bullet for one reason: to kill a werewolf.

CHAPTER TWENTY-ONE

Logan

"A regular blade will work, right?" one asks. "It doesn't actually need to be silver."

"So I hear. Anything that can hurt us can hurt them."

The second voice comes from the other end of my bed. I feel a tug, as if he's lifting the sheet from that end. Cool night air slides over my foot and calf. I force myself to stay perfectly still even as my heart pounds.

"You know what you're doing, right?" the first one says.

"My dad's a doctor. I've had to work for him since I was twelve. Padding my pre-med application. One nick to the Achilles tendon should do it."

Did he say cutting my Achilles tendon?

This is a nightmare. It must be. I *have* actually drifted off, and everything from today is whipping through my mind, spinning crazy scenarios where the other campers find out what I am and decide to maim me while I sleep.

The blade nears my skin. It doesn't touch, but I feel the chill of it. Every cell screams for me to leap up. What the hell am I doing? Even if it is a nightmare, *do* something.

What if it's real?

All the more reason to get off your ass, Lo, and kick theirs.

No, because if this is not a nightmare, then I need to be sure they're going through with it. I need to feel that blade, let it cut my skin, proof of what they attempted.

Are you crazy?

No, I know how guys like this act. If I leap up, they'll say it was a joke. They'll make me feel paranoid, the new kid who's overreacting and trying to cause trouble.

I know this because I've seen it. Some of my so-called friends have done it to other classmates, and I didn't participate, but nor did I say anything, and that makes me just as guilty, doesn't it?

Kate would have said something. She always says something.

And you know what, Lo, that's an awesome moment of self-revelation, but now is not the time for epiphanies. Get off your ass!

The blade presses against my skin. My attackers have gone silent, but I swear I smell them salivating. There's something unnatural here, something dark, a tension and a predatory anticipation.

I remember what Elijah said.

Then there's the actual aggression—the shouting matches and fistfights. People snapping over anything. It's as if everyone's looking for an excuse to fuck or fight, you know? I can feel the tension. My hackles go up and stay up for no reason I can tell.

My hackles are up. They're up as high as they go.

The blade presses and—

There's an *oomph*, the blade skating across my skin.

"What the fuck?" Mason roars. "A knife?"

I scramble up. He's got the guy in a headlock and has

given him a bloody lip. It's Hayden, the blond prep-school guy Kate told off earlier. I register that as his two buddies rush Mason. I leap in front of him, facing them.

"You don't want to do that," I say.

Mason lets out a hiss of pain behind me, and I look over to see a gash in his side. Hayden's still holding the knife, blood painting the blade. He goes to slash again, and I kick, hitting his right arm. The knife clatters to the floor. I scoop it up and hand it to Mason.

"First step," I say to Mason. "Disarm your attacker."

As I release the knife, it flies out of my hand before Mason can take it. I grab it again and turn to the other two.

"Telekinetic half-demon, I presume?" I say.

They both charge at me. One grabs me, his fingers cold as ice. Mason yanks him off me. I drop the knife and stomp on it as the telekinetic demon tries to pull it to him. I knock him flying with a right hook, the dull thump of my fist hitting flesh seconded by the crack of a rib. Hayden casts a knock-back spell. I dodge and grab both his arms, effectively killing his ability to cast.

When Hayden spits curses at me, I say, "Next time, learn witch magic. Otherwise, it's far too easy to shut you down."

More curses. Sadly for him, they aren't actual curses.

The telekinetic demon stays on the floor, doubled over, gasping for breath.

"You're winded," I say. "Give it a minute. If you still have trouble breathing, that rib may have pierced a lung."

"What the—what the fuck?" the half-demon says, voice rising.

"You attacked a werewolf," Mason says behind me. "Did you expect him to rap your knuckles and call you a naughty boy? Stop whining and be thankful you *can* still breathe."

Under my foot, the knife wiggles, but the guy can't summon the power to wrest the knife out.

Mason has his target—the ice demon—against the wall, wrists pinned. One of Mason's forearms presses against the half-demon's windpipe. "How about you? Can *you* still breathe?"

The guy gasps.

"Good enough."

Blood streams from Mason's side, but it doesn't seem to bother him. He holds his target easily. While vampires don't get extra strength, Mason's big, and he's muscular, and he had the sense to avoid those ice-wielding fingers.

"This doesn't concern you," Hayden says to Mason.

Mason sneers. "Seriously? That's the best you can do? Next you'll be calling me a meddling kid. Vowing revenge on me and my dog." He jerks his chin at me.

Hayden sniggers. "Is that why you're defending him? He's your pet dog? Do you hump him? Or does he hump you? One of the counselors saw your intake form. He said that's why you went off on Mackenzie when she hit on you. You don't like girls, do you?"

"Fuck you." Mason makes a face. "No, on second thought, I'd really rather not. But if guys like me make you nervous, you might want to watch your buddy here." He jerks a thumb at one of the half-demons. "He was definitely checking me out."

Hayden throws off a few homophobic slurs, followed up with threats.

"Yeah, yeah," Mason says. "You gonna come after *me* with a knife next? Might wanna rethink that. I can't change into a wolf but . . ."

Mason throws the ice demon aside. Then he runs a finger through the blood dripping from Hayden's busted lip. He licks it off and then bares his teeth. He doesn't have fangs, but the meaning is clear, and Hayden's eyes go wide.

"What the fuck? Vampires *and* werewolves?"

"Yeah, it's such bullshit, being forced to associate with the sub-races." Mason looks at me. "Right, Logan? All these half-demons and sorcerers and necromancers. Call themselves supernaturals, but they piss their pants when we come around. Like rabbits freaking out over wolves crashing their party. Guess what?" He grins again, that flash of teeth. "The predators are in the building."

He gives Hayden a hard shove. "Now go run back to your rabbit hole."

"This—this is—"

"Unacceptable? And you're going to tell your daddy, some middle-aged nobody with a fancy job title? Skip the tattling, little boy. Send Daddy straight to me. I'll show him how important he is. Doesn't matter who you are. Blood tastes like blood."

I should mediate here. Sand the edges off Mason's threats. Tell the guys we won't bother them if they don't bother us. But blood pounds in my ears, the thrill of an easy takedown fading under the outrage at what they'd tried to do, and I'm afraid if I open my mouth, what comes out will be the opposite of mediation. So I settle for shoving the ice demon toward his friend with "Help your buddy up and then go."

The ice demon turns and glares at me, and then helps his telekinetic friend stand as Hayden stalks out.

"Can you believe those fucking guys?" Mason slaps the

door shut behind them and flicks on the light. Then he wheels on me. "And *you*. What the hell were you doing?"

"Let's see. First, I retrieved this." I pick up the knife and hand it to him. "Potentially saving your life *again* because you forgot the first rule of fighting an armed opponent. Then I disabled the other guys. I believe I did my share."

"I mean before that. They were going to cut your goddamn tendon. Do you know what that means?"

"I'd be unable to walk and would require prompt surgery to repair it or risk a lifelong serious disability. Even after surgery, I might have difficulties. Also, there's the risk of cutting more than they intended, after which I could bleed out."

He shakes his head. "So you know exactly what it means. And yet you were lying there, listening to them plotting to maim you, letting them put the damned knife to your leg."

"I was waiting for the first cut. I wanted proof of what they intended. Otherwise, they could have claimed they were joking."

Mason shakes his head and thumps onto his bed.

I look at the closed door. We've made enough noise to bring someone running, but no one has. People heard the fight. They must have. And they're ignoring it.

"I need to warn my sister," I say.

I'm heading for the door when I see the blood on Mason's bare torso. "First, though, let me look at that."

Mason waves me off. "It's fine. I thought he got me good, but I barely feel it."

"Still, it's a long gash. It'll probably need stitches." I manage a wry smile. "At least that's one thing you won't have to worry about when you go full vamp. You'll get insta-healing. Have you ever seen that?"

He shakes his head as he grabs a discarded T-shirt from the floor.

"Wait!" I stop him as he's about to wipe off the cut. "Blood doesn't come out easily. Trust me. I know."

"That's okay. It's not my shirt."

I say nothing. He mops the blood and then stops, looking down at the red-smeared shirt. "Fuck."

"Yep, that *is* your shirt. Mine wouldn't be on the floor." I point to where my clothing is neatly folded on the dresser.

I expect another curse. He's just staring down, not at the shirt, but at his wounded side. The shadow from his arm hides the injury.

"Is it worse than you thought?" I ask. "We should notify the counselors anyway. At the very least, it'll need cleaning. My sister has a first-aid kit—she's the future doctor—but the counselors should . . ."

I trail off as he pulls back his hand. Underneath the faint wash of wiped blood, I can see his skin where it'd been sliced open.

The gash is gone.

CHAPTER TWENTY-TWO

Kate

I'm asleep when Logan taps on the door. I don't wonder for a second who it is. I know that tap.

For the first years of our lives, Logan and I shared a room, right up until that became awkward. Awkward for everyone else. That was the only time in my life I wished I were a boy, and only because if I had been, no one would have insisted on separate bedrooms until we wanted them. But there comes a time—too soon, in my opinion—when opposite-gender siblings are not supposed to share a room.

Mom made it seem like a celebratory rite of passage. We were old enough to have our own bedrooms. Wasn't that special?

No, it was not.

I had shared a crib with my brother. I don't remember it, of course, but I've seen photos, and I've heard the stories, how they'd bought two cribs, but I'd scream until Mom and Dad put Logan in mine. Even if they tried keeping me up and putting him down alone, he'd fuss softly until I was beside him. When it came time for beds, one of us always crawled in with the other until Mom and Dad gave up and shoved them together into a double.

While Mom said we'd "earned" our separate rooms, we knew it was more about them than us. They wanted us in our own rooms because that was "proper." So we didn't complain, but if we couldn't sleep, we'd creep to the other's door. While I'd slip into Logan's room, he'd always tap on my door, and when he did, it sounded just like this.

I slide from bed and crack open the door to see Logan with a burly dark-haired guy.

"There's been an incident," Logan whispers. "May we come in?"

I lift a finger. I'm wearing a T-shirt, which is decent enough with Logan, but I'll pull on sweatpants for the stranger. I also rouse Holly, whispering that Logan needs to talk to me and asking whether she'd like us to go outside. She says no and rises to put on her own clothing.

I let Logan in. When the big guy starts to follow, I block him.

"Are you Mason?" I ask.

He nods and steps forward again, presuming that's the ticket to entry. I grab him by the shirtfront and say, "Outside. Now."

His brows lift. Behind me, Logan says, "Kate, he's—"

"Having a conversation with me. This won't take long. Now move, asshole."

Those brows rise higher, but I march him to the exit by the stairs. The entrance door is only secured with an internal deadbolt. I undo it and push him outside. When we're far enough from the building, I swing in front of him.

"You must be the sister," he says, looking amused.

"And you must be the jerk roommate who's been hassling my brother. Who stomped off when he saved your ass from your blood-sucking afterlife."

"Kate," Logan says behind me, his footfalls swishing over the dew-damp grass. "It's fine, Kate."

"Has he thanked you yet?" I ask.

"There's no need—"

"The hell there isn't." I turn on Mason. "You can't treat people like shit and expect them to stick their neck out for you. You're lucky Logan didn't just run to camp, yelling for help, telling them you were dead. By then, you would have been, and let's hope your family knows enough not to embalm you or you're going to have the worst vamp-life ever. Logan brought you back to *life*. And you walked away without letting him know you were okay, let alone thanking him."

"I didn't ask him to save me."

I sputter. "What the hell? I bet you told your parents you didn't ask to be born, either. Seriously, you need an image makeover. Emo-vamp is so 1990. Wear bright colors. Smile once in a while. Say thank you."

Mason starts to walk away. "As amusing as this is, I don't have time—"

I haul him back. "Oh, you'll make time. Logan might not get into a pissing match with you, but I will. You want to compare fangs?" I lean into his face. "Trust me, mine are bigger."

From behind me comes soft laughter that must be Holly.

"Just apologize," she says. "Kate's not letting you go until you do."

"I'm sure I've already thanked him."

I turn to Logan, who shrugs.

"That's a no," I say.

"Fine." Mason calls a too-bright, "Thanks, roomie!" He turns back to me. "Better? I'm not sure he actually saved me, though, considering this."

Mason yanks up his shirt. It's awash with smeared blood.

"You two got in a fight again?" I say. "Well, I'm sure you started it, and I don't see any damage, so quit whining."

"Whining?"

"He was slashed with a knife," Logan says.

Logan doesn't need to clarify that it wasn't him—we don't use weapons.

"Where?" I ask.

"Here." Mason points to unmarked skin under the smear of blood. "Asshole split me open a good six inches. Bled like a son-of-a-bitch. That was ten minutes ago."

"You healed," I say. "Like a vamp. You're obviously alive, though." I peer at the spot and then straighten. "Logan mentioned you were part of an Edison Group experiment. I know they played with side effects. They might have given you pre-vamp-life healing abilities, but I'm sure you'd have noticed by now."

"Kinda."

"Huh." I glance at Logan. "So the death-and-resurrection cycle triggered a partial change to vamp-hood."

"That's what I presume," Logan says.

I turn back to Mason. "If you start craving blood, do not ask my brother to donate. He's done enough for you already. Start with the guy who stabbed you. Unless you deserved it."

"He didn't," Logan says. "It was that kid you talked to in the dinner line. The blond. Hayden."

"You mean the Aberzombie who talked *at* me. Let me guess: you mouthed off to him. I've heard you like to do that.

"I didn't. He came for your brother . . . to cut his Achilles tendon while he slept."

I may be somewhat incoherent for the next few minutes. Logan explains once I'm calm enough to listen, but every sentence only reignites my rage. It doesn't help that my brother stays completely cool, as if these guys really had snuck in for a camp prank as he first presumed. I'll be angry for him. That has always been my role in our relationship. I rant and stomp and throw things, channeling his rage in a way he cannot.

They tried to lame my brother. If this asshole's dad is really a doctor, he'd have known exactly what he was doing. It's called the Achilles tendon after the Greek Achilles, whose mother had protected him by dipping him into the River Styx while holding that part of his body, meaning it was his only vulnerable spot. Like most myths, it has a deeper meaning. We are all vulnerable there. It's a necessary tendon for walking, running and jumping. Cut that and my brother would have been sent home with a serious injury, perhaps never able to run or jump properly again. For a werewolf, that would be catastrophic.

This was no prank. It was malicious and cruel, and the only thing my brother did to "deserve" it was to be born a werewolf.

"There really is something going on," Holly says. "Those guys are jerks, but this is insane."

Logan explains the hormone-overdrive theory to Mason.

When the vampire rolls his eyes, Holly says, "*You* were a real jerk the other night. Are you telling me that's normal for you?"

"Yep. Sorry. No excuse for my behavior except that I don't want to be here, and if I have to be here, I want to be left alone."

"I introduced myself," she says. "I wasn't hitting on you. Wasn't asking for your life story. Wasn't trying to make a new BFF. I said, 'Hello, I'm Holly.'"

He shrugs, but color touches his cheeks in a look that says it's a whole lot easier to be nasty to a stranger.

"I'm an asshole," he says.

"And proud of it," she mutters.

"Should we warn Elijah?" I say. "Regardless of what's causing this, these guys have a batshit crazy issue with werewolves, emphasis on the *crazy*."

"Elijah?" Mason says. "Wait, that's the dude with the dreads, isn't it? He's a werewolf, too? Fuck, maybe Surfer Boy had a point. You guys *are* taking over."

"We are," I say. "So please feel free to jump onto Team Surfer."

"Let's leave Elijah out of it for now," Logan says. "No one else knows he's a werewolf, not even the counselors. We can quietly warn him in the morning. I don't want to call attention to this."

"You were attacked with a knife," I say. "In your *bed*. At the very least we need to tell the counselors."

"Do you trust them to handle this?" Logan says. "Or will they make it worse?"

He's right. I remember Tricia when we got back from the cabin walk. Earlier today, she didn't want to tell others what we are. Now she's openly talking about it herself.

The cheerleading counselor has vanished, replaced by a petulant and testy babysitter.

Something hormonal is sparking aggression and libido, increasing both tension and mood swings. Yet we *are* teens. Sometimes I want to just slam my fist into the wall for no reason. Sometimes I want to invite random cute guys into the nearest dark hallway and make out with them. Other times, I want to go in my room, shut the door and cry. And all three impulses can take place in a single day . . . or a single hour. Yet the situation here is exaggerated. It's as if someone went looking for a teen-movie scriptwriter and hired a sixty-year-old who hasn't spoken to an actual teen in thirty years.

Worse, whatever's going on, the counselors aren't immune to it.

"Paige will be here tomorrow," Logan says.

"We keep saying that."

"I know, but it's true. Do you think we're in serious danger? If you do, then let's pack our bags and head into the forest. We can hike to the nearest town."

I shake my head. "No, you're right. As angry as I am about what happened to you, it's three guys, not a lynch mob."

"We're on alert now. We'll stick together until Paige gets here."

"What about calling her?" I say. "The cell phones are in the office, and I know where that is."

"Wake her in the middle of the night to say weird stuff is happening? That some guys came after me, but I'm fine? It's . . ." He checks his watch. "Three in the morning here, which makes it midnight in Portland. Too late for her to catch a flight. She's due here around noon tomorrow, so she must already be booked on the first flight out. If you *are* really concerned, we can call Mom and Dad."

"If I was really concerned, I'd do what you said, grab my bag and head out. I'm not there yet, so you're right. Hanging tight and waiting for Paige is the best option. I just really don't like it."

"Neither do I."

CHAPTER TWENTY-THREE

Kate

The next morning, Holly and I head into the dining hall for breakfast. We've decided to play this cool, not hang out in our little "pack" as Tricia called it. That would signal fear, closing our ranks. Whatever is happening here, not everyone is affected. I'm not sure I'd know if I was—I'm already prone to mood swings and making out with guys I've just met. Logan's testosterone is definitely spiking, but only around Elijah, which is normal for werewolves. Maybe as adolescent werewolves, we're already too high on hormones to notice an increase. I don't see anything with Holly and Allan, though. Whatever is happening, it only impacts some campers. Why? Well, that's the question, isn't it?

"You can have breakfast with Elijah if you want," Holly says as we walk to the dining hall. "You two don't need a third wheel."

"You're not a third wheel," I say. "You're a second wheel. Unless that's a polite brush-off . . ."

"Definitely not."

"Then it's you and me for breakfast. I want to hear about your Sabrina training."

As we walk through the dining hall, I spot Elijah.

Damn it.

I just told Holly I was going to have breakfast with her —just her—but I do need to speak to Elijah about last night

I'm still figuring this out when he looks over. He goes still, as if trying to decide whether to join us or hang out with others. I glance his way, ready to motion that I need to speak to him a moment. Yet as I turn, he wheels, and I'm left looking at his back. Then he makes an exaggerated show of checking his watch and stiffening in a "Shit, I forgot something" way before he lopes off down the other hall.

Did Elijah just dodge me?

Did he duck out before I could pounce and insist on eating with him?

Annoyance darts through me. I've done nothing to suggest I'm that kind of girl. Sure, I hauled him to talk to Logan when I first discovered he was a werewolf, but after that, he was free to leave. Logan made it clear he'd *like* Elijah to leave. It was Elijah who tagged along. It was also Elijah who invited me on the kitchen raid. I'd been the one watching the time, not wanting to make Holly stay up late waiting for me. He'd been the one delaying my departure until the last possible moment.

I'm overanalyzing this, aren't I?

Elijah wants to have breakfast with someone else, and rather than say so, he pretended not to see me. That isn't cool, but he doesn't know me well enough to realize he could just say, "Catch you later." He overreacted, and now I'm overreacting.

I do need to speak to him about what happened with Logan, but my brother's right—no one realizes Elijah's a werewolf, so he's in no immediate danger. I'll warn him later.

I forget Elijah and gather my breakfast. No one comments on my overflowing plate this time. I hear the whispers, though, snaking down the line.

She's a werewolf.

The Alpha's daughter.

Her brother's here, too.

Oh, did you hear about the vampire?

Vampire?

I also catch other whispers.

I'd do her.

Oh yeah, I hear werewolves like it rough.

She's cute, but have you seen her brother? Damn . . .

Whatever is happening here, the heightened sex drive is at least as strong as the heightened aggression, and so far, those two haven't overlapped, thankfully. I've barely even formed that thought before a guy says, "Hey, I thought you were coming to my room last night."

He's talking to a girl ahead in line, who's giggling with another girl. When she doesn't respond, he surges forward.

"Hey!" he says. "I'm talking to you."

He grabs for her arm, and I'm setting my plate down, ready to run interference, but the girl tosses his hand off easily.

"I changed my mind," she says. "Especially since you apparently found company elsewhere."

"I don't know what you're talking about," he says, in that fake belligerent tone that says he knows exactly what she means and he's wondering how he got caught.

"You found someone else," she says, "and so did I."

"What? Who?"

The girl puts a hand behind her friend's neck and kisses her. The guys nearby break out in hoots and cheers, and even her would-be suitor eases back with, "Hell, if you'd told me that, I'd have said bring her along."

There's a round of laughter.

Holly shakes her head, and we break from line to find a table.

"Why do I feel like I've stumbled into a bad teen sex comedy?" I mutter.

"Better than a bad teen horror movie," Holly says.

"True enough. I just hope the camp supplies condoms."

"They covered that in the orientation. They're with the bandages, insect repellent and other first aid supplies."

"Excellent."

From the sounds of it, whatever's going on with the girls is heating up, and the ring around them grows as others walk over to watch and yell encouragement.

"Not my idea of breakfast entertainment," I say. "Dinner theater, maybe, but it's too early for that shit."

Holly laughs. "Agreed. Want to see if we can sneak outside to eat?"

I do.

On the way out, I spot Logan, but he's with Allan on the other side of the buffet table fracas. I catch his eye just long enough to wave. Then I follow Holly out. No one comes after us, and we eat at a picnic table outside.

I want to get to know Holly better, so I ask questions. I don't get much. She said earlier that she has the most boring, happy family imaginable, and she sticks to that. Her family is great, very close and loving. She's just an average girl with an average life. Nothing else to say, really.

That could be true but . . . I feel as if she's dodging and deflecting, and that stings a little. I'm not asking for her life story. I'm not trying to intrude. I'm just reaching out, showing interest because I *am* interested, but a door has been slammed, in the nicest, politest way.

So we talk about the Sabrinas. If I'm hoping for insight into Holly and her life that way, I don't get it. Maybe there's nothing to tell. Or maybe I haven't earned it yet. I accept that.

After breakfast, other campers wander outside. Apparently, scheduled activities for the morning have been canceled while the counselors call an emergency staff meeting to discuss behavior issues. To me, that sounds a whole lot more like the prison guards retreating to a locked room and letting the inmates run wild until the warden shows up. They're waiting for Paige.

Despite the counselors retreating, it's a quiet morning. Allan comes out around ten and says Logan's in his room, talking to Mason, and most of the campers are holed up organizing a party, judging by what he overheard.

It's nearly eleven when I go inside to hunt down a midmorning snack. Holly says they put out bowls of granola bars and fruit for us to graze on, and I am in serious need of grazing.

I'm looking for the bowls when I catch a familiar scent. I turn to see Elijah poised just inside the doorway.

"Hey," I say, heading over to him. "I'm snack-hunting right now, but you and I need to chat."

He backs up fast, his hands rising to ward me off.

I stop short. "What the hell's that for? Do I look like I'm running over to throw myself on you?"

"No, no."

My annoyance from earlier surges. "I didn't fail to notice you running from me this morning, Elijah. I was turning to say hello. That's it. Say hello and let you know I planned to eat breakfast with Holly. I'm not a leech. I don't cling to real boyfriends, let alone fake ones."

"Yeah . . . about that . . ." He inhales, not meeting my eyes. "I don't think the girlfriend stuff is a good idea."

My heart stutters, and I have to remind myself I wasn't really dating Elijah. Don't take this personally. It was a relationship of convenience, and if it's no longer convenient for one party, that's fine. Even if it doesn't feel fine.

"You're great, Kate," he begins, "but—"

"Whoa!" I lift my hands. "You're my fake boyfriend. You don't need to dump me for real. You've changed your mind. That's cool. Done. We are no longer a pretend couple. Now, I really do need to talk to you. Help me find a snack and—"

"No," he cuts in. "I . . . It's not just the dating thing. I . . . I don't think any of this is a good idea. I'm sorry."

He turns and strides into the hall. I stand there, stunned. Then I jog after him, staying well back, so it's clear I'm not chasing him.

"Elijah," I call. "I need to talk to you. It has nothing to do with us."

He shakes his head and breaks into a lope.

"Elijah!" I call.

"Take a hint," a voice says behind me, and I turn to see a counselor. Behind her, the others stream into the dining hall as if their meeting is done.

"You got dumped," she says. "Deal with it. Don't humiliate yourself by chasing him."

"No, I—" I blink hard, forcing myself to change mental gears. "When is Paige coming?"

"That's Ms. Winterbourne to you."

"Paige is a family friend." I force a smile, trying to sound casual.

"Well, aren't you special."

I swallow a retort and ask, calmly, "When is Ms. Winterbourne arriving?"

"She's not." The counselor starts walking off. "Her kid woke up puking sick, and apparently, he needs his mommy. She's coming tomorrow."

"Wait." I jog after her. "I really need to speak to her. Can I use my cell? I'll skip my evening call."

"Will you?" She turns to me. "You might be special where you come from, Miss Werewolf Princess, but to me, you're nothing but a spoiled little bitch-dog. One who needs to be taught a lesson."

I stare at her. Just stare as she wheels and swans off to join the others.

Okay, something is definitely wrong here, and it's getting worse.

The whole *situation* is getting worse, and Paige isn't coming.

I need to find Logan.

CHAPTER TWENTY-FOUR

Logan

After I was attacked, the rest of the night passed without incident. I rigged up a makeshift alarm for the door to alert us to entry. Mason looked at it, snorted, and shoved the dresser in front of the door, instead. Even with that, I don't think either of us slept. I rest until a bell signals breakfast, and then I ask Mason whether he's eating, but he only rolls over and grunts. As soon as I leave, though, I hear the dresser being shoved back in front of the door.

Allan's also heading for breakfast, so we fall in step together. I tell him a bit about what happened last night. We're still talking as we join the line for the breakfast buffet, and it takes a couple of minutes to realize something's happening up ahead, a commotion that has guys gathering like they do when a fight breaks out. I stiffen, ready to leave. Until Paige arrives, I'll force myself to retreat from any situation that looks as if it could erupt in violence.

I hear catcalls and whoops, which don't sound like audience reactions to a fight. I ask Allan, who only shrugs and says, "I don't even want to *know* what it is. I'm starting to feel like I'm living in a zoo. Except those who are *actually* part animal aren't the ones acting like it." He pauses. "That didn't come out right. I don't mean you're less human." Another pause. "How do you guys think of it?"

"In the Pack, we do consider ourselves part wolf and part human. Just as you might say you inherited certain characteristics from your mother and certain ones from your father. That doesn't make you two people. It's a seamless blending."

I realize I've switched into lecture mode and scoop up a forkful of bacon as I say, "The short version is that we'd be insulted if you said we were *sub*human, but not if you call us part human. To us, the wolf doesn't negate the human."

"Makes sense. Oh, there's Kate and Holly. Looks like they've got their food, and they're ducking whatever's going on."

I catch my sister's eye, and I'm going to ask what's happening, but she only smiles and waves and then continues for the door. She's obviously heading outdoors to enjoy breakfast with Holly, so I won't interfere. My sister never had a wide circle of friends, but in middle school, she'd had no end of girls *wanting* to befriend her, and she'd had a decent group of pals. In high school, that slowly constricted. I know my sister misses that female friendship, and I'm glad to see her hanging out with Holly.

After breakfast, the staff disappears into a meeting, and a bunch of the campers do, too, planning some kind of party.

While the counselors are away, the campers will play.

The buffet is still out. I decide to take food for Mason, and Allan decides that's the point at which we part company.

"I'm sure he's secretly a great guy," Allan says.

"No, he's not. But he should still eat."

Allan smiles and shakes his head. "You'll make a great dad someday. However, not being nearly so charitable, I'll skip the company of the brooding vamp and go find Holly and Kate."

I take the food to Mason and then immediately wish I hadn't. I could have foreseen that, couldn't I? While I'd love to believe he'll accept the gesture for what it is— simple consideration—if asked to predict his response, I'd have said he'd see the food as a bribe or a solicitation for friendship . . . or a solicitation for more than friendship, the werewolf equivalent of bringing him flowers. Admittedly, had I predicted the last one, I wouldn't have brought it.

Last night, our attackers said Mason is gay. That doesn't jibe with his seemingly homophobic comments from earlier, and I suppose that could mean those guys were wrong. However, Mason didn't argue the point, either. Does that mean his comments *weren't* homophobic but rather like a female roommate warning me about sneaking into *her* bed in the middle of the night?

I don't care what Mason is. I could just do with a little less of him acting as if every friendly word and gesture is a come-on. It's exhausting. I wasn't lying last night. My sexual orientation remains a mystery even to me. Maybe that suggests I'm bisexual. Maybe it just puts me somewhere on the spectrum, and I won't know which way I lean until I have an actual romantic encounter, and I'm in no rush to do that. For me, it isn't a question urgently requiring an answer, and I don't appreciate being grilled on it by a near stranger.

So Mason hints that I'm bringing him flowers, and I ignore him. That seems the best defense. I leave the food, and I grab a book and plunk onto my bed—only because I don't want to walk out and seem like he was right and I'm fleeing in embarrassment. I read for the next hour. He eats the food and then plugs in his earbuds.

After an hour, I head out, planning to join Kate and the others. I decide to grab snacks from the dining hall first, and I'm heading for the stairs when I see Elijah. He glances over his shoulder, as if for an escape route. Escaping me? Afraid of me? I'm fine with that—it just surprises me.

At school, I'm the quiet, studious kid who never makes waves, never causes trouble, certainly doesn't scare anyone. Even if I have the physique to fight, no one has any reason to start one with me. In the last twenty-four hours, I've fought Mason and those guys last night, and I won easily. I threatened Elijah, and now he's obviously trying to avoid an encounter. Here, I am someone new. Here, I am a guy you don't cross.

Here, I am Clayton Danvers's son.

Even as I recoil from the thought, a frisson of satisfaction runs through me.

Hell, yeah, I'm Clay Danvers's kid.

What, no, no. That's Kate, and she can keep it. I'm the thoughtful one, the careful one. The brains. Not the brawn.

Except Kate has her own brains, and I have my own brawn.

Dad has a freaking PhD. He *is* the brains and the brawn.

Yet Dad is not the calm and reasonable one. He's the homing missile, the smart weapon, but a weapon nonetheless, and I'm . . .

I'm standing here, trapped in the web of my anxieties, while Elijah is about to breathe a sigh of relief and retreat.

I walk toward him, on an angle that means his only escape route is straight through a gaggle of the popular girls. The same girls he's apparently avoiding.

Is he really avoiding them? Or did he use that as an excuse to get close to my sister?

I saw how he looked at her yesterday. Kate isn't some random girl he asked to help him out. He's interested, and she's oblivious to that, just happy to hang out with a cute guy who also happens to be a werewolf.

Seeing himself cornered, Elijah plasters on a fake smile. "Hey . . . you. Good morning."

"We need to talk."

"Uh, sure. Later, though. Right now—"

"Don't worry. It isn't about Kate. We need to talk about what's going on, your theory. Wait here while I grab some fruit."

As I walk away, one of the girls giggles and says to Elijah, "Hey, *you*? Forgot his name, didn't you?"

"Nah, I know it," Elijah says. "Can't forget it—it was also my brother's. Which is awkward."

I slow as I listen.

"It *was* your brother's?" the girl says. "Your brother's dead? I'm so sorry. That guy is such a jerk."

"For daring to have the same name?" another girl says. "Don't be stupid. Elijah, I'm so sorry to hear that, though. What happened to your brother?"

"Uh . . ." Elijah seems to be struggling for a polite way

to say *none of your business*. Instead, he says, "He fell in with a bad crowd, and it got him killed."

"A gang?" one girl says breathlessly.

Another girl's voice rises as she says, "Oh my gawd, did you actually say that?"

Elijah laughs softly. "It actually kinda *was* a gang. Now, if you will excuse me, ladies, I'm going to duck out before he comes back."

They cluck sympathetically as he flees. I don't pursue. I'm standing at the table, still littered with the remains of breakfast, looking more like an abandoned pig's trough than a buffet. My mind whirs as I stand with my hand poised over an apple.

I know it. Can't forget it—it was also my brother's.

Fell in with a bad crowd, and it got him killed.

It actually kinda was *a gang.*

I turn to see Elijah taking off at a lope. He glances sideways down the hall, and his profile . . .

The girls notice me watching and fan out, as if to block him from my view. I still see him, though, in my mind. That profile. That face.

I knew I'd seen it before. Now the answer hits with a rush that sets my heart pounding, my brain shouting that I'm being silly. Worse than silly. I'm being racist, seeing a Black werewolf and jumping to an imagined resemblance to one of the few I know.

I reach for my phone. It's not there, of course. But I can pull up what I want from memory.

When we got our first cell phones, Kate and I had taken pictures of the Pack. Kate played amateur photographer, sneaking around like a paparazzi, wanting "real" people, not their smiling photo-ready faces. I wanted the same, but I got it another way. I took pictures of pictures, photographs of Jeremy's sketches and paintings of the Pack.

I'd started with the two portraits in his studio. The ones of my parents. In it, Dad wasn't much older than I am now. He'd been leaning against a wall, talking to Jeremy, with his mouth full of . . .

I look down at the apples under my hand.

Dad, talking, with his mouth full of apple, his head bursting with some idea that couldn't wait until he chewed and swallowed. Like Kate. But now, in that painting, I see something uncomfortably close to a mirror.

The portrait of Mom is very different. In it, she looks dangerous, almost feral. That was Jeremy capturing sides of my parents seen only by those who knew them best.

I have other paintings on my phone, too, of Pack brothers, some gone before I was born, like . . .

I mentally zoom in on one portrait. It's Mom in her twenties, sitting on the sofa. Her legs are drawn up, and she's leaning sideways in deep, almost conspiratorial conversation with a Pack mate, her best friend. He's laughing at some inside joke, the kind that best friends have, the kind I used to have with Kate. His head is thrown back, and I see him and . . .

Elijah.

That's who I see in his profile.

I don't just see Elijah in that painting, either. I see Kate as she'd been last night with Elijah, the two of them laughing at some joke the rest of us didn't get.

I remember the first time I saw that picture, and I hear Mom's voice.

"That's your namesake, Logan. I met him just after I met your

dad. He died a few years before you were born, and your dad knew it would mean a lot to me if we named you after him."

"You were friends," I say, and it's not a question—even as a kid, I could see the answer in that painting.

She smiles. "We were very good friends."

Logan Jonsen.

When I focus on that mental image of the portrait, I see the differences between Logan and Elijah. Logan was lighter skinned—his mother was Caucasian. Their features aren't an exact match, either. In the first portrait, Logan also has locs, longer than Elijah's, and that could mislead me, make me jump to a conclusion, but I've seen photos of Logan Jonsen taken long after he'd shorn off the college-era locs and become a lawyer, yet another reason I've leaned toward that occupation. I can pull up those later pictures and still see the overwhelming resemblance to Elijah in his profile, in his eyes and mostly in his smile.

Elijah is Logan Jonsen's half-brother.

And Elijah knows it. He knows who his brother was. Knows Logan was Pack. Knows he was murdered in a war between mutts and Pack. Yet that's not how Elijah sees things, is it?

It actually kinda was a gang.

Elijah knows who we are. He also knows who we are in relation to his brother, and it is very clear how he feels about that.

Elijah blames the Pack for his brother's death. He tried to hide from Kate, tried to hide the fact he's a werewolf, and now that we know, he's hiding the connection to his brother.

I had good reason to be suspicious. Elijah is up to something.

I take two steps in the direction Elijah disappeared. Then I stop short.

I *will* confront him. I *will* get to the bottom of this. But first I need to tell Kate. Otherwise, if I go after him, she'll think the worst of me, and we don't need that. We really don't.

CHAPTER TWENTY-FIVE

Logan

I'm heading outside to talk to Kate about Elijah when one of the counselors stops me. It's a guy I haven't met before. He's wearing a Team Necromancer shirt that looks slept in. Judging by his face, though, he hasn't slept at all. That could mean he was up all night partying, but his face sags, making him look ten years older, his eyes dark with deep exhaustion.

I remember what Kate and Elijah said about whispers in the woods. Werewolves don't usually hear ghosts, but it's possible that a whisper or two could break through if the ghosts are strong enough . . . or if there are enough of them.

That might explain this necromancer's exhaustion. Ghosts often pester them to deliver messages, as if a necromancer's sole purpose is to play spirit-world FedEx.

"Is everything all right?" I ask him.

"Hell if I know," he mutters, low enough that he probably doesn't mean for me to hear it. Then he says, louder, "Tricia needs to speak to you. I'm supposed to escort you to her office to wait."

In other words, she's heard about the trouble last night. Well, I knew I'd need to deal with this. Best to get it over with. And I won't mind having access to her office while I wait. Maybe I can find my cell phone.

The necromancer takes me upstairs and down a hall to an unmarked door. He opens it and waves me inside.

The door shuts, and I look around. This isn't the office. Not the main one, at least. It's walk-in-closet sized with a desk and a few chairs. The empty coffee mug on the desk proclaims, "Life is short. Do stuff that matters," and there's a laptop cord hanging from the sole outlet. The laptop, however, is nowhere in sight.

I cock an ear to the door. I can hear the voices of what might be counselors. Before I can make out words, footsteps stream into another hall. Their meeting seems to have broken. I wait for Tricia, but all the footsteps move on toward the dining hall.

When this end of the building goes silent, I ease open one desk drawer. Empty. Another reveals a notebook with a watercolor mermaid and an Anaïs Nin quote on the front: "I must be a mermaid . . . I have no fear of depths and a great fear of shallow living." I crack it open to find what seem to be Tricia's notes on the camp. A quick leaf through fails to divulge any dastardly experimental plan. Nor does it hint at the disorganized chaos I'm seeing today. It's the polar opposite, in fact.

Within these covers, Tricia has the conference organized in a way that would make Paige proud. It is meticulously detailed with the kind of schedule I'd hoped for, discussion and debate and education, mixed with outdoor excursions and activities. She even made changes yesterday morning to accommodate Kate and me. For example, orienteering had been changed to us leading a lesson in wilderness tracking, showcasing our skills in a way that suggests she actually knows something about werewolves.

Yet if that was her plan, why did she tell us to keep our supernatural race a secret?

Something changed after she wrote this. It must have.

I look at yesterday's schedule. When we arrived, the group was supposed to be listening to a panel discussion on half-demon subtypes. Instead, they'd been doing a team-building exercise. When I skim the schedule, though, I don't see *any* team-building exercises.

After dinner yesterday, small group sessions were indeed on the schedule. I look at the list of groups, and something about it niggles the back of my mind. When I can't make the connection, I file it and move on.

Following the group sessions came a bonfire and marshmallow roast. That didn't happen. Everyone had been in bed by ten, yet according to this schedule, the bonfire went from nine to eleven, and Tricia had added a note that if the counselors weren't too tired and discussion was going well, the fire could extend to midnight for those who wanted to stay.

I'm so engrossed in the notebook that I don't hear footsteps until the last second. I shove the notebook into the drawer, and I'm still sliding into my chair when the door opens. It's not Tricia, though—it's the exhausted necromancer.

I get to my feet. "If Tricia's delayed, I'd like to speak to my sister. I'll come right back."

The necromancer shakes his head. "If I see Kate, I'll send her up, but I have my orders, and right now, I think we'd better just do what Tricia wants."

"What's up?" I say. "This isn't the conference I expected." I pause and then meet his eyes. "I don't think it's the one you expected, either, nor the one Tricia planned."

He hesitates, and he seems on the verge of admitting it, but then suspicion sparks behind his eyes. Whatever's going on here, I'm still a werewolf, possibly the cause of the trouble.

I open my mouth to speak, but he turns and says, "Come on," to someone I can't see. Mason appears, his jaw set. When the necromancer reaches out, as if to prod him in, Mason only has to look at the guy's hand, and the necromancer pulls back.

Mason walks in. The door shuts behind him.

That's when Mason sees me. "Fuck."

"Yes, I'm here. If this is about last night, though, those guys tattled. Not me."

Mason grunts and slumps into the chair beside mine. When our arms brush, he shoots me a look, as if that's my fault. I rise and walk to the desk, slide open the drawer and remove the notebook again. Then I lean against the edge of the desk.

"This conference isn't going according to plan," I say.

"You just figured that out? I thought you were some kinda genius."

"I mean it's literally not going according to plan. I have the schedule here. It was off-course before Kate and I even arrived. If I ask what activities took place yesterday morning, is there any hope you actually participated and would know if they're different than what's here."

"No." A beat. "And yes."

"No or yes?"

"The conjunction was 'and' not 'or.' You asked two questions. I gave two answers."

I think that one through. "No, you didn't participate. Yes, you'd know if they were different."

He only grunts, which I suppose is as close to agreement as I'll get. I rhyme off yesterday morning's five activities.

"Yes, yes, yes, no, no."

"Did you participate in any of them?" I ask.

"No."

"Remind me why you're here?"

"Never told you why."

When I wait, expectantly, he groans, as if I'm a five-year-old pestering him incessantly.

"Bribed," he says.

"Bribed?"

"Yeah, that thing where someone has something you want, and to do that, you gotta do something you don't want to."

"You agreed to attend the conference as a vampire representative, but whoever bribed you didn't specify that you needed to actually attend any sessions."

The hint of a smile plays on his lips, one of self-satisfaction. "Yep."

"So you're in self-imposed solitary confinement," I say. "That must be a fun way to spend a week."

"It's not solitary anymore," he shoots back. "Unfortunately."

"Then go back into the forest. I fixed the tent for you. Well, mostly. And, no, I'm not giving you our room no matter how much you grumble and glower. Feel free to try throwing me out again. I could use the exercise."

I don't look up from the book as I talk. I'm thumbing through it, sure there's a clue here. It isn't anything obvious. It's just a random note that my mind made, analyzing the data and extracting a nugget of information that surfed past on a brain wave before I could snatch it. I keep skimming, hoping to see that wave rise again.

Then it does.

"Half-demons," I murmur as I skim the list of small group sessions. "There are a lot of half-demons here."

"Because there are a lot of fucking half-demons. Randy bastards breed like rabbits. And how come no one's concerned about *them*? Their daddies are demons. *Demons*. But no, the ones you need to watch out for are the overgrown puppies and the overgrown mosquitoes."

"It's a matter of population infiltration and familiarity. As you said, there are a lot of half-demons. They take up an inordinate slice of the supernatural population pie, and therefore other supernaturals are familiar with them in ways they aren't with the much rarer werewolves and vampires. Familiarity may breed contempt, but the lack of it breeds fear."

"Thank you, Professor Danvers."

I continue as if he hadn't spoken, still flipping pages, my words more musing aloud. "Given their overall population density, it isn't surprising there are so many half-demons at this conference. All the subsets must be represented. Of the small group sessions, there's one for witches, one for sorcerers, one for necromancers, and four for half-demons. That suggests fifty percent of the campers are half-demon."

"More like sixty-five."

He's not being sarcastic. I don't comment on the fact he obviously paid more attention to his fellow campers than he let on.

"I'm curious about the staff," I say. "Tricia is half-demon, and I saw a couple others—"

"One witch, one necro, four half-demons. There was supposed to be a sorcerer, but he started a new job or something. And, no, I wasn't taking notes. I have a photographic memory." A pause. Then he glances over. "Not going to correct me and say photographic memory is a myth?"

"That would be rude."

He snorts a laugh and shakes his head. "You were thinking it, though."

"I presumed you meant eidetic memory, and I would never correct you. You know what you have. I don't."

"It's not eidetic memory, and yeah, I know what that is —when the brain takes a snapshot of an image and stores it in memory. It appears sometimes in children and disappears as they grow up. True photographic memory—the ability to recall text and images—has never been proven. It's a myth." Another snort, disgusted now. "I wish."

I say nothing. I just wait.

After a moment, he continues. "They were supposed to remove side effects. That's what the experiments were for. For the werewolves, that meant easier shifting and a lower predatory instinct."

While he may have heard this, I'm initially surprised he bothered to remember it. If he does have the fabled photographic memory, though, he'd remember whether he deemed it important or not.

"That's where I got it from," he says. "My memory. It came from the experiments. I bet they thought it was a feature. If you live for hundreds of years, what tweak might make life easier? An improved memory. So you don't forget things. So you don't forget a goddamned thing. Fucking amazing, right? All the mistakes you make, all the things you wish you could forget? You won't. All those people who come and go in your life? All the people you care about who die? Hell, yeah, you don't want *them* to fade into pleasant dreams. Let's keep everything right there. Front and center."

I open my mouth and then realize he won't want sympathy or even understanding. The bitterness in his voice tells me that nothing I can say will help.

The hell of a vampire's life is outliving everyone they know, everyone they care for, everyone they love. Eventually, those memories do fade, and there's mercy in that.

There is no mercy in this. Giving Mason a photographic memory is the cold practicality of science, devoid of any consideration or empathy. Everyone wishes they had a better memory, so wouldn't that help vampires in their long lives? No. No, it would not.

"What's this half-demon nonsense you're babbling about?" Mason says into the awkward silence.

It takes me a moment to reroute my mental train. Then I nod and say, "Whatever's going on here, you and I aren't affected. Neither is Kate or Elijah, who are both werewolves. Holly is a witch. Not affected. Allan—a guy we knew from years back—isn't affected, either, and he's a sorcerer. Last night, that one guy who attacked us was also a sorcerer, but the other two were half—"

Footsteps tap along the hall. I shove the book back into the desk, but the footsteps head down the other hall, instead. They're soft, barely audible. The steps stop. A moment later, someone taps on a door, and it's definitely in the other hall. Probably a camper hoping to speak to the counselors, knocking tentatively, knowing they're in no mood to hear complaints.

I check my watch. "It's been nearly an hour since they brought me in. I'm going to speak to Kate. If they find I'm gone, would you say I ran to the bathroom, please?"

He shrugs, which I take for agreement. I listen at the door. When I'm sure the hall is empty, I turn the knob. It doesn't budge. I jangle it, in case it's sticking. It isn't.

We're locked in.

CHAPTER TWENTY-SIX

Kate

After Elijah dumps me, I go to find my brother and let him know Paige isn't coming today. Logan isn't in his room—I knock and no one answers, so I say, "Yo, Mason. Is my brother in there?" I don't get an answer. I knock again, and I know that if Mason was there, he'd tell me to fuck off and stop knocking. He doesn't.

I head outside next. Holly's still there, Allan having wandered off.

"Snacks!" Holly says and puts out her hand. Then she catches my expression. "What's wrong?"

I open my mouth to say that Paige isn't coming, and instead hear myself say, "I just got dumped by my fake boyfriend."

She scrambles to her feet. "What?"

I force a laugh. "No big deal. It was a joke anyway." That's where I want to leave it. Instead, I hear, "I'm doing something wrong, aren't I? Giving off a . . ." I wave my arms. "Anti-boy vibe or something. Scaring them away, and I have no idea how or why." I rub my face. "Sorry, I don't mean to get angsty. Not over a fake boyfriend. It's just . . . The way he did it, I still feel dumped." I suck in a breath. "Shit. Stop that. Sorry."

"Don't apologize. He obviously hurt you. What'd he say?"

"That it's over. Then he practically ran from me when all I was trying to do was warn him about what happened to Logan last night. The situation is getting worse, too, and now Paige isn't coming until tomorrow."

I explain. Then we split up to hunt for Logan and Allan. I go back inside while Holly circles the building to check all the various groups out here. Inside, it's practically empty, and I wonder whether we've missed the call for a group meeting. The distant murmur of voices suggests we have.

I'm standing at the top of the steps, ready to start tracking my brother's scent when I realize that everyone who isn't outside seems to be in that meeting, which means the other end of the hall is silent. The end of the hall where our cell phones are kept . . .

I creep in that direction. If I hear so much as a cough, I'll retreat.

I continue to the office and put my ear to the door. Silence. I step back into the hall, close my eyes and listen, focus everything on that.

Silence. Complete silence.

I rap on the office door as softly as I can, but the sound still seems to echo in the silence. When no one answers, I turn the knob. It's locked, which surprises me because I thought Elijah broke it last night. I twist firmly, and it doesn't snap—it just disengages. Nice security. A credit card probably would have worked just as well.

I slip into the room. It's brightly lit, the sun streaming through the skylight, which I'm sure is awesome for the electronics. With the door shut and the sun blazing down, it's got to be ninety degrees in here. Who the hell designed this place?

I wipe away a bead of sweat and look around. There's a desktop computer—the one Elijah tried breaking into. There's also a printer with paper in the output tray. I flip it over to see a stack of sheets for a workshop we were supposed to have this morning. The printer menu screen tells me they were printed late yesterday afternoon. No one even bothered collecting them.

That's troubling, but it isn't why I'm here.

Elijah said they keep the phones in a locker. I find three lockboxes. One's too small to hold phones, so I ignore it. The other is unlocked—it's a long, narrow container that's open and empty. I strike gold with the third. It's a phone-charging cabinet. I've seen simple versions in libraries and airport lounges, a box a couple of feet square with pull-out shelves for the devices.

I open one drawer and see . . . Nothing. It's empty. I open the next. Same thing. I keep opening.

The charge-box is completely empty.

Maybe this is one of those devices that seem supercool until you actually use it and realize a simple shelf with plugs would have worked better.

I leave the box and look for anything big enough to hold two dozen cell phones. There's nothing, really. The office isn't that big. I open drawers and glance into the shallow closet, but it's mostly office supplies and a nest of tangled device cords. The only boxes are for printer paper. They're big enough, but no one's going to dump twenty cell phones into a cardboard box. There's no better way to ensure mutiny than to hand teenagers back their devices with scratches and dings. Sure, they already have scratches and dings, but we know every last one of them, and we'd better not find new ones.

There's a metal container under the printer paper cartons. I'm moving aside the first cardboard box when the contents shift in a way that paper *doesn't*. I open it to see the phones. Two dozen cell phones, tossed into a cardboard box as if headed for recycling.

That must be what these are. Recycled phones. Maybe for a game or some kind of cool tech project. As I pull them into the light, though, I see a phone case that looks like Doctor Who's blue phone box. Anime characters decorate another.

Not recycled phones.

I dig until I find a bubblegum pink leather cover with a Mexican sugar skull sticker. I open it to see my phone.

I stare down at the box.

What the hell?

There must be fifteen grand worth of tech here. Dumped into a cardboard box.

I stifle a surge of indignation and turn on my phone. Nothing happens, because it's been unplugged for the past day, and I'd handed it over with ten percent battery, assured by Tricia that they'd charge them for us.

I dig through the box until I find a plain black leather cover. Logan's phone. As usual, my brother had the foresight to charge his in Nick's car, and it's at eighty-five percent. The facial recognition fails, of course, but I know his code. We've always known each other's codes.

I enter it and wade through the inevitable barrage of text notifications. There's a goodnight one from Mom, who is thrilled that we're having such an excellent time we didn't call.

You have no idea, Mom.

As I look at the texts and messages, I notice the last one came in early yesterday evening. Odd, considering how many notifications he was getting until then. I see one from my ex and flip past, my stomach clenching even without reading it.

The last message—a group text from a schoolmate—came in at eight last night. A little earlier, there's one from Paige.

Hey, Logan. You've probably already had your phone confiscated. Sorry about that. I'll talk to the counselors when I get there. I understand the basic principle, but you guys need to be in touch with your parents. For now, have fun, and I'll see you tomorrow!

I hit Reply on her message and type.

It's Kate. I know Benny is sick (tell him I said hi!) and you're delayed, but seriously weird stuff is happening here. My phone's dead. I'm going to recharge it, and then Logan and I might head into the forest to wait for you. Yeah, stuff is THAT weird. Please don't tell Mom! Just text when you can, and I'll explain once we're out of here.

I hit Send. Then I return to the closet unit, where I saw a shoebox filled with cords. As I dig through the box, I listen for a reply from Paige. Sure, she's caring for her sick six-year-old, but Paige is always plugged in. She'll see my text pop up on her watch, and even if she's in the middle of giving Benny medicine, she'll let me know she'll reply ASAP.

I find the right cord and then check my text to see the exclamation mark signifying that it wasn't sent. My gaze rises to the cell service bars. We must *have* service. Otherwise, we wouldn't be given phone time every night. Yet there isn't a single bar.

When I hit a couple of buttons, a message pops up.

SIM card not installed.

I hurry back to the box and pull out a couple of older phones without thumb or facial recognition. After a few tries, I find one that isn't passcode protected. On the opening screen, it says the same thing. No SIM card.

They removed the SIM cards. Took them out and chucked all the phones into a box. That's why there's no message from Mom. They pulled the cards yesterday evening.

I stuff my phone, Logan's phone and the charge cord into my pockets. Then I start searching for our SIM cards.

I'd spotted a small locked box across the room. It'd been too small for all the cell phones, so I hadn't bothered snapping the lock. I do now and open it to find prescription bottles. I check a few. Adderall, Tylenol with codeine, Ambien. In other words, the counselors confiscated any medication that other campers might steal for recreational use.

I dig through the box, in case the SIM cards are at the bottom. They aren't. I see a couple of other small boxes down by the floor. I bend, and as I'm picking up one, air wafts through a vent in the wall. With it comes a very distinctive smell.

Blood.

CHAPTER TWENTY-SEVEN

Logan

The fact that they locked us in the office is troubling, but it isn't as if I'm trapped here. I'm a werewolf. I snap it easily. I'll probably regret that, but I really need to find Kate.

I'm heading outside when I spot Holly making her way toward her room. I call a "Hey," but like me, Holly is one of those people who hear a hail and presume it's for someone else. By the time I call her name, she's at her room. She sees me, and I motion her inside, where we can speak in private.

"Do you know where Kate is?" I ask.

"She went looking for you."

I bite back a growl of frustration. Before I can comment, Holly says, "Paige isn't coming until tomorrow," and explains what Kate heard.

"Do you know where Allan is?" I ask.

"Sure, outside with some other sorcerers."

I pause. "Who's all outside? Mostly spellcasters?"

She frowns as she thinks. "Actually, yes. Spellcasters and a few minor races."

"Any necromancers?"

"One, I think. I heard most are still sleeping. Partied hard enough to raise the dead, I guess. Let's just hope they didn't *really* raise any."

I manage a small smile at the quip, but I'm considering what she's said. The spellcasters and minor races are hanging out, killing time. The necromancers are all exhausted, like the counselor.

"Can you do me a favor?" I ask. "Find Allan and stick together. Maybe stay in your room." I raise my hands against her protest. "I know that sounds like an odd request, but whatever's going on here, I believe it mostly affects the half-demons. I'm still working it out. We can talk once I find Kate."

Before I can go, she taps my arm. "About Kate. She might be distracted, and just . . . go easy on her. Elijah broke it off. Yes, I know it wasn't a real relationship, but he was weird about it, made her feel like he was actually dumping her. She really didn't need that, especially after what happened with her last boyfriend."

I pause. "Brandon? No, he was definitely on the receiving end of that breakup. Believe me. I've been dealing with him ever since, blowing up my phone trying to get back with her."

She stares at me.

"What?" I say.

"You're still *talking* to him?"

"Why not? It didn't have anything to do with me. He's taking it really hard. Kate can be . . . tempestuous." I smile. "I'd say she gets it from our dad, but it comes from both parents, really."

Holly's staring as if I've just sprouted hair and fangs, and I almost reach up to be sure I haven't.

"Tempes—?" She bites the word off. "Are you actually

siding with the asshole who screwed around on your sister?"

"What?" I'm sure I've misheard. Or she's misunderstood something Kate said. "By screwed around, are you implying he had sex with another girl?"

"No, I'm implying they built a bookshelf together. Yes, he had sex with another girl because Kate wasn't ready. Then he told her what he did, thinking that'd make her see the error of her ways. And when she didn't give him another chance? He told *everyone* about it, and now she's dealing with crap from him and from your local cast of *Mean Girls*."

Now I'm the one staring. "Who told you this?"

"Who do you think told me? You can't tell me you haven't noticed. You guys go to the same school."

"I . . . "

"She's your sister, Logan. Your *twin* sister. Did you even ask why they broke up? Maybe find out before you decide to play Cupid getting them back together."

"I didn't—"

She lifts her hands. "Never mind. This isn't the time. Now you know, so when you see Kate, try showing a little compassion. I know you didn't like her with Elijah, but he still hurt her. And she did absolutely nothing to deserve it." She shakes her head. "Go, Logan. Your sister needs you."

I'm trying very hard not to think of what Holly just told me. She's right—we have more pressing concerns right now. But I keep thinking of Brandon texting me and pestering me at school, and me brushing him off politely, giving no sign that I had an issue with him, perhaps even showing enough consideration to suggest that I sympathized with his plight.

His *plight*.

His failure to harangue my sister into having sex with him.

Harangue?

I almost laugh at the word. He did more than pester and plead, which would be bad enough. He screwed around with someone else and then told Kate.

See, other girls will have sex with me. Better get on this now, 'cause I am in demand.

I clench my fists and struggle against the urge to put one through the wall.

A little voice whines that Kate should have told me, and now I feel sick for hanging out with him, but that's not my fault because I didn't know what happened.

Bullshit.

I knew Kate was upset. I saw her sinking into what we called her "blue" moods. Not depression, but depressive states, retreating to her room when Mom and Dad weren't around, because they'd notice.

I'd been there, though. I noticed. It was my responsibility to go to her and say, "What's wrong?"

I knew she was upset over the breakup, but deep inside, I rolled my eyes and called her dramatic. Just Kate being Kate.

I can say I didn't know about Brandon, but Nick hinted at it yesterday. I remember his shock on hearing I was in contact with Brandon. I might not have had a chance to pursue it with him, but I could have pursued it with her.

Hey, Kate. Nick seems to know something about Brandon I don't. Can we talk about that?

Nope, instead, I was busy worrying about my roommate stomping off. A total stranger who didn't even want my help. It made me feel good to be concerned for him. Virtue signaling. See what a nice guy I am? How considerate? Not the sort of brother who rolls his eyes at his sister's pain and dismisses it as teenage-girl drama.

I bend at my bedroom door. Kate's trail is there. I focus on that. It leads me upstairs and down the hall toward the office.

I remember those light footsteps. That careful rap on a door.

Not someone timidly approaching the counselors; Kate staging a break-in. Unable to find me, she'd taken matters into her own hands.

Off on an adventure by herself.

Giving up on me. While this is a small thing, it symbolizes so much more.

Logan isn't there for me. He's been hanging out with my ex, not even asking why I broke it off. He's been hanging out with the girls who are bullying me.

She'd hate that word: bullying. But that's what it was, and I can say I didn't know, but I remember catching the odd snarky remark and dismissing it as jealousy. When she refused to join the popular clique at school, they took offense and twisted that into contempt. From "Who does she think she is?" to "Don't you think she's kinda weird?"

I thought it'd been a few backbiting comments, just typical stuff that Kate would ignore as she always did.

How much worse had it gotten?

Hint: she shut down her social media accounts.

Faint movement sounds inside the office. Footfalls hurrying to the door. I turn the knob and push, and Kate lets out a soft gasp, her mouth opening with, "I was looking for Tric—" Then she sees it's me and grins, and it's the grin I know so well, the grin I don't get nearly as much these days.

I slide into the office and let the door close. Then I catch her up in a hug so sudden and fierce that she yelps before covering her reaction with a chuckle.

"Nice to see you, too, Lo."

"Elijah is an asshole," I say as I back up.

There's a flicker of consternation that I know. Or maybe because I know and thought she would need that hug. She makes a face, such a Kate face. It's a Mom face, too, throwing off concern, not wanting to be seen as the type of person who needs it.

She shrugs. "I'm not sure about *asshole*, but he's something, that's for sure."

"He's—"

I start to tell her that he's Logan Jonsen's half-brother. But this isn't the time. It's also not the time to say I know about Brandon, and I'm going to kick his ass. Well, not literally kick his ass. I'd like to—both his and Elijah's—but Kate wouldn't want that, and I'm not sure once I started kicking that I'd stop. I'll tear a verbal strip off them, instead. Not as satisfying, but safer.

"Forget about Elijah," I say.

"I have," she says. "For now, at least. I was just coming to find you."

"I know. I heard about Paige."

"And it seems that's the least of our worries." Kate holds up my cell phone and shows a text she sent Paige, undelivered. My gaze shoots to the signal-strength indicators. There aren't any.

"They're blocking the signal," I say. "I'm not surprised. That's Draconian, but if they really want us offline this week, they need to do that. Someone's bound to have smuggled in a cell-ready device."

"It's not a blocker," she says. "They've removed the SIM card." She walks over and picks up a printer paper carton. Inside is a jumble of cell phones. "They removed all the SIM cards and dumped the phones in here."

Okay, this is different. This is worse.

"We need to find those SIM cards," I say.

"Agreed, and I was doing that, before . . ." She tugs me to the far wall and motions for me to crouch and inhale. It takes a moment. Then I detect the unmistakable odor of blood.

Kate's already heading for the door. I follow. She checks the hall. It's still silent, so we creep to the next door. Kate tries the handle. Then she snaps it and pushes open the door.

Inside is a dorm room like ours except this one is brightly lit from that windowed ceiling. Despite the light, though, someone is still in bed, and Kate draws back, as if to retreat. Then she inhales and audibly swallows. I know why. I tap her hip, saying I'll go first, but of course she ignores me. She slips forward. I step into the room and shut the door behind me.

Kate continues to the bed. Despite the stifling heat, the covers are pulled up to the sleeper's face. Kate stops, her nose wrinkling as she rubs it, banishing a smell.

She stands there, looking down, and I know she's fighting the urge to check for vital signs. There's no need. She realizes that from the smell. Not the blood—that only signifies injury. It's the other smell, that one from a corpse left in a sweltering hot room.

Kate draws back the comforter. It's a female counselor, one I remember seeing at the counselors' dining table yesterday. She'd sat near the end, focused on her meal, quiet as I spoke to the others. I'd presumed it was my presence making her uncomfortable. Perhaps not.

As Kate pulls off the comforter, the smell of decomp rises, freed from the sheets. Kate exhales, as if expunging it from her nose.

The bloodied top sheet sticks to the young woman's body. Kate peels it back as I pad forward to see no signs of injury. There's blood on the counselor's T-shirt, but when Kate discreetly tugs that up, the young woman's torso is nearly clean. I'm reminded of Mason's fast-healing wound, but the real answer is the blood drying under from her nose. That's the only sign of injury.

Like Mason yesterday when he'd been attacked in the forest. Dead, his only injury a bleeding nose.

Just like Mason.

Except, no one was here to revive her.

CHAPTER TWENTY-EIGHT

Kate

The counselor is dead. I don't even know her name, don't remember speaking to her, and now she's dead.

As Logan watches, I check her torso and arms more carefully, and then lift her hands, turning them this way and that. I'm looking for defensive wounds and seeing none. Then I finger the woman's wrist, and I see bruises there. More bruises on one shoulder and her opposite side. Scratches on her arm.

Signs she'd either been restrained and beaten or beaten and then restrained.

I think of what Logan said had happened to Mason. His bloodied nose. His heart stopping. Did something similar happen here? Had an otherworldly *whatever* killed the counselor? Then her roomie—not being a werewolf—hadn't noticed the smell and just let her sleep?

That's what I want to believe. An outside force killed this counselor. Not anyone here.

Logan moves forward and checks the young woman's shirt. Through the blood, I read "Team Witch."

Logan murmurs, "One witch, one necro, five half-demons."

"Hmm?"

He opens his mouth, but before he can get out a word, footfalls thunder down the hall. I freeze, but they're at the far end, where the meeting had been. They only sound loud because there are so many of them.

The meeting is out, campers charging from the room as if they're thundering from last class. Logan moves to the door to listen. I look for a hiding place. When steps come our way, I yank the sheets over the dead girl again, and we both duck and roll under the beds.

The steps continue past the door. More follow, and the doorknob turns. I hold my breath. Across the way, Logan's gaze follows the sound. He's tensed and ready for trouble. But the door only opens a moment as someone reaches in and grabs an item from the dresser top. Then it shuts again, and the footsteps retreat.

When I start to slide out, Logan motions for me to wait. Seconds tick past. Then the other footsteps pass, as if they'd only gone to a room temporarily. Now they head over to the other hall. I catch the click of a door.

"'Bout time," a voice growls. It's Mason. "The pup went to lift his leg on a tree somewhere."

"He's outside?" Tricia says.

Mason snorts. "Maybe. You can't tell with werewolves. I think he planned to just use the regular facilities, though."

"José?" Tricia says. "Go get Logan. Has anyone found his sister?"

"Still looking," José says. "She's around. She's been hanging out with that witch and that guy with dreads." A pause. "I didn't see him with the other HDs."

HDs? Half-demons. Right, that's what Elijah is posing as.

"Just find the curs. The sooner we're rid of these parasites, the better."

Parasites. That's a common insult for vampires. But Tricia obviously is including werewolves in that.

Across the way, Logan tenses. My gaze shoots to him. Through the wall, I hear Mason say, "What the fuck?"

"Someone's coming to take you and your canine buddies out of here. Unless you'd rather walk."

"I might. Could use the exercise. But if you want me gone, just say the word and let me grab my shit."

"It's packed and outside. Now come on."

I relax. Okay, the situation isn't as dire as it seemed. I have no idea what happened to the poor girl rotting in the bed above me, but I'm going to guess no one here is to blame.

Whatever happened to Mason also happened to her, and this morning, her roommate presumed she was sleeping off a late night.

That means others are in danger from whatever's going on, but Paige can resolve that tomorrow. Right now, we're being kicked out, and considering I didn't plan to stick around, that's fine with me.

"You heard all that?" Logan says as we slide from under the beds.

"I did. It's the excuse we need to leave and get someplace where we can notify Paige. I'd like to see whether Holly and Allan will join us. We should probably warn Elijah, too, in case they realize he's a werewolf."

"He isn't coming with us," Logan says, face darkening.

"Nope, he's not. But he deserves a warning. Now let's get out of here.

. . .

On the way to the stairs, Logan whispers his theory. Whatever's happening here, it's affecting the half-demons. Well, the hormonal part, that is. Something else is up with the necromancers, and it's probably connected to those ghostly encounters we had in the forest. I suspect they're being pestered or harassed by ghosts, and they're too exhausted and distracted to notice what's going on with the half-demons.

"Could it be possession?" I whisper. "Half-demons are more susceptible to it. I've never heard of mass possession, but that could be the answer."

"Except they don't *seem* possessed. They aren't acting like themselves, but they aren't *not* acting like themselves, if that makes any sense."

It does. Tricia is no longer the bubbly young woman we met when we arrived, but it's been a gradual change, not the sudden one of possession.

"What about the guy who tried to cut your Achilles tendon?" I say. "He's a sorcerer."

"Mob mentality. He's not actually affected, but seeing the rest act out gives him an excuse to do the same. There are others like him, I suspect, who've joined in."

And there are some who won't join in even if the half-demons try to convince them. Some who will rebel in horror.

I think of the dead counselor's Team Witch shirt.

Had she realized something was wrong, and they murdered her for it? I don't want to think that. I can't. Literally cannot. It goes too far.

Cutting Logan's tendon is crazy, but it's the sort of thing that does happen when a mob gets out of control.

Murder goes beyond that, and if that counselor was killed because she was interfering with plans, I don't even want to know what those plans are.

I need to believe that, whatever's happening here, it's manageable insanity, which we will manage by gathering Holly and Allan and any other spellcasters who want to come with us, and then we'll get Paige and her resources to truly squelch this fire before it spreads.

We can hear voices outside. Once, I catch a snarl from Mason. Seriously, the guy missed his supernatural calling—he snarls and growls and grunts more than any were-wolf. Whatever he's bitching about now, it's only a snarled word that I don't catch, and then he falls silent. Probably some token protest against being kicked out. He doesn't want to stay, but he won't like leaving at the end of a boot, either. Can't say I blame him. If I didn't suspect we were dealing with something more than paranoid teens, I'd argue the point, too.

But whatever has gone wrong, it's otherworldly. Demonic. Ghostly. Something else altogether. This is not the sort of thing you can treat rationally. It's time to get the hell out and look forward to having a lifelong excuse to never attend a supernatural leadership conference again.

We sneak down the stairs, moving quietly despite the empty and silent floor below. When we reach the bottom, someone clears a throat, and I spin. It's one of the counselors, flanked by two campers, all three in Team Half-Demon tees.

"Hey," I say. "I heard you guys were looking for us."

"Outside," the counselor says with a jerk of his chin.

"Did I hear you want us gone?" I continue. "I didn't mean to eavesdrop but . . ." I point at my ear. "Werewolf hearing. Can't help it. You can imagine how much fun that was for our parents—we heard all the grown-up conversations, and we didn't need to put a glass to the door."

"Outside," the counselor says again.

"Sure," I say. "We don't want to be anywhere we aren't wanted. But I left my notebook under my bed. Just let me grab that and—"

One of the campers steps forward. He'd been partially hidden by the counselor, and as he moves, I see something in his hand. It rises, and I fall back against Logan with, "Holy shit!"

It's a gun. A hunting rifle. I remember the long, empty lockbox upstairs in the office. This is what had been inside it.

"A gun?" Logan says, bristling with mere annoyance, as if the guy pulled a water pistol. "I can assure you this is not necessary. Kate asked politely to retrieve her notebook. If that isn't possible, then just say so. Now lower the gun—"

"No."

Logan's voice hardens. "We are the Alpha's children. You are threatening us with a rifle when we are complying with your orders. Unless you want to invoke the wrath of the werewolf Pack, please show a little respect and lower—"

The guy raises it to my chest. "No."

Logan rocks forward. The guy's finger moves to the trigger.

"Lo," I whisper, and he stops.

"It's okay," I murmur under my breath, heart pounding. "We're fine." Louder, I say, "Take us outside, and we'll go."

The trio leads us down the hall. At a noise down a side

passage, I glance as discreetly as I can. It's Elijah. He's half out of his room, poised there, as if spotting me, ready to retreat. Then he sees the rifle. His eyes widen.

Hand at my side, I gesture for him to go back into his room. Do I hope he'll stand firm and refuse? Stride down here and demand to know what's going on? Better yet, sneak down and wrest the gun away from this guy?

Yes, I do. But I also know that isn't the smart move. Elijah makes the smart move. He eases back into his room and closes the door quietly, and I try not to be disappointed.

"I heard you say someone's coming for us," Logan says as we reach the door. "That isn't necessary. We'll walk out. We know the way."

They don't even acknowledge he's spoken. One pushes on the door, and the noise from outside rushes in. Hoots and hollers and jeers. Clearly, the half-demons are looking forward to seeing us banished.

Fine by me.

We'll give them their show. It'll sting, but we'll do it. We'll walk away knowing this will be resolved later, and every adult half-demon in any position of power will be tripping over themselves to assure the werewolves and vampires no insult was intended—it was all a mistake. That'll give Mom plenty of political ammunition. We'll get concessions from this fiasco, and that'll help our standing in the supernatural world.

I keep telling myself this as they push us through the door at rifle point. I pay little attention to our surroundings, caught up in my own thoughts of the future. Keep my mind on that, and I can endure this humiliation. In the end, we will win.

There's a crowd ahead, at least a dozen campers

ringed around a campfire. It's not lit, thankfully, because one of the idiots is standing in the middle of it.

"Mason?" Logan whispers.

I frown over to see Logan staring at the firepit. I follow his gaze back to it and realize the idiot standing in the middle of the piled wood is Mason.

No, he's not *standing* in the middle.

He's bound to a pole in the middle. With wood and kindling stacked at his feet and a gag over his mouth, he snarls and writhes as the half-demons jeer and catcall and wave lighters and matches over their heads.

And beside him? Two other firepits. Two other poles.

Two funeral pyres.

Waiting for us.

CHAPTER TWENTY-NINE

Logan

I am a werewolf. You may not need a silver bullet to take me down, but the threat of a mere hunting rifle is not enough for me to step into a firepit to be burned at the stake. I cannot be taken that easily. I'm a trained fighter with superhuman strength.

That is the thought screaming through my mind as I go down under the barrage of blows and kicks.

This is not going to happen.

The moment Kate and I saw what lay ahead, we swung on our captors—and a half-dozen campers jumped from their ambush spot by the door. The others around the fire join them, and we are swarmed by twenty supernaturals. We fight as if we're the ones demon-possessed, but ultimately, we fall under those blows, under the very crush of our attackers' bodies.

Even when they have us down, we still fight, but it does no good. We're bound and dragged to the firepit, and all of our struggles only earn us more blows, only sap our strength, until we're hauled onto a pyre. They don't bother with the third stake. They put us both on one, back to back, and the last view I have of my sister's face is blood and dirt and impossibly wide eyes. Eyes wide not with terror but with shock. Those eyes scream three words: *I don't understand.*

I know my sister, and I know what she's been telling herself. That no one here killed the witch counselor. She was not silenced. She was murdered by a ghost or demon or other supernatural force. That makes sense to Kate. This does not.

"Why?" she croaks as they tighten the nylon ropes around our wrists and ankles. "Why?"

She isn't asking why this is happening to us.

She's asking why it's happening at all.

How it *can be* happening. How twenty fellow supernaturals could want to kill us in the most terrible and symbolic way possible.

Burned at the stake.

It's the fate of so many of our kind—*all* of our kinds. Sorcerer, witch, necromancer, werewolf, vampire, half-demon. We have all been burned at the stake for the "heresy" of our powers. Such a death rings with symbolism to every person here. It is what humans have done to us. It is not ever what we do to one another.

Kate asks why, and they don't answer. They sneer, and they mock her, but they don't answer.

If forced to respond, they might say they fear us. They might say we are a danger or an abomination.

None of that is the reason, though. It's just the excuse. It's what they tell themselves, while the truth blazes from their eyes, rings from their laughter. They're doing this because they want to. Whatever fills them, that adrenaline and rage, this is how they'll exercise it.

Exercise it, not exorcise it, because they don't want to

be rid of it. This rage is exciting. It makes their hearts beat faster, their adrenaline pump. It makes them feel powerful.

And all that, while a lovely little revelation, does not resolve the fact that we're bound to stakes in a laid firepit. Reflecting on it, however, is only a way to keep me calm while I do something about it.

When we were first bound, we tried the ropes, of course, but they aren't anything we can snap. They've been careful about that. Now Kate's working at the knots while exhorting the non-demons in the crowd to do something.

"You're surrounded by half-demons," she's saying to someone. "Doesn't that tell you something?"

A chorus of catcalls drowns out any response.

"Whatever this is," she says, voice rising, "it's affecting demon blood. They have an excuse. *You* don't. You're about to commit murder."

"No," a girl yells. "We're about to exterminate parasites. Kill you before you kill us."

Kate keeps arguing. Trying to reason with those in the crowd who should be open to reason. Those uninfected by whatever has ignited the blood of the half-demons. Normally, that would be what I'd do. Right now, though, I'm working on a backup plan.

My mom has a trick she taught herself, one my dad can do but less expertly, lacking the patience to learn it. Mom can localize her Change, specifically her hand, allowing it to shift to a stage between human and wolf. It seems like a parlor trick, yet it comes with one very useful advantage: her fingers become claws. With it, she can pin a werewolf to a wall with nails sharp enough to rip out their throat. The fact she's still human means she can threaten or negotiate.

I've been practicing this mostly to improve overall control of my shifts. Now, as Kate engages the crowd, I focus on shifting my hand, feeling hair sprout on the back of it. I keep my fingers cupped away from the crowd so they won't see what I'm doing.

Sweat beads, and I blow upward, trying to unstick hair tickling my forehead.

You think it's warm now, just wait until they light that fire.

Slowly, my fingers begin to Change, thicker, stubbier, the nails thickening, too. I pluck at the nylon. My nails aren't sharp enough to cut through the rope, but I can slice threads. It's slow going.

Kate's still shouting at the non-demons in the group, trying to make them see reason, but they're caught up in the fervor, mocking her "nonsense." To them, there's nothing wrong with the half-demons. They've just had enough of parasites like us.

They're feeding on the frenzy of the others. It validates their own rage.

See? I'm not wrong to feel this way. Others do, too.

What will they do when they realize they're wrong? That the half-demons have an excuse . . . and they do not?

That's the true horror here. Not the infected half-demons but the handful of others who have joined in, ready to light us on fire because it's the rare opportunity to indulge their worst instincts.

I've been worrying about what *I'm* becoming. How much I am like my father. How my own instincts are rising up and shutting down common sense.

What am I capable of?

Not this. Never this. Whatever lurks inside me, it's dark and it's frightening, but it's not this.

My darkness is cold steel. Dangerous and deadly, and I

need to learn to control it. But it's a weapon. Not a fire that consumes, a fire willing to set anything ablaze on the flimsiest of pretenses.

My darkness is my father's. And my mother's, too. It's the werewolf instinct to protect and defend at any cost. Yet they could never get caught up in what's happening here. They don't have a fire that needs feeding, a rage that demands an outlet. They'd be the ones trying to stop it.

Well, they'd stop it to save Kate and me. Mom would fight for Mason if it wasn't obvious suicide, and Dad would help because she'd want it, not because he gives a damn about a stranger.

Just as I think that, Holly peeks around the far end of the building. She pulls back quickly and then Allan looks. I shake my head, trying to motion them back with my chin. They withdraw.

Like I said, Mom would fight for strangers if it wasn't suicidal.

This is suicidal.

Better Holly and Allan stay back and stay safe.

They peek out every few seconds. I keep shaking my head, warning them not to do anything stupid. And I keep snapping these threads. When I've weakened my bindings, I do the same for Kate. She tenses as the rough pad of my finger brushes her. Then she feels the hard nail working at her rope.

"Mom's trick?" she says.

"Yep."

"Damn, when'd you learn that?"

The words sound like Kate, taking this whole "burning at the stake" problem in stride, but her voice wavers, telling me she's struggling to stay calm.

When I've weakened her rope, I tap her arm with

three fingers. Then I tap two, starting the countdown. Her fingers close around mine.

"No," she says. "Not yet."

"Why? You got more to say?" one of the half-demons yells. "We're getting a little tired of your voice, blondie. Time to break out the marshmallows."

Hoots and hollers sound, and Holly peeks again. She motions something I don't catch, and then she withdraws.

Kate's "not yet" wasn't for the crowd—it was for me. After a burst of pique—what the hell are we waiting for? —I answer my own question. If we break free now, we're right back where we were when we got jumped coming out of that door: facing this entire mob.

I should have thought of that. Kate should have been the one leaping in without thinking it through.

And does that matter? I keep putting things in terms of which of us "should" do them. This is a Kate move; that's a Logan one, as if our roles are clearly delineated, as if I lose something by failing to do the "Logan" thing, and she steals from me by doing it herself.

We are not children. We're leaving those old roles behind. I have no idea what we'll become, but it does no good to keep fighting the changes.

My sister is correct. We need a distraction, and I'd love to be able to ask Holly and Allan to provide it, but there's no way of doing that. We can only rely on each other.

"Start with the vamp!" someone shouts.

I can't see Mason's pyre. It's behind me, and he's facing the opposite way. The wood creaks as he struggles, and I'm sure every one of his grunts is a muffled expletive. He's terrified, too. The stink of sweat and fear wafts from him, overpowering Kate's lighter musk of anxious sweat.

If Mason dies, he'll come back to life. That doesn't

matter. I saw his terror when he thought he'd risen as a vampire. That is a fate to postpone for as long as he can.

Then I remember the cut on his side, the one that healed instantly. And I remember a story in one of the council books I'd been too young to read: the eyewitness account of the burning of a vampire.

You cannot kill a vampire by burning. Nor by a stake to the heart—that makes no more sense than needing silver bullets for a werewolf. The only way to kill a vamp is to inflict the one injury that cannot heal: decapitation.

In that account, the mob did not decapitate their victim before lighting the pyre, and I had nightmares for weeks afterward, of imagining her torment, able to burn but unable to die, her flesh constantly healing.

When I confessed to Mom what I'd read, I'd half expected to be banned from that library for life. Instead, I no longer had free access to it, needing to run my selections past Mom or Dad.

I think of that story, and I smell Mason's terror, and I know he's realized the same thing. He will heal. Burn and heal.

I swallow hard, and I open my mouth to say something to the mob, to convince them to start with us. But if they start with him, is that not the distraction we need? He'll heal.

How cold does that feel? To let him suffer so we can get free? Yet it's the logical choice. He will suffer, but he will heal, and we will have the chance to free all three of us.

"Burn the vamp!" someone yells, and others take up the chant, and I clamp my mouth shut.

"Sure!" Kate yells. "Burn the vamp. So he can come back and slaughter every last one of you. You do understand that's how it works, right? He's still human. He hasn't died yet. But if you kill him, he comes back, and then you have a real vampire to deal with."

I squeeze my eyes shut. She's drawing them to us. Protecting Mason because even if he's been nothing but an asshole to her, that's who she is. He's defenseless. We are not.

"Why the hell isn't she gagged?" someone yells.

"Because some of you know I'm right," she says. "Some of you want to hear what I have to say. You want to listen to reason."

"Shut that fucking bitch up!"

Someone lights a match. Another lifts a lighter. Kate hooks her pinky with mine, and we wait. We grit our teeth, and we wait. One of the counselors lowers a lighter to the kindling at our feet.

A cry goes up. Kate's pinky tightens on mine, but she stays perfectly still. Waiting.

A piece of crumpled paper catches fire. I watch it, my heart hammering, smoke wafting to my nose, every primitive survival instinct screaming for me to break this rope.

Fire. They're setting us on fire.

I will myself to be calm. We are waiting on purpose. Waiting for the fire to catch and the mob to relax, and then we will break free.

They dare set us on fire? We'll use it against them. We'll fight them off with the very weapon they sought to use against us.

They light another piece of crumpled paper. As soon as they do, though, the first goes out, having never come close enough for me to feel heat. The second piece ignites, and they light a third, right beside my sneakers, but both only burn to ash, the wood below untouched.

Someone shouts in the distance. A cheer and a cry goes up as others turn. Kate gasps, and I twist to see Tricia running toward us. In her hand, she carries a familiar red canister.

A gas can.

"This will get the job done," Tricia says, hoisting the can.

"Oh shit, oh shit," Kate whispers. "Now, do it now."

I flex, preparing to snap the rope, knowing it's too soon. They're not distracted, and there's no fire to use against them.

Someone has grabbed the can from Tricia, and he's twisting it open as he runs, lifting it to slosh onto the wood, the others ready with matches and lighters, their faces glinting, teeth bared, as predatory as a starving wolf that scents prey.

"Three," Kate whispers. "Two—"

"Hey!" a voice shouts. "Did I hear something about a werewolf-killing party? I think you guys forgot my invitation."

I look up as Elijah walks around the building.

"You're just in time," someone says. "Come join the party."

"Don't mind if I do. I presume that other pyre is mine?"

The rumble of the mob subsides as all eyes turn his way.

"That other funeral pyre," he says. "The empty stake. That's mine, right?"

He pulls a length of steel construction rebar from behind his back and lifts it over his head.

"'Cause if you're burning werewolves?" He bends the rebar. "You forgot one."

CHAPTER THIRTY

Kate

I hear the voice behind me. I can't see who it is, even when I twist, but I know that voice and my heart leaps. Then Elijah says something about not getting an invitation, and I realize he's not here to help—he's joining in, hiding what he is in case they wonder why he didn't participate.

Survival of the fittest, baby. Can't blame a guy for trying.

Yes, actually, I can, and when I start to stifle my rising outrage, I stop.

No, use that. Get angry.

I channel my fury at Elijah's betrayal and flex, snapping my bonds just as the crowd goes quiet, and I think, "Oh, shit." They've noticed. They see that I'm free, and there's a moment of surprise before they'll attack.

Then Elijah's voice penetrates the blood pounding in my ears.

"'Cause if you're burning werewolves? You forgot one."

I twist to see him bending something metal over his

head, a feat of strength that proves his claim. That's when I realize Logan's still bound.

"Lo!" I say as the mob rushes for Elijah.

Logan snaps the rope as I drop to claw at the one binding our feet. Someone notices. A shout goes up. Logan's already bending, his hand still misshapen with those very useful nails.

Once he's working at the rope, I leave him to it. I have my fists free, and I use them, slamming the first half-demon within range. Without thinking, I strike full-strength, and the sickening crack of his jaw rings out, echoed by his scream of pain.

I swing at the next one, hitting lighter, but not holding back the way I should. I cannot afford to truly hold back. They need to see what they're up against, as I couldn't demonstrate earlier in the melee that knocked me down before I managed more than a few clumsy blows.

Now they get the real Kate Danvers.

With every blow, every scream of pain, a couple of those rushing at us falter, something deep in their infected brains still aware enough to fear. Others, though, rush in howling, the cries of pain and the crack of breaking bones only setting their fevers aflame.

A smell hits my nostrils. Acrid and sharp. Something splashes onto my jeans.

Gasoline.

The rope binding my legs finally falls free. I twist and kick the guy with the gas can as more sloshes onto me. He falls back. Someone throws a match. I dive out of the way just in time.

I grab the gas can and swing it, contents spraying across the mob. A few cry out in agony as the gas splashes into their eyes. I empty the canister as Logan stumbles free of his foot bindings.

A half-demon rushes in. Logan swings, but the guy teleports just out of reach. Another charges my brother with a penknife raised. I wheel, grab his arm and wrench the knife from his hand.

My brother keeps fighting. I don't worry about him. He has this. As I run for Mason, fog billows up around me. I slow, thinking a sorcerer is casting against me. Then I see Allan on the forest's edge, his fingers raised as he casts fog to hide me.

I wave my thanks and bend behind Mason, using the penknife to cut him free.

When he's loose, he rips off the duct tape gag with, "What the hell are you doing?"

"Setting you free, asshole. You're welcome."

He turns, sees me and blinks. "You? I thought . . ."

He thought it was Logan, and I don't mistake the disappointment that flashes through his eyes. He might have been giving Logan shit for coming to his rescue, but he'd been pleased, too. Seeing his mistake, he switches gears with, "I thought you didn't like me much."

"You're an asshole. Not a hanging offense. Or a burning one." I take his hand and slap the penknife into it. "We'd appreciate some help."

"There are two dozen supernaturals. You can't fight—"

"Eighteen, but who's counting. We're not trying to take them down. We're trying to get out of here and maybe give them a reason not to follow. Now—"

A half-demon charges. I hit him with a right hook that sends him yowling into the fog.

I turn back to Mason and point at the knife. "Use that.

Put a few holes in them. Remember you can heal. Try not to die."

I take off before he can respond.

I'm racing through my fog cover when a girl stumbles in. It's Mackenzie, still wearing her Team Witch shirt.

I lift my hands. "Just stay out of my way. I know you can hear me and understand me. This has gotten way out of hand, and I hope you see that. I don't want to hurt you."

"Well, I want to hurt *you*, parasite."

Her lips move in a spell. I rush her, but she launches a fireball. It's a small one, barely worthy of the name, and I mentally laugh.

Then the fireball hits my shirt. It ignites, and my brain freezes, still thinking, *But it was just a tiny fireball.*

That's when I remember the gasoline splashing.

Fire scorches me. Mackenzie laughs. She throws back her head and laughs, and all I can think is, *She's not infected. This is her. All her.*

I yank up my shirt, biting back howls of pain. I manage to get it off, and I'm still holding it by one corner when I see her grinning at me, and I whip the shirt at her. She yelps and flies back. That's all I meant to do—scare her—but she must have been in the path of that gasoline, and her own shirt catches fire. She screams.

I run at her. Run, and shove her to the ground and hope she has the sense to roll out the fire, because I cannot stop to help. Cannot pause to care.

I race through the fog, hitting anyone who appears in my way. The fact I'm wearing only a bra seems to help—it gives my attackers pause. Still, I pull on my scorched shirt.

When a figure stumbles into me, I grab him by the

shoulders, ready to throw him aside. Then I see his short locs.

"It's me!" Elijah says as he twists and sees who has him.

I let him go, and he steadies himself, turning with a wry smile as blood drips from his mouth. "You might *want* to hit me, but I'm on your side."

"Move," I say.

"What?"

I gesture that he's between me and the fighting ahead.

"Oh, right," he says. He does not, however, move. He wipes blood from his mouth. "Look, about earlier—"

"Do you know why I wanted to talk to you then? To warn you about this."

His gaze drops. "Yeah, I'm sor—"

"And I don't actually care. My brother is in there." I point toward the sounds of fighting. "That's what I care about. Mason's free. We're fine. We'd appreciate your help, but that's your choice."

I start to go around him.

He catches my shoulder. "Kate." He pauses, seeing my expression, and murmurs, "Okay. Not the time. Go on. I'm right behind you."

I run, protected by Allan's fog. Once I reach the locus of the fighting, though, the fog hinders more than it helps, and he dissipates it. The mist clears, and I see . . .

I stop short, my breath catching.

My brother is fighting, but he's not overwhelmed, as I feared. He's facing off against three guys. Holly is just around the corner of the building, casting spells to help him, mostly sorcerer knock-backs to keep him from being jumped while he's midswing.

Off to the side, Mason has indeed joined the fray,

fighting two half-demons. And the rest of our attackers? Some have fled. Others are tending to their injuries. At least a half-dozen, though, aren't standing around watching Logan and Mason fight. They are fighting each other.

At first, I think some—maybe the non-demons—have come to their senses and are trying to shut this down. Then I realize that's not what I'm seeing at all.

This is blind frenzy. Powers flying and spells flying and blood flying. The air seems to sizzle with electricity and sets even my nerves ablaze. A hyperawareness that raises my hackles and makes me want to wheel on Elijah and tell him what I think of him.

No, it makes me want to hit him. Slam my fists into him and say I don't care if he came to our aid—he is not forgiven for hurting me.

But he knows that. I've made that clear, and whatever I'm feeling, it affects me only enough to sense that rising rage while knowing it's unfounded.

Around me, some of the snarls of rage and howls of pain have taken on a different note. Calls for help. Cries for mercy.

It's the non-demons, realizing at last that something is wrong, that this isn't just a way to indulge their most socio- pathic impulses. They realize they're in actual danger, and that's what flips the switch in their heads. They're under attack from crazed half-demons, and they're screaming for rescue, and to be bluntly honest, I'm a lot more worried about the half-demons themselves. They're the infected ones. They have an excuse.

Yet even when I see a fire demon grab a gasoline-splat- tered half-demon, her shirt igniting, I can't stay to help. I will have nightmares about that. Against all better judgment, I will look her up later, see her smiling school photo and say to myself, "This is the girl who caught fire. This is the girl I couldn't help."

But I can't. As horrible as it feels, I must take advantage of this madness and let them attack one another because it keeps them from attacking us.

An ice demon grabs my bare arm, his fingers burning as much as any fire. I hiss in pain and spin, my fist raised, but Elijah rips him off me and throws him aside. Another camper jumps on Elijah, and I wrench that one off, and Elijah says a quick, "Thanks," but I ignore it and barrel on toward my brother.

The three of us make quick work of Logan's attackers. These may be supernaturals, but the half-demons' powers aren't mature enough to be a serious threat, and the spellcasters are too busy shouting for someone to come to *their* rescue. No one does. No one will.

Once Logan's free, we help Mason, but he's only fighting one guy. As Elijah and Logan run to help, I notice Allan at the edge of the fray, casting his fog spells. A figure is advancing on him. It's Hayden, the sorcerer who tried to cut Logan's tendon. He's homing in on Allan, who's too busy casting to notice.

I leave my brother and Elijah to help Mason, and I jog over as Hayden shouts, "Bitch!" Or that's what he must be saying, because it sounds like *witch* but only Allan and I are around, and Hayden sure as hell knows what I am, which is—in canine vernacular—technically a bitch. But his gaze stays fixed on Allan. He grabs Allan's shoulder and whips him around.

"I'm talking to you, witch," he says. "Do you think you're fooling anyone?"

Allan hits him with a knock-back. Hayden staggers. Then he recovers, his face gathering in a sneer.

"Just because you can do sorcerer magic doesn't make you one, witch."

Hayden's fingers rise. I charge and knock him flying, whereupon Hayden proves that he might look like a jock and act like a jock, but he's sure as hell *not* a jock. He tries a few weak spells and weaker punches, but I only need to land a few blows of my own for him to take off, yowling like a scalded cat.

"I'm thinking we were wrong about whatever's infecting people," I say to Allan. "Or else that guy is high as a kite. Calling you a witch?" I shake my head.

Allan looks at me, his gaze searching mine. Then he grins. It sparks just for a moment before he sobers, eyes still glittering as he says, "Don't worry about him. He's fine—just a grade-A asshole. But you and I need to talk later."

Holly comes running over. "Logan's looking for you, Kate."

"Is he okay?"

"He's fine. They're clear and ready to get out of here."

I glance at Allan. "You were saying?"

"Later," he says. "Time to flee this shit-storm."

We run back to the others. Holly casts blur spells and Allan casts fog, and between the two, we escape the melee and make it into the forest.

"Tell me you found cell phones," Elijah says, panting.

"Yes, but they took out the SIM cards," I say. "We're going to need to get to the highway and flag down a car."

"The three of us will Change forms," Logan says. "If they come after us, we'll be better able to fight as wolves." He looks at Elijah. "How fast can you shift?"

"Uhh . . . I haven't had my first Change yet."

"Kate?" Logan says.

"I'm not nearly as fast as you."

"Can we just *go*?" Mason says. "You guys fight just fine in human form."

"Yes, but—" Logan begins.

I wheel, cutting my brother short. From somewhere at the edge of the fog comes a noise. A snuffling.

"Lo?" I say.

"I hear it," he says, tracking the sound.

"Allan?" I murmur. "Can you kill the fog?"

With a wave, Allan cancels his spell. Holly casts a cover spell. As long as we stand still, we're covered. Or that's the theory though I'm not sure how well it works on a group this large, even huddled together.

When the fog dissipates, I see . . . nothing. We're in the forest, the chaos of the camp behind us, and around us there are only trees.

The snuffling comes again, like a giant wolf. But nothing is there.

No one speaks. We're all peering around, trying to figure it out. My mind flips through possibilities. The only one even remotely plausible is a werewolf covered by a cover spell. Yet the snuffling doesn't sound like a wolf's. It's too wet, too . . . My skin prickles. I can't even name what I hear in that snuffle, only that it isn't human, isn't wolf, isn't natural.

Elijah taps my arm, and I follow his finger to see grass swaying, as if something is moving through it. I glance over to see Mason, predictably not huddled close to us, like a kid who doesn't want to be seen with his uncool parents.

"Mason!" I hiss under my breath.

He glances over. Then he jerks back with a yelp, his arm flying up, blood drops flicking. Logan yanks him closer to us.

"Something *bit* me," Mason says, the puncture wounds already closing. "I felt—"

The invisible thing lunges, hitting Mason so hard he falls against us. We yank him back, but the thing has his arm, fangs raking through flesh. Mason kicks, and his foot makes contact, hitting with a thud.

I kick as hard as I can. My foot strikes something solid, and a yelp rings out, weirdly pitched. Then a growl and a snarl, and I kick again, and the thing must have been leaping at us, because my foot hits it full on, and it yowls as it flies back, setting a maple sapling shaking.

The wind whips up, and in that wind, I feel what I sensed earlier, something cold gripping at my heart, fraying my nerves, infecting me with rage.

"Run!" I say.

"Where?" Elijah says, shouting to be heard over the wind.

"The cabin!" Holly shouts. "It's warded. Get to the cabin."

Someone reaches for my hand. Even before I look over, I know that touch. I glance toward Logan. His hand tightens on mine as that horrible wind becomes the howls of a dozen beasts on our heels.

And we run.

CHAPTER THIRTY-ONE

Kate

I'm glancing over my shoulder when I trip. In my defense, I was making sure the damned vampire kept up. Everyone else runs behind me in a tight knot, but Mason has to hang back, as if we're strolling through a mall and he doesn't want anyone to think he's part of the group.

If the guy is that survival-averse, I should let him dawdle. It's not as if he'll die. In fact, the Machiavellian thing to do would be to *let* him lag behind as a chew toy for the hell beast. But Mason's behind Logan, and there's a chance—a good one actually—that his "lagging" is actually "staying between Logan and the hell beast." I think someone has a crush. Which is terribly sweet. So, I cannot help but worry about him, and I glance back . . . and trip over a vine.

It isn't more than a stumble, but I'm in the lead and when I trip, arms flailing, it ripples through the ground, everyone pulling up short. Everyone except Elijah, who dives to my unneeded rescue, damn him . . . and slams into my side instead. With his werewolf strength, it's like being hit by a bag of cement. We both go flying and crash into the undergrowth.

When we stop bush-surfing, Elijah looks down at me, his eyes dark with worry. "You okay?"

"I was . . . until I got body-slammed by an idiot who thinks I need"—I throw him off, his landing thump punctuating my words—"rescue from a killer vine."

"I was just—"

A growl reverberates around us. Elijah and I both look around, seeing nothing but thin air. Thin air that growls and likely has fangs big enough to skewer us whole.

"Logan?" I whisper. "Run."

My brother's behind me, and I don't dare turn to look, but when I tell him to run, there's no answering thunder of footfalls.

"Take the others," I say, my gaze fixed on that low growling. "I've got this."

"*We've* got it," Elijah says.

Brave words, but I don't think he has any choice in the matter. We're lying on the ground, and when he goes to rise, there's a chomp, as if the beast lunged at him, jaws snapping in warning. Telling us to stay down.

"Take the others, Lo, please," I say, my voice low. "Elijah and I will keep the hell beast distracted."

"Hell hound," Logan says.

"What?"

"It's a hell hound. They can materialize but—"

"Really?" Mason says. "Does this seem like the time for a bestiary lesson? Fuck this." He charges. "I'll keep it busy while—"

The hound snatches his arm before he can finish. Blood flies. Mason flies too, a six-foot-three quarterback of a guy whipping through the air like a rag doll.

I vault to my feet and rush the hound, or where I presume the hound is, given that it still has hold of Mason, jerking him by the arm as blood spatters the trees. I hit the beast in the side and slamming a wall of coarse fur.

Elijah and Logan leap into the fray. They miss the beast—easy to do when you can't see it. I'm gripping fist-fuls of fur, feet flying as I try—and fail—to kick the beast.

"Here!" I shout.

Logan understands what I mean: hit *here*, where I'm clutching the hound. He slams his fist into it. Behind us, the spellcasters do their thing.

Elijah roundhouse kicks the beast as Logan punches again, and his foot doesn't come near Logan's arm, but my brother still snarls at him.

I throw myself on the hell hound, and as I hit the beast, it shimmers. I blink. It's definitely shimmering, revealing a ghostly outline of a black-furred flank.

"Hit it harder!" I shout.

I grapple the hell hound as I haul myself onto its broad back. I can see the midnight black expanse of fur. I can also see the beast's head, jaws still clamped tight on Mason's arm, his flesh ripping beneath massive jagged teeth.

Mason lashes out, smacking with his free hand, but while he might not be screaming, his eyes are doing it for him, bright blue wells of agony, his face contorted, his jaw wired shut. He's in too much pain to focus his blows, and his fist only swings blindly at the beast.

Holly pauses her casting. Her spell must be failing. I'm certainly not seeing any magical assistance as the guys pummel the beast, I grip its back and poor Mason is whipped from side to side, his arm shredding.

"Just repeat after me," Holly's voice is sharp with frustration. "Say the words."

She begins casting again, and this time, Allan's voice chimes in, falteringly saying the words after her.

The hell hound continues to take shape, opaque now, a huge, black thick-furred beast. From my vantage point, I can only see its back and hound-like ears. Even that's a blur. Yet its attention is on the vampire in its jaws, as if the werewolf on its back is little more than an annoying flea. That's what I feel like, too, clinging here.

Grabbing one fistful of fur at a time, I haul myself up the hound's back. I almost fall twice, but I finally reach its huge skull and bash my fist down on its muzzle.

The hell hound barely flinches.

I snarl a curse. That's a sensitive spot on a canine, but apparently hell hounds don't quite fit the genus. When I curse, though, Elijah shouts, "No, keep at it! You're making it materialize."

"That's not—"

The hound's head jerks back, hitting me in the chin, my teeth snapping shut. Blood fills my mouth. I spit it out, and say, "It's the casters."

That's what Holly's doing. A witch spell to make the hound materialize, with Allan repeating her words, throwing his sorcerer magic into the mix.

"Doesn't matter," Logan says. "Keep—"

The beast spins, Mason dragged behind as it turns on the annoying werewolves. There's a horrible tearing sound, and Mason howls in rage and pain as he goes flying. Blood spurts, hitting me full in the face. I gasp and rub my face against the hell-hound's thick fur. Then I slam my fist down on its snout again, just as it snaps at Logan.

I strike again, this time aiming my fist at one red eye.

Contact. The beast yowls and bucks. I grab it by the ears, my fingernails digging in. Its head whips back and forth, and I grab its ruff again before I lose my grip. I ram my fist into its eye. As it yowls in pain, Elijah runs in front of it, wielding a tree branch, twice as thick as a baseball bat.

"Duck!" he shouts as he swings the branch back.

I bury my face in the hound's fur. A tremendous blow rocks through the beast as the wood cracks, and then I'm flying, still on the hound, both of us sailing through the air as Elijah shouts, "Kate!"

We hit the ground, the huge beast atop me. I start to scramble out. A snarl as the hound twists. I see my foot, right next to those massive jaws. I pull away, but it's too late. The beast grabs my foot, and I sail into the air.

CHAPTER THIRTY-TWO

Logan

Hell hound. We're fighting a hell hound.

That isn't possible. Hell hounds exist only in demon dimensions, and whatever is going wrong here, we have not crossed over into another world. And, yes, when my sister is clinging to the back of a giant monster, standing back to muse on the implausibility of it doesn't help anyone.

In my defense, while pondering, I'm still pummeling the beast with everything I have. Also, the impossibility of the situation is only a fleeting thought, carried along on a rush of all my data on hell hounds, my brain sifting through the minutia, searching for something that will help. Clearly this hound isn't going to stop because a few teenagers are beating on it.

Kate's clinging to the hound's back like a cowgirl on a bull. Holly and Allan are casting together, forcing the beast to materialize. Elijah is . . . I don't know where Elijah is, and I don't really care. He was fighting alongside me, and I want to grumble and say he was only getting in my way, but that would be a lie. He's a werewolf, and apparently he knows how to fight, so even if I'd rather we'd left him behind, I was grudgingly glad for the assistance. Now, though, he's taken off. As reliable as ever.

Elijah's gone, and Mason . . . I'm trying not to think about Mason. I saw him whipped by the hound, heard that terrible sound as his arm tore free of the beast's teeth. I keep telling myself he's all right. No, he'll *be* all right, once he heals, and he *will* heal.

Do I know that for certain?

I do not.

My concern right now, though, is for my crazy sister riding atop a hell hound, bashing its snout and ramming a fist into its eye as the beast bucks and snarls.

Someone yells, "Duck!" and I spin to see Elijah swinging a massive branch at the hell hound. The hell hound with my *sister* on its back.

I lunge to stop him, but it's too late. Kate ducks, and Elijah smashes the branch into the beast's head. The beast topples back *onto* Kate.

I'm running for the hell hound as Kate scrambles to get free. She kicks . . . and the beast spots that foot, flying straight for her head. She sees her mistake, eyes going wide as she yanks her foot back. The hound chomps down on it.

Elijah makes it to the hell hound first. I snarl at him to get out of my way. He ignores me, of course, and dives in to Kate's rescue.

Elijah grabs the hell hound's snout, one jaw in each hand as he pries them open. His face screws up like a weightlifter trying to pump twice as much as he should. Sweat breaks out on his forehead. His fingers accidentally slip into the beast's mouth. If Kate *does* pull free, he's liable to lose a finger or two. For reckless heroics, he's as bad as my sister.

"Grab the top!" I shout to be heard over the beast's snarls. I lock my fingers around the bottom of the hound's jaw. "Grab the—"

Elijah lets go of the lower jaw, grabbing the snout instead. I hate to give the guy any credit, but he's probably saved my sister's foot. The hound's teeth haven't done more than break the skin.

Elijah and I struggle to pry the beast's jaws open, but we can only keep them from clamping down.

"Hold on, Kate," I say between gritted teeth. "Just let us—"

She yanks her foot free, scraping over sharp canines, blood welling. Then she shouts, "Let go!" and I see her foot pull back for a kick.

I release the top of the hound's snout. Elijah hesitates until he sees her foot slam out, and then he lets go fast as Kate's foot plows into the hound's jaw. The beast tumbles back.

The hell hound barely skims the ground before it's on its feet again, slavering as bloody froth drips. It has fully materialized now, and I'm looking at a beast twice the size of a wolf and triple the weight, with four-inch fangs and glowing red eyes. It's canine, but grotesque, like a toddler mashing a dog-shaped figure from raw clay, features askew, thick legs and lumpy torso and misshapen head.

Kate inches closer to me, and Elijah glances over sharply, as if surprised she's taking refuge. She's not hiding behind me—she's moving *beside* me, shoulder to shoulder, facing off against the hound. Elijah grabs the fallen branch and steps Kate's way, flanking her.

The hell hound lowers its head between its shoulder-blades and snarls at us.

"Yeah, we can see you," Elijah says, wielding the branch. "You aren't hidden anymore."

The hound snaps and snarls, but it takes a slow step back. Elijah starts to lunge, and Kate grabs his sleeve, murmuring, "Let it retreat."

Those red eyes fix on Elijah as the beast steps back again. It's watching him, ready to charge us if he so much as test-swings that branch. If he does, the hell hound won't need to take him down. I'll do it myself.

The beast takes another two careful steps backward. One final snarl, and then it wheels and runs into the forest.

"Keep watching in case it changes its mind," Kate says.

Then she runs to Mason, and pride surges in me. My sister can be the most impulsive, reckless person alive—jumping onto a hell hound, really? I grew up trotting along in her footsteps as she barreled into danger, expecting me to follow. I do follow, though, because she's always the first person throwing herself into battle, *and* she's the first one checking afterward to make sure everyone is okay.

As Kate runs to help Mason, I scan for any sign of the hell hound returning. It seems to be gone. I don't like that, though, and when Elijah says, "I'm going to scout," I don't stop him.

"Don't go far," I say.

He turns a cool look on me. "I'm not a child. I'm not a Pack wolf either."

He means he doesn't need to obey the Alpha's son, but I snort and say, "Yeah, I can tell."

His dark eyes narrow. "What's that supposed to mean?"

"It means you nearly got my sister killed, flinging that around." I nod at the tree limb in his hand. "I know you two aren't fake dating anymore, but I'm going to warn you to stay away from her. She doesn't need a guy who'd sacrifice her to save himself."

"What?" he sputters. "I almost got killed by those crazy half-demons—" He shakes his head. "Forget it. I might not be Kate's favorite person right now, and I earned that, but I would never do anything to hurt your sister. I knew she'd duck when I told her to. I'd have stopped swinging if she didn't. I don't know what your problem is Logan—"

"I think that's the first time you've used my name."

He flinches before barreling on. "I've barely spoken to you so yeah, I haven't—"

"I know who you are, and I know why you don't like using my name."

His mouth opens. Shuts.

"Tell her or I will," I say as I walk away. "And I'm going to, as soon as I get the chance. She needs to know you're up to something, and you cannot be trusted."

I jog to where Mason sits propped against a tree as Kate examines his arm. I'm surprised he's letting her do that . . . until I see she's not giving him a choice. He's still grumbling, like we're all making too big a fuss over this, and please, can we just go away and let him brood in peace?

"Take the others and get to the cabin," Kate says, not looking up from her ministrations.

"No," Mason growls. "Tell your sister to stop playing doctor with me. She's really not my type."

Kate manages to flash him a finger, while still working on his arm. "He's still bleeding. Just take the others and go."

I shake my head. 'The hell hound's gone, and we need to stick together. We'll leave as soon as he's ready."

"Can you make him sit his ass down?" Kate says. "Before I kick it down?"

"Can you make her let go of my arm?" Mason says. "Before she snaps it off?"

"The bone isn't broken," she says. "Your arm won't come off that easily, which is unfortunate, because I've always wondered how that works with vamps. Do they regrow a new limb? Or do they lose it for good?" She looks up at Mason. "We could answer that question right now, for the sake of supernatural medical science."

He only snorts and rolls his eyes.

"I think they lose it for good," Holly says, standing nearby as she and Allan scan the forest for the hell hound. "That's what the lore suggests."

"It doesn't grow back," I say. "But the arm can reattach itself if you hold it against the stump."

"Really? Cool. Where'd you read that?"

"Jiskani's medieval treatise on the healing properties of vampires."

Holly sighs. "I've been looking for that one."

"God save us from the geeks," Mason mutters.

"No," Holly says. "The geeks will save *you*. Next time a hell hound attacks, you can let it take your arm, knowing you can reattach it. Well, as long as it doesn't run off and eat it for dinner."

Mason mutters under his breath. I pace around, squinting into the bushes. Kate's right that we need to keep moving. There's no way I can leave her behind, though, so I'm playing along with her, joking and acting like everything's fine, and we're safe here. We are not safe here. Not one bit. Yet the others are taking their cues from us, and we need to keep them calm.

The woods remain silent and still. If I strain, I can hear shouts from camp, and I try very hard not to think about that. We can't go back. We need to keep moving. Stabilize Mason and then run for that warded cabin.

"Everything okay?" Holly asks.

"All quiet," I say. "A hell hound is like any other predator. Once it realizes you're not easy prey, it backs off."

Kate's look calls me on the lie, but she nods, satisfied with it.

I lean in to look at Mason's arm. Allan stays off to the side, gaze averted, and I don't blame him. It's not a sight for a weak stomach. Even Mason, as cool as he's acting, doesn't look down at the mangled mess of flesh.

It is healing. That's the only reason I can look at it, witnessing a fascinating phenomenon without feeling like a ghoul. Let my inner geek flag fly at this rare opportunity. I still cannot do it with completely scientific dispassion. I'm horrified by what I see, the flesh ripped, white bone showing, Kate clamping down to keep Mason from bleeding out.

"How are you doing?" I ask, lowering my voice so the spellcasters can't hear.

"Peachy, thanks, pup."

"He's a gem," Kate says and she clamps harder on Mason's elbow, making him wince and shoot her a glare, to which she returns a sunshine-bright smile. He snorts, but there's no anger there. I might even detect a glimmer of amusement, granting her a point.

"Logan?" Kate says, gaze on her work. "We're going

to be done here in five minutes. If that gives you time to Change . . ."

I curse under my breath. I should have thought of that. In fact, I should be Changed by now.

"I'll—" I begin.

"Kate!"

We all jump at the shout, echoing from deep in the forest. I'm confused at first, thinking whatever is out there is calling my sister. But her head jerks up and she says, "Elijah?"

She looks at me. "Where's—?"

A crashing through the forest cuts her off. Elijah shouts, "Kate!" again. Then "Kate! Run!" and Kate grabs my hand, clamping it onto Mason's arm as she leaps up.

I see Elijah through the trees. He's at least a hundred feet away. Then he's in the air, hoisted by an invisible hand. He dangles there a moment as Kate runs into the forest, shouting, "Elijah!"

The invisible hand whips him back and then hurls him through the air as Kate screams.

CHAPTER THIRTY-THREE

Kate

"You're a very brave boy," I say to Mason as I adjust my hold on his arm, using my werewolf-tight grip as a tourniquet. "If you keep this up, I'll need to find you a lollipop."

"Fuck off," he says, but there's no rancor in it, and I can tell I've guessed right—he appreciates flippancy more than sympathy.

He's in agony right now, blue eyes nearly black with pain, teeth gritted, sweat running down his broad face. The fact he's not rolling on the ground—or sinking into shock—tells me the tough guy act isn't entirely an act. It's a wall, too, though, one that keeps everyone else firmly on the other side and lets him hide behind it, while pretending he's not hiding at all. I know that feeling. I've been living with it all my life. In my case, my school-yard defense is a carefree in-your-face brashness that hides the fact I'd really rather run home to my Pack.

"I'd suggest you don't look at it," I say.

"Fine by me. My insides are not my best angle."

I snort at that. Then I glance over to where Logan and Elijah stand guard, watching the hell hound's retreat. My mind flits in that direction—a hell hound? Why? How?—before I yank it back making sure Mason doesn't lose his arm.

The only thing holding the limb is cartilage, and I'm trying not to feel ill at that. As a werewolf who also wants to be a doctor, I'm fine with gore. The nausea comes from knowing that I'd been willing to let Mason get tossed around to distract the hell hound, while not considering that it could have done permanent damage.

Holly slides over to help, but I ask her to stand guard instead.

"You hanging in there?" I ask Mason.

"I dunno. Is my arm still hanging in there?"

I chuckle. "It is, and it's healing. I can literally watch it heal. It's fascinating really."

"I'll take your word for it."

It is indeed fascinating. The tissue stitches itself together, blood vessels and muscle finding their torn edges and healing before my eyes. I tuck a few pieces in to aid the process, and I do murmur an apology to Mason for that, but he only shrugs and grunts, "Whatever," which might sound like he's rejecting my apology, but really only means I can do what I must. He trusts me, and I'd like to think I've earned that, but I suspect I've won it simply by being Logan's sister.

I've seen the way Mason looks at my brother when he thinks no one's watching. He might snark and insult Logan, but I see a guy with a crush he's desperate to hide from everyone, especially the subject of that infatuation.

As for whether Logan is interested back, honestly, I've never known my brother to be more than mildly intrigued by anyone, and when he is, his target is as likely to be a guy as a girl. That's just Logan. He'll find the right person when he's ready, and if the past is any indication, he'd need to know Mason a lot better before his attention turns in that direction.

Mason tenses, his entire body going still, and when I glance up, he's looking at something behind me. Then his gaze drops fast, his features hardening to implacable stone, and I know who's walking over.

"Can you make him sit his ass down?" I say to Logan before he even steps into view. "Before I kick it down?"

"Can you make her let go of my arm?" Mason grumbles. "Before she snaps it off?"

I snark back at him, and Holly joins us as she and Logan discuss the finer points of vampire healing powers. I stay out of the conversation and keep my attention on clamping off the blood flow and nudging pieces into position.

When they're done talking, though, I do bring up an important point—the fact that the hell hound almost certainly didn't just magically appear here on its own.

A voice booms, shouting my name.

I look up sharply. "Elijah? Where's—?"

Something crashes through the forest.

No, not something. *Elijah* crashes through the forest.

What the hell is Elijah doing there? He was just with Logan, standing guard.

"Kate!" Elijah bellows. "Run!"

I grab Logan's hand and clamp it onto Mason's arm. Then I race toward the crashes, squinting to see into the thick forest.

There!

I see Elijah, running. But he isn't running toward us. He's going in the opposite direction. Leading something away from us.

I start to run. Then, suddenly, Elijah isn't running anymore. He's dangling in the air.

"Elijah!" I shout.

His eyes widen his limbs windmill as he flails to get down. Then whatever has him throws him through the trees. I let out a scream of rage as I race toward him.

"Kate!" Allan shouts behind me. "Don't—!"

The rest is cut off by the thunder of running footfalls. I glance back to see Logan coming after me, Holly now clamping down on Mason's arm as Allan follows Logan.

I race to where Elijah lies crumpled in a twisted heap, not moving, and my heart slams against my ribs.

"Elijah!"

Movement. Excruciatingly slow movement, as he lifts his head, blinking at me. Then, his eyes go wide, head whipping up as his mouth opens.

Something hits me in the side and knocks me flying into a tree. Logan snarls in rage, and I dimly hear Holly shouting, "Get *back* here! Do not—"

"Hey," Mason yells. "You want a plaything? Come get it."

"Demon," I whisper as I push up. Arms grab me, my brother tugging me to my feet. I whisper "Demon" again, still winded, every breath searing through me.

"I know," Logan says grimly.

He doesn't say more. He doesn't need to. My brother might be the expert when it comes to our supernatural world, but even I know that if there's a hell hound where a hell hound should not be, that can only mean one thing. It's been brought here by a demon.

I push to my feet and look around. The forest has gone quiet. Mason's striding around the clearing, his face set in grim determination. Holly's there, and Allan, too, fog wafting from his fingertips, ready to cast it and hide us. But there's nothing to hide us from. All is quiet.

"Too quiet," Logan murmurs, as if reading my thoughts.

I nod and stagger to Elijah on wobbly legs. He's doubled over, retching. When I approach, he waves off my concern. I reach out and he stands, putting an arm around my shoulders, letting us prop each other up.

The others reach us, and we instinctively cluster, spell-casters in the middle. When a growl sounds in front of us, Elijah stiffens, his arm tightening around my shoulders.

"That you, mutt?" Elijah says. "You really think that's a good idea? We kicked your ass—"

Another growl sounds, this one off to our left. I'm turning that way when the hell hound behind us snarls again.

"Please tell me hell hounds can teleport," Elijah whispers.

"Sorry," I murmur.

"Don't move," Logan says. "Holly?"

She's already casting her spell to materialize the hounds. Allan joins in. Two forms begin to appear. Two massive hell hounds.

"Ideas?" Elijah murmurs.

"Run like hell?" I say.

He gives a strained chuckle. "Yeah, I'm thinking that's all we've got."

I glance at Logan. He nods. When I look toward Holly, she points in the direction of the cabin, our initial destination.

"Okay," I murmur. "On the count of three. Logan, Elijah and I will move toward Holly and Allan. Mason?" I look at him, the farthest from the group as always.

"I'll distract them," he says. "Give you guys a head start."

"Let them each grab an arm and rip you in two?" I say. "I don't think you can recover from that."

"I'll be—"

"Go on, Kate," Logan says to me. "I'll stay with Mason."

Mason scowls his way. "I don't need a guard dog, pup."

"Too bad. You stay, I—"

"For fuck's sake, are we running?" Mason says. "Get on with it."

I reach and squeeze Logan's hand. Then we run.

CHAPTER THIRTY-FOUR

Logan

Two hell hounds. As Kate would say, of course there had to be two. One just wasn't challenging enough.

We run in a group, with the werewolves on the outside. Mason tries to lag behind, but he doesn't try very hard, and I only need to look over my shoulder for him to glower and grumble and catch up. Even he isn't keen to put himself in the path of *two* hell hounds.

As the hounds pursue, the spellcasters hide us with fog and blur spells. They don't bother forcing the beasts to materialize. We can hear them crashing through the forest. That's all they do, though, and I feel like a rabbit being run to ground. They could catch up. I'm sure of that. But they don't.

I catch glimpses of Kate's sweat-streaked face, and I know she's in pain. Elijah is, too, when I bother to look his way. Whatever his initial game plan with Kate, I grudgingly admit he's carried his weight in battle. The rest can be tackled later.

So the hounds could catch up. They're toying with us, and one of the first things we learned from our parents was not to toy with prey. Yes, the chase and the hunt are fun. Exhilarating, adrenaline pumping fun. But you must enjoy that part while your prey still has an actual chance of escape. Once they're cornered, it doesn't matter if it's a mouse or a rabbit or a coyote—you do not prolong the torment.

"I see the cabin!" Kate calls. "Logan? Elijah? Grab sticks if you see them. Allan and Holly, we'll need your casting."

The cabin appears, rising from the forest. We all bear down, finding that last bit of energy as we barrel toward it.

We clamor onto the porch, and Kate starts hammering on the door, trying to smash it down. We form a knot around her, with me and Elijah in front, both brandishing sticks. Mason has one, too, and he's backed against the spellcasters, letting them work their magic. Fog spells, cover spells, knockbacks and fireballs—they unleash their entire arsenal as the hell hounds snap and lunge at us.

"We're going to run out of juice soon," Allan warns.

"I know," Kate says. "This damned door isn't budging. Logan?"

I flip around and dodge between the two spellcasters.

"Count of three," I say, and we ram our shoulders against the door simultaneously. Pain shoots through me . . . and the door doesn't budge.

"Son of a *bitch*," Kate snarls.

"Window," I say, and I shove past Mason to get to the nearest front window. It's boarded from the inside with simple plywood. I slam my fist into it, pain arcs through my hand while the wood only cracks down the middle.

Okay, not simple plywood. It's reinforced with two-by-fours. I lift my hand again.

"Stand back," Kate says, lifting a branch.

She smashes the stick into the wood. It cracks more . . . and the branch snaps in half. She starts battering with the broken branch.

A hiss of pain behind us. Allan staggers, blood dripping from his arm. I grab him as Kate yanks on the broken boards, clearing enough for Allan to scramble through. He falls inside, cursing, but I'm already hefting Holly.

"Mason!" I shout.

"I got this."

"Forget him," Elijah calls. "Get yourselves inside. That fog is about to disperse and when it does——"

Elijah flies back into the wall with a thud and an *oomph*, and Kate dives to his rescue. Inside, Holly and Allan must be casting, because I catch a glimpse of black fur, a flash of monstrous fangs. My sister is makes contact with the latter. Elijah and I grab Kate at the same time, and we heave her, still fighting, through the window.

As Kate tumbles into the house, Elijah turns to me with a wide smile and a hand lifted for a high five. I shove him toward the window. He shakes his head and scrambles through. Then I turn to Mason.

"Go on, pup," he says, not looking my way. "I've got this."

I hoist him by the back of his shirt, ignoring his "Hey!" and his struggles, and I shove him through the window. Inside, Kate hauls him through.

"Let go——" Mason begins, and she does, tossing him unceremoniously aside. Then she reaches through the window, wraps her hands in my shirt front and heaves. As I fly up, the four-inch fangs of a hell hound clamp down on my foot. Pain sears up my calf as I tumble through the window.

"Shit!" Kate drags me away from the window and drops over my leg as red rivulets run down it.

I grit my teeth and pull my leg in, waving off her concern as I push to my feet. We all turn toward the window. Outside, the hounds snarl, and when I ease closer, I see them, half materialized, pacing.

"You know why I wasn't in a hurry to get inside?" Mason calls from across the small room.

"Because you love us and want to keep us safe?" Kate says.

He snorts. "Because I'm not stupid enough to trap myself in an old wooden house, especially after the big, bad wolves busted open a window big enough for those things to squeeze through. But thanks, pup, for trapping me in here to die with you. I appreciate that."

Kate pats his shoulder. "Don't worry. You won't die, big guy. You get to come back as a giant mosquito."

He lifts his middle finger in front of her face.

"Truth," she says. "However, as you may have noticed, the hounds are not at our door. Or our window. Remember that night you died?"

"You mean *last* night?"

"Time flies, huh? Well, after you slunk off on Logan—"

"I didn't slink—"

"After you *slunk* off, the rest of our Scooby gang went exploring. We found this place, which is warded. Now we know what it's warded against." She waves outside. "Voila. Thou shalt not cross, hell hounds."

"Yeah? Well, you know what? We can't cross either,

not with a couple of hell hounds out there. You think demonic beasts get tired? Take naps?"

"You are such a ray of sunshine. You're lucky my brother feels responsible for you or I'd toss you out for the hounds to chew on."

"Feels responsible for me?" Mason sputters.

"You didn't think he was letting you hang around for your charming personality, did you?"

She grins at Mason, who scowls back, and I feel like I've missed a joke. Clearly Kate is teasing Mason, and I'm not sure why.

She walks over and grabs his good arm, and I tense, ready to intercede if he gets pissy. He can mistreat me all he wants, but he'd better not try that with Kate. Especially not when she's been much more considerate than he deserves.

When she grabs his arm, though, he only shoots me a glare, like this is all my fault. She hauls him to the window and waves out at the prowling hounds.

"You really think you'd be better off out there?" she says. "If you do, be my guest. I'll keep Logan from stopping you."

He grumbles, nothing intelligible.

"Yeah, that's what I thought," she says. "You're just being a pain in the ass for the sake of being a pain in the ass."

"No, I'm pointing out the flaws in your plan, Goldilocks. Those wolves are at the door, and they're not going away."

"Goldilocks is bears. The three bears."

"Either way, you're gonna get eaten. We all are. So is anyone who comes to rescue us."

"Well, then, it's a good thing no one will come to

rescue us. Did I mention we found our cell phones? They took out the SIM cards. We're stuck here until we come up with a plan. So how about you brood on that for a while, big guy. Find yourself a corner, and we'll all stay out of your way while you pretend to be thinking up a plan."

He glances at the window. "You're sure it's safe in here?"

"No, we are not," I say. "We presume that's what the warding is for, given that it seems to be working. Time to catch our breath and, as Kate said, come up with a plan."

"Uh, guys?" Allan says. "I hate to interrupt but . . . I think I know why Kate couldn't break down the front door."

"Is it barricaded?" I ask.

"You . . . could say that."

We follow him into the hall. Holly peeks out from a room where she's been poking around. Elijah is right behind Allan, and he sees the front door first and stops short.

"Holy shit," he says. "Is that . . .?"

"The reason why we couldn't get in?" Allan says. "I think so."

I round the corner into the entry way, and my shoes squeak as I stop. The door is indeed barricaded—thick planks are nailed across it. There's something nailed to the planks, too. Long white bones.

"Tell me those are deer," Elijah says.

"No," Kate says, her gaze rising to the ceiling where human skulls grin down. "I don't think they are."

Thank you for reading!

I hope you enjoyed
Wolf's Bane!

Kate & Logan's adventures conclude in

Wolf's Curse

Coming spring 2020

ABOUT THE AUTHOR

Kelley Armstrong is the author of the *Rockton* thriller series and standalone thrillers. Past works include the *Otherworld* urban fantasy series, the *Cainsville* gothic mystery series, the *Nadia Stafford* thriller trilogy, the *Darkest Powers & Darkness Rising* teen paranormal series and the *Age of Legends* teen fantasy series. Armstrong lives in Ontario, Canada with her family.

Visit her online:
www.KelleyArmstrong.com
mail@kelleyarmstrong.com

facebook.com/KelleyArmstrongAuthor

twitter.com/KelleyArmstrong

instagram.com/KelleyArmstrongAuthor